"What do you want, Mallory?"

She knew exactly what she wanted. With her fingers wrapped around Jake's tie, she forced him to lower his head until she could whisper in his ear.

"Orgasm."

The effect of that word was visible. Jake's chest rose and fell with a ragged breath and a shudder rocked his body.

Mallory remembered exactly why she'd kissed him ten years ago instead of escaping. She couldn't resist his dark blond hair, tanned skin and brawny body. She had a plan to bring this man to his knees. But right now, with the steam caressing her body until she felt every inch of her skin ache beneath his strong fingers, her plan was less about satisfying vengeance than desire.

She wanted to press against him, feel the contrast of fine silk and hard muscle against her naked skin. She wanted to feel the vibration when his breath rumbled deep in his chest.

And she always got what she wanted.

Dear Reader,

My travels often take me into cyberspace to discuss my love of red-hot romances. These trips are always interesting, often thought provoking, touching, educational or just plain fun. And sometimes—when I'm very lucky—a trip can be all of the above, which is exactly what happened when I hosted my first message board at eHarlequin.com. Wow! I found inspiration, emotion, ingenuity, humor, intelligence and community with the visitors to the board. Above all, I confirmed something I've suspected all along—romance readers are very, very special people.

Mallory Hunt is also a special woman. She lives life by her own rules and doesn't make apologies. She believes that Jake Trinity owes her big, and she plans to collect. The funny thing is Jake feels exactly the same about her. When he reappears in her life to collect his due, Mallory discovers he's grown into a man used to getting what he wants—and he wants her.

Blaze is the place to explore red-hot romance and I'm delighted to be among the ranks of the wonderful Harlequin authors who share their journeys to happily ever after. I hope *Over the Edge* brings you to happily ever after, too. Let me know. Drop a line in care of Harlequin Books, 225 Duncan Mill Road, Don Mills, Ontario M3B 3K9, Canada, or visit my Web site at www.jeanielondon.com.

Very truly yours,

Jeanie London

Books by Jeanie London

HARLEQUIN BLAZE

OVER THE EDGE

Jeanie London

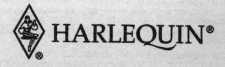

TORONTO • NEW YORK • LONDON
AMSTERDAM • PARIS • SYDNEY • HAMBURG
STOCKHOLM • ATHENS • TOKYO • MILAN • MADRID
PRAGUE • WARSAW • BUDAPEST • AUCKLAND

For my very dear friend Judith Pich. This one is significant.
It's number six, which means I'm—gasp!—*real.*

Special thanks to Cyber-Aunt Karen, DianaP, Andee, Queen April,
Cheryl the Angel, Marcy, Nammy, Esjai, Krazkim55, MeriG, Latesha, Jerry,
Riza, Aurelene, JenO, Audrey, Dee and all the visitors to my message board at
eHarlequin.com. Your professional expertise, creative input and love of happily
ever after inspired the Princess of Paperback while she wrote this story.

ISBN 0-373-79114-3

OVER THE EDGE

Copyright © 2003 by Jeanie LeGendre.

This edition published by arrangement with Harlequin Books S.A.

Visit us at www.eHarlequin.com

Printed in U.S.A.

Prologue

The kiss—ten years ago

THE WOMAN moved as if she were making love, slim curves gathering and unfolding in a sinuous display as she descended a rope using nothing more than the strength of her upper body to lower her, long sleek legs to anchor her. She wore all black, from the top of her ski-mask-covered head to the tips of her soft-soled boots.

Jake Trinity stopped short in the doorway leading from the offices to the warehouse, the two sides of his brain colliding at the impossibility of the sight. One side absorbed her smooth descent as she shimmied down and dropped to her feet without a sound, her body absorbing the impact with an effortless motion that brought to mind a cat landing on all fours.

This had to be the testosterone-filled half of his brain. The more rational half observed that she'd landed neatly out of reach of the infrared sensor beams zigzagging across the opening of the warehouse doors.

No one should have been in the building.

The night watchman who'd let him in earlier must have gone to sleep on the job because Innovative Engineering had a state-of-the-art security system, barbed-wire fences and steel-reinforced doors and windows to avoid exactly this occurrence.

Jake knew this for certain. For the past two years he'd

been conducting his internship with Innovative, the largest electrical engineering firm on the eastern seaboard. He'd made it his business to learn everything about the company he was establishing a career with while earning his degrees.

He'd only stopped by this late on a Saturday night to retrieve some account data so he could continue work on a project for his newest boss, the company president.

He remembered his father's parting words as he'd left home earlier. *College students should spend their weekends dating, playing golf and watching football games, in that order.*

Had Jake put any stock in his father's opinion, he wouldn't be standing inside a building watching a burglary in progress.

Not that this particular thief would present much of a problem. *She* wouldn't, but Jake didn't believe for one second that this woman was alone. No way.

He stood shadowed in the doorway as she raised her hand to punch numbers onto a keypad, presumably to disable the beam sensor. He searched for any identifying features to report to the police—if he survived the meeting with her accomplices.

Five feet four inches, maybe five-five, most of which comprised long, long legs...

A body that was all slim lines and sleek curves...

Liquid movements that reminded him of...sex.

Something about her, and Jake wasn't sure what, struck him as young. Around his age maybe. Not quite twenty. With effort, he shrugged off the thought as plain stupid. Why would any young woman be breaking into a commercial warehouse that stored millions of dollars of electrical equipment, not to mention a high-security vault that housed several invaluable prototypes?

Jake didn't have a chance to consider the possible answers because the mystery woman suddenly spun and looked directly at him. She could have only sensed his presence. Her back had been to him and he hadn't moved, had barely *breathed*.

The black mask covered her face and neck. He couldn't make out her eyes but got the impression they were light, that she must be Caucasian, although he couldn't see even a sliver of skin to support the impression. Something about her suggested she was as surprised to find him as he'd been to come across her. Something about the way she squared her shoulders and raised her chin…

He stepped into the foyer that connected the offices with the warehouse, expecting her to run. He'd catch her and deal with her accomplices later.

But his mystery woman didn't run. She only lifted a gloved finger to her mouth and gestured him to silence as she approached. She clearly wasn't worried that he'd hurt her, and Jake thought that said a lot about her confidence in her abilities. Though she couldn't know he'd wrestled through high school and still made time for the sport in college, he was a full head taller and outweighed her by at least eighty pounds.

But her hands were free. If she was armed, she hadn't gone for a weapon.

He stopped and waited, the more impulsive side of his brain noticing how she even walked as if she were making love, all toned muscle and sleek grace. There was no panic about her, or violence. He had the feeling she was challenging him. As if she dared him to play a dangerous game.

So what was his next move?

Jake wasn't sure about anything except there were other

burglars around somewhere, and he wanted very much to see what this woman's next move would be.

The eye slits in the ski mask were wider than he'd realized, but she'd blackened the skin below, like a television cat burglar. He could see two pale-green eyes, so clear a green they seemed to laser through the darkness.

She didn't utter a sound, though he half expected her to say something. The occasion seemed to warrant a verbal exchange, but she only assessed him with a challenge in those eyes.

Jake assessed her as carefully, calculated that she stood just out of his reach. A few inches closer and he could've taken her down with a leg drop that she wouldn't have seen coming. He still could, but he'd have to spring on her to cover those extra few inches.

Holding her gaze, he tensed for action....

In one sleek burst of motion, *she* pounced, covering the distance between them while dragging up the edge of her mask. A glimpse of clear ivory skin, a daintily pointed chin and a kissable red mouth stopped him short.

He could see enough of her face to shoot sparks through him even as the rational half of his brain recognized that she hadn't revealed enough for him to identify her to the police.

That was his last thought before she slipped leather-clad fingers around his neck, raised up on tiptoes...

And kissed him.

Her moist mouth slanted across his and parted enough so their breaths literally collided.

Jake gasped, but she only laughed, a sultry sound that gusted against his lips, a sound that annihilated reason beneath a blast of testosterone that made his bones melt and his glasses fog.

He should take her down and restrain her for the police.

But that thought dissolved the instant she swept her warm silk tongue into his mouth, prowling inside boldly, engaging him in a kiss so hot that she shut down the rational half of his brain as if it had never existed.

Her fingers anchored his face close. She thrust her body against his, a sleek motion that caught him in all the right spots…firm breasts against his chest, her stomach cradling a hard-on that shouldn't be happening given their situation. Everything about her was daring him to take what she offered.

Jake practically vibrated with his reaction, a hunger unlike anything he'd ever felt. Instinctively, he lifted his hands, slipped his fingers along the ski mask and forced her to tilt her face back so he could drive his tongue into her mouth.

The hot taste of passion chased away any worries, any reasonable thoughts…including all awareness of the surveillance camera that was angled at them, recording every second of that incredible kiss.

1

MALLORY HUNT wanted a piece of Jake Trinity's ass.

Literally.

The way she saw it, the man owed her for some very good reasons. For one, he'd sent her dad on a four-year stint in prison. For another, he'd sent her on a six-month stint in foster care. *And* forced her dad's burglary crew into retirement.

All because of one lousy kiss.

Well, the kiss hadn't exactly been lousy. If it had been, she might have forgotten it after ten years. She hadn't.

Of course she wouldn't admit that to her dad, so she simply said, "You heard right. Jake Trinity contacted me about a job."

An understatement if ever there was one. The man ha blasted back into her life with the force of a gunshot, in sisting she drop everything to consult with him.

And Mallory intended to consult…oh, yeah, she in tended to do a lot more, too, but she wouldn't tell her da that, either. She didn't want to invite any questions whe she knew for a fact that her dad didn't know Jake Trinit had been the informant who'd gotten him busted on th Innovative Engineering job all those years ago.

As far as Mallory was concerned, if her dad had su vived the past decade in the dark, dredging up memorie of that painful time in their lives would serve no good purpose.

She'd handle Jake Trinity herself. And she had some *very* specific plans to pay the man back for his interference in their lives. *Very* specific. She'd make him regret the day he'd taken the moral high road by triggering the silent alarm that had changed the lives of everyone she cared about forever.

She'd make him pay for being the reason that her dad had lied to her for the first and only time in her life.

Yes, Mallory had it all under control…but she didn't want her dad around to interfere with her plans, or to get any wrong ideas. He'd been dropping way too many hints about her finding a husband lately. He wanted her to settle down in a house with a white picket fence, and the last thing she needed was for him to decide Jake Trinity might make an acceptable candidate to share her happily ever after.

No, her dad didn't need to know this job was anything more than a normal troubleshooting gig.

Which meant she wasn't answering any more questions.

As a diversionary tactic she glanced to where he was perched precariously on the wall beside her, and asked, "Are you doing okay? How are you holding up? This is a long climb."

Her dad peered down the sixty feet of man-made rock-climbing wall separating them from their belay partners below. "I'm going all the way today, babe. How about you?"

"If there's no challenge, I don't see the point."

Today's rock-climbing challenge had limits. She and her dad both were harnessed and roped with their belay partners clinging to their lines, ready to control the descent if either one fell. As she barely tipped the scales at one hundred and ten, a fall wouldn't be much of a challenge for her belay partner, either.

Following her dad's gaze down to the high-tech foam floor far below, she experienced a rush of vertigo that made her tighten her grip on the handholds and suck in a tight breath to chase the thrill that coursed through her.

She smiled.

While indoor rock climbing might not be the greatest of challenges, it was a *great* workout.

"That's my girl," her dad said. "No guts, no glory."

"No risk, no reward," she agreed.

"No pain, no gain."

That comment made Mallory slant her gaze his way again. Her dad winked, alleviating any cause for worry with one charming glance.

Although Duke Hunt had been scaling man-made walls with her three times a week ever since the Vertical Playground rock-climbing gym had opened in their hometown of Atlanta, the fact still remained that he was a man on approach to his sixtieth birthday. Like her dad, she wasn't one to dwell on impending maturity, but Mallory did have to face the occasional reminder that he was getting older. With a lifestyle as active as theirs, it would have been impossible to ignore the fact.

Though her dad was just as healthy and attractive as he'd always been—a man who women routinely went to pieces over—the passage of time had marked him physically. Distinguished silver shot his black hair at the temples. Laugh lines around his mouth and eyes scored his olive skin more deeply than ever.

But despite this evidence of age, Mallory only saw her dad, a timeless, larger-than-life man who laughed easily, lived life on the edge and loved her more than anything else in his world.

"No risk of failure, no fun." She contributed a new addition to their collection of motivational sayings.

Lifting her gaze to the remaining thirty feet of wall shooting above her head, she reached for her next handhold.

Each time she planted a booted foot on a hold, she shifted her weight and thrust her body upward. Her muscles strained, and she forced herself to concentrate so she didn't misstep.

As a sport, rock climbing was half technique and half muscle. Though she was barely of average height, the muscle part of the equation wasn't an issue. The more Mallory practiced her technique, the more strength she built.

Which didn't mean squat at seventy feet.

The muscles in her thighs had rebelled a good while ago. Of course, she'd arrived at the Vertical Playground earlier than her dad to warm up by bouldering—challenging climbs that she made without the benefit of protection or aids. She relied solely on her technique and strength to get her to the top and down again.

The top in that instance had only been twelve feet, but the activity had contributed to the sweat now soaking through her shorts and ribbed T-shirt.

"Well, tell me what Trinity said." Her dad steered the conversation right back around to the one subject she didn't want to discuss.

"I haven't talked to him yet. We're consulting after I'm done in the gym." She didn't sound much less winded than her dad, each word coming out as sort of a breathy grunt.

"Did he detail what he's looking for in his proposal?"

"He wants me to pinpoint the holes in the prototype of a new security system he's designed."

"How does his new system look? Anything interesting?"

Interesting meant cutting edge. Staying on top of the

latest security developments was a crucial aspect not only of Mallory's security consulting business, but of her dad's.

They were two sides of the same coin. Both their business cards read Hunt Security Specialists. Both their business cards had a phone number. Anything more would have been overkill since their reputations grew each year, a tribute to the power of client satisfaction and word-of-mouth referrals.

But that was where the similarities ended.

Mallory handled only *legitimate* jobs, so she didn't have bars looming in her future. She consulted about security for commercial businesses and worked as a troubleshooter for the engineers who designed the systems. She'd also been working with several law-enforcement agencies recently, projecting how professional burglars might have entered various properties to carry out crimes.

Irony at its finest.

Her dad…well, for Duke Hunt, old habits died hard. Like Mallory, he consulted about security, but he consulted for professional burglars while they planned their heists.

On the fringes of the law, but not prosecutable. And there was no denying that her dad's consulting business was a natural fit. Before his forced retirement, he'd spent his adult life working as a professional burglar, specializing in infiltrating commercial properties and cracking safes.

He'd trained Mallory at his knee from as far back as she could remember. By age thirteen, she'd taken her place as a member of his crew, starting off by scouting egress routes and disabling telephone lines. Eventually she'd graduated to disarming motion and heat sensors and had been training to monitor video stations when they'd been busted.

As Duke Hunt's only child, she'd had an unconventional

upbringing that she wouldn't have traded away one second of—except for the four years her dad had spent in prison.

All because of her run-in with Jake Trinity.

"How'd Trinity hear about you?" her dad asked.

"From the work I did with Triple Safe."

Duke shot her a smile that epitomized a pride in her abilities that far surpassed normal parental standards. "You were prime on that job, babe."

She returned the smile. She *had* been prime on the Triple Safe job. The company had lucked into a chance to bid on a large account here in Atlanta. They'd contracted her to consult, and she'd blown meteor-sized craters in their proposal and helped them redesign their entire system. They'd won the account, established themselves in the industry and generously added to her portfolio and reputation in the process.

"Trinity's prototype has a few new features. Of course I won't have a bead on how new until I see the specs," she said, hoping a minimum of information would satisfy his curiosity. "I did notice in his proposal that he was minimizing the risk of false alarms by using passive infrared and active microwave sensors together in the same units."

"Sounds good. Nothing worse than a twitchy alarm."

"You're right about that." Twitchy sensors could activate an alarm at the most inopportune times—a major inconvenience.

"Think you'll accept the job?"

"Don't know until I talk to the man." The lie tumbled off her lips easily, considering she didn't usually lie to her dad.

"Well, here's hoping he offers you a challenge, then. No doubt you'd love the chance to blast holes in his new system."

No doubt. And while Mallory appreciated her dad's vote of confidence in her abilities, the simple truth was there was no such thing as a fail-safe security system. People designed the systems, and people weren't fail-safe. Clever burglars—and accomplished security specialists like herself and her dad—could always find ways around new precautions.

Jake Trinity, CEO and founder of Trinity Security Services, known throughout the industry as TSS, might be Atlanta's golden boy in the security industry, but he wasn't any more fail-safe than his systems.

Mallory intended to prove just how fail-safe he wasn't.

"Did Lance ever make it home last night?" she asked to divert her dad from his interrogation.

"How'd you hear?"

"Polish Paul called me on my cell. He wanted to know if Lance had contacted me."

"Had he?"

"No."

Duke frowned, and Mallory knew he was worried about their friend's seventeen-year-old son. Polish Paul had been part of her dad's crew since long before Mallory had been born, and he'd crossed the line to become family-by-love somewhere along the way. He'd stuck by her dad's side through thick and thin, through flush years and lean, and was still sticking around ten years after Duke had retired from burglary.

Mallory wished Lance had contacted her. Once upon a time, they'd been close, too. Or as close as a young boy could be to an older almost-sister. While they weren't related, they had lived together for a few years after Polish Paul had sprung Mallory from foster care during her dad's incarceration.

"Well, don't worry, babe. Paul promised to call as soon

as Lance shows up." He exhaled heavily. "Damned kid is going to be the death of him yet."

Mallory wished she had some reassurance to offer, but she didn't. Lance had grown into an angry teen who was determined to buck his father at every turn. He'd shut out all the people who cared for him, all of Duke's crew and her, too. Once upon a time, they'd all been one big happy family—the only family she and Lance had ever known. But time and circumstance seemed to be pulling them all in different directions.

"Just call me when he shows up, okay?" she said.

"And you let me know if you accept Trinity's offer. Working with TSS will look good on your résumé."

"You think?" She swallowed back a sigh. They were back here again. "I kind of thought my endorsement on Trinity's new system would look good on *his* résumé."

Her dad gave a hearty laugh, tossing his head back in a gesture that would have knocked most climbers off their center and sent them gliding toward the floor.

Her dad wasn't most climbers.

"Opal was right. You're getting cocky."

"And that surprises you? I'm *your* daughter." Mallory didn't care for the word *cocky,* but she'd earned the right to be satisfied with her work, as both her dad and Opal knew.

"Watch out, babe. Arrogance has been the downfall of too many good men."

"And women?"

"Job hazard," he said, a little too seriously.

"Is that why you've sicced Opal on me? Are you worried I'm heading for a fall?"

Opal was another of her dad's crew who'd been around for longer than time—although Mallory would never have dared to phrase it that way to Opal. On the down side of fifty-five, Opal liberally contributed to her plastic surgeon's portfolio in an effort not to look older than forty.

So far she was succeeding admirably.

But even more importantly, Opal was the closest thing that Mallory had ever had to a mother. Not that she would have ever said that to Opal's face, either. The term connoted an age difference that simply wasn't part of Opal's vocabulary.

Nevertheless, she'd graciously played the role through the years, stepping in whenever Mallory had needed some motherly advice that Duke's never-ending, constantly-changing stream of girlfriends couldn't provide.

Mallory's own mother had abandoned her husband and infant daughter for an opportunity to perform in a Las Vegas show—her first stop on the road to stardom. Unfortunately, life hadn't cooperated, and she'd wound up dead in a car accident before leaving Vegas for Hollywood.

"I'm not worried you'll take a fall," her dad said. "And I haven't *sicced* Opal on you, as you so eloquently put it. She's just helping you out with your administrative tasks."

"And keeping you informed about the clients I take."

"A job perk."

He delivered that one so matter-of-factly Mallory rolled her eyes. Her dad had never been one to pull any punches.

"Are you telling me you don't need the help? With all the work you've been juggling lately…from where I'm standing, it looks like you should open a real office and hire a staff."

"I have a *real* office. Just because it's in my house doesn't mean it isn't real."

"You have voice mail, a pager and a computer."

"Okay, a *small* office. My space is much better put to use in the workshop." She chanced a glance away from the wall to look at him, suddenly realizing what this conversation was really all about. "The police work is bothering you, isn't it?"

He looked away from the wall, too, meeting her gaze with those inky-black eyes that shouldn't have been able to look warm when he smiled, but did.

At the moment he wasn't smiling.

"You're worried," she said.

"Let's say I'm reserving judgment about your latest career move. You've been consulting for *law enforcement.*" He spoke the words as though they scraped over his tongue.

"I'm a consultant, Dad. I consult."

He still eyed her stoically.

"I have no intention of turning down perfectly good money. Besides, I like the work. I feel like Nancy Drew solving mysteries." She didn't say that she also got a kick out of the police relying on *her.*

"You also enjoy being one of the 'experts' that prosecution calls on for testimony in court?"

She smiled, hoping to lighten the moment. "It makes me feel…*expert.*"

"I'd rather see you focus on normal jobs."

She might have argued that consulting for Jake Trinity wouldn't be anything resembling normal. She didn't. Her dad didn't need to know she'd been so preoccupied with the man that she could see him in memory without even closing her eyes.

Though, in all fairness to her, Jake Trinity had been a good-looking guy with tawny hair and a sculpted bone structure that would look handsome whether he was nineteen or ninety. Ten years ago he'd screamed clean-cut good breeding with his wire-rimmed eyeglasses and preppy name brands.

Mallory remembered thinking he'd been too good-looking to be allowed. Then again, she'd been sixteen at the time and impressionable. Had she not been so impressed with the gorgeous young man who'd popped up on the job unexpectedly, she might never been tempted to approach him.

Nope, time hadn't dimmed that memory. She still recalled every detail of that night with perfect clarity.

The Commercial-Cam Monitoring Network Prototype.

Ten years ago this video surveillance system had been state of the art. One of Innovative's major competitors had paid her dad big bucks to acquire the prototype before the system officially launched onto the market.

The job had been meticulously planned and about as fail-safe as any job could be—they were sort of like security systems and people, never one-hundred-percent perfect. But this particular job had been going off like clockwork, until a very handsome man who shouldn't have been in the building showed up while she secured the egress route for her dad's escape.

Mallory should have hightailed it back up the rope to her own egress route on the roof. She should have radioed Polish Paul and told him she'd been made, so they could have aborted the job. That had been the backup plan. They *always* had a backup plan. Getting out of a building was just as important as getting in, Polish Paul always said.

But Mallory hadn't done either of those things. She'd confronted that handsome young man instead, thinking she could stall him long enough to buy her dad the extra minute and a half he needed to complete the job. And she had. *Almost.*

But *almost* hadn't been good enough. In this instance, *almost* meant that Jake Trinity had gotten to the silent alarm and changed their lives forever.

Almost everyone had gotten out of the building by the time the police had arrived.

Except for her dad.

He'd *lied* and said he'd tripped the alarm. She hadn't believed him, of course. Neither had anyone else. Duke Hunt didn't make those kinds of mundane mistakes. Mallory knew he simply hadn't wanted her to feel guilty about ignoring the backup plan. He hadn't wanted her to feel responsible for him going to prison or for the crew being forced into retirement. And his lie hurt almost as much as knowing she was responsible.

Almost as much as watching him handcuffed and thrown into the back of a police cruiser.

Almost as much as learning that the world she'd always believed perfectly normal wasn't normal at all. To hear the police and the child welfare people tell it, her world was an illegal and morally ugly place.

That had confused Mallory at sixteen.

At twenty-six, it still did.

She was Duke Hunt's beloved daughter, well-loved and cared for. She'd always thought being loved was a good thing whether she'd grown up on the fringes of the underworld or not.

With maturity, she'd come to understand that the real world wasn't quite as black and white as the authorities painted it. The real world was an unpredictable place filled with good guys and bad guys. Not the classic depiction of white hats and black capes, either, but a place where the boundaries between right and wrong were often blurry and the bad guys could be more charming and gallant than the good guys.

No, her upbringing hadn't been conventional, but burglary aside, it hadn't been morally bankrupt either.

Which had led to another life-altering change.

During a visit to the prison where she'd gotten to see her dad through a four-inch-thick sheet of protective glass, she'd been informed that they were all retiring from the family business. The way her dad saw it, four years in prison wasn't such a raw deal after an illustrious twenty-odd-year career. He'd made Mallory and all of his crew promise to turn their lives around and go legitimate.

Thanks to his business acumen and foresight, he'd provided the means for her and his crew to do exactly that. Nowadays, his crew was sitting pretty with legitimate businesses. Polish Paul owned a tattoo parlor; Eddie Gibb a pawn shop. Only Opal, who'd opted to spend her share of the nest egg on a nice house and expensive plastic surgeries, didn't own a business. She worked as Eddie Gibb's office manager instead, squeezing work for Mallory into her free time.

All in all, life was good.

Except for this love-hate thing she had for Jake Trinity.

She loved the fact that she and her friends had gone legit. Well, *reasonably* legit. She hated being responsible for making the decision that had changed all their lives.

Both occurrences began and ended with a very self-righteous man she couldn't seem to get out of her head no matter how much time passed. He'd had a dramatic impact on her life, and Mallory had never been able to decide whether to love him or hate him for his interference. Taking this job for TSS would give her the perfect opportunity to decide which it would be.

The way she saw it, Mr. Straight-and-Narrow would benefit from being knocked on his holier-than-thou ass. And if he wound up taking a hard look at his own morals to see if they held up under temptation, then she'd be honored to provide the temptation.

"Damn." Her dad's voice blasted away the image of

Jake Trinity quicker than a bait pack exploding in a rigged safe.

Mallory smiled, released the last handhold and tagged the ceiling to end her climb. ''Hunt Junior rules the day.''

She didn't signal her belay partner, waited instead while her dad scaled the last few feet between them, muscles bunching in his powerful arms, sweat pearling at his salt-and-pepper temples, black eyes flashing.

''Great climb, babe.''

''You, too.''

She liked that about her dad. She'd kicked his butt fair and square, and he appreciated a job well done. Although, truthfully, his chances of winning today hadn't been good. Not only did Mallory have the advantage of thirty-plus years on her side, but her adrenaline was pumping double-time in anticipation of her upcoming consultation.

''You will give some thought to what I said about working for law enforcement.'' He didn't ask, just leveled a steely expression her way. ''Don't let them become your full-time job.''

She nodded.

His expression softened, and she knew he was satisfied. ''Shall we?''

''Let's do it.''

After signaling her belay partner, Mallory kicked off from the wall, stomach lurching at the rush of a ninety-foot drop. The air whizzed past her ears, and she laughed, the excitement as thrilling as the prospect of seeing Jake Trinity again.

2

THE WAY Jake Trinity saw it, Mallory Hunt owed him one
and the time had come to collect. Angling his sport utility
vehicle into a parking spot along the street in front of her
upscale brownstone, he glanced at the dashboard.

Ten fifty-seven.

Three minutes to get upstairs and he'd be right on time
for their eleven o'clock appointment.

Grabbing his briefcase, he stepped out of his SUV into
the bright morning sun just as a low-slung black convertible cruised past him, the driver's ponytail whipping out
on the wind behind her. He quickly pulled in his door so
she didn't take it off as she wheeled into the driveway and
came to a sharp stop with a flash of red brake lights.

Mallory Hunt.

Jake knew her name. He knew a great deal about her,
in fact, mostly from his preliminary research and references from industry associates who'd contracted her services. But he'd never seen her without a ski mask.

Even if he hadn't known her address, he'd have known
instinctively that this was the woman who'd boldly kissed
him ten years ago. He wasn't exactly sure how he knew,
but he did. Even with a sidewalk and a neatly kept yard
between them, he felt the same awareness he had on that
long-ago night, that same chemistry, as if every nerve in
his body had been wired to react to her just by being in
the same vicinity.

It was crazy, really, but the moment slowed to a crawl, his every sense heightening as her door swung wide and his mystery woman emerged.

A slim booted foot touched the pavement, and Jake's gaze traveled up the very shapely length of bare leg as she stepped from the car, the shorts she wore giving him a choice shot of sleek thighs.

She was as delicate as he remembered, but that was where memory ended—the black coveralls she'd worn ten years ago hadn't molded her curves anywhere close to the way these khaki short-shorts and skin-tight T-shirt did now. The thin—wet?—cotton hugged a trim waist and full breasts in a way that made him drag his gaze over her appreciatively.

Her hair had been pulled back from her face in a thick black ponytail that fell halfway down her back. She swung the door shut, an efficient, graceful motion that brought the memory of the sensuous way she moved crashing back in vivid detail. Then she turned to him....

Jake stopped breathing.

A decade had passed since he'd crossed paths with this woman. She'd blown into his life for a few minutes and the fallout had left him stunned for years. And yes, resentful of her intrusion into his meticulously planned life.

But he'd never had more than an impression of the woman herself, a faceless memory of bold confidence, a lithe body and sensual movements....

And those eyes.

His breath burned tight in his chest by the time she gazed over the rim of her stylish black sunglasses and looked at him with those clear green eyes.

Eyes that had haunted him for a decade.

Eyes that reminded him of...*the kiss.*

Just the memory sucker punched him in the gut, made

him look deep for some clue whether she knew who he
was, whether she remembered, too. Something about the
way she sized him up convinced him that she did.

After their accidental encounter on that night long ago,
he'd made every effort to find out who she was, but he
hadn't known if she'd done the same. He couldn't predict
what a woman like Mallory Hunt would do in any given
situation, because she was unlike anyone he'd ever met.
He hadn't made the acquaintance of any professional
thieves at the private schools he'd attended, nor anywhere
in his upper-middle-class upbringing. Mallory Hunt was
an enigma to him. She had been ten years ago. She was
today.

Forcing himself into action, he slammed the door shut,
engaged the alarm and circled his SUV, fiercely containing
his reaction to this woman. He'd been down this road before and the consequences had turned his life upside down.

He probably shouldn't have contacted her, should have
realized their past history would interfere with his agenda.
But contacting her had been the only logical thing to do.

His latest security system had the potential to launch his
company into the big leagues. Trinity Security Services
employed a staff of top-notch engineers who could only
test his system from the viewpoint of top-notch engineers.
But meeting Mallory Hunt had taught Jake that security
systems weren't about securing a premise, but about keeping the bad guys out, which meant he needed a bad guy
to test his system.

Or a bad girl.

He stared at one right now and couldn't help feeling as
though he'd come full circle. After all, Mallory Hunt had
been the reason he'd become interested in the field of security and commercial protection in the first place.

Given their history, Jake supposed he shouldn't be surprised to find himself so curious to see her up close. She was exquisite, with features as delicate as the rest of her and a face dominated by that lush mouth and those clear eyes.

Meeting him at the corner of her driveway, she extended a hand. "Well, you've certainly grown up, Jake Trinity."

He'd never heard her speak, and her voice filtered through him, richer and more sensual than his imagination could have invented, a sexy voice that fit her to a T.

What was it about her that kept bringing to mind sex?

"So have you." There, the situation was on the table. She recognized him. He recognized her. They were on level ground.

"Are you always so punctual?"

"Yes." He glanced at his watch as he reached for her hand. A minute to spare. "Do you always cut your appointments so close?"

"I'm always right on time."

He supposed perfect timing would be a necessary skill in her line of work, but he didn't comment as she slipped tapered fingers against his, and the feel of her warm skin connected.

As an electrical engineer, Jake knew about conductivity, and Mallory Hunt's touch flowed through him like a current. They'd only touched once before and sparks had flown then, too.

He thought he saw a flicker of surprise in those thickly fringed eyes, but her expression never changed. He wanted to feel detached, professional. He didn't. The urge to lift her hand to his lips and press a kiss to her soft skin was strong, even though such an absurdly romantic gesture had no place in a business meeting.

Especially this meeting.

If she noticed how he seemed to be drinking her in, she

didn't react, simply withdrew her hand and said, "I shouldn't get too close. I smell like a goat."

He laughed. Even in a sweaty T-shirt and wrinkled shorts, there was nothing goat-like about this woman. "A workout?"

"Of sorts. Come on in."

Jingling her keys, she trod lightly up the stone steps to her front door, and try though Jake might not to focus on her gently rounded bottom and the toned muscle playing along her thighs, he found himself staring.

And wondering what she'd done to work up that sweat.

He might no longer be a testosterone-filled teen who'd gotten a hard-on from kissing a sexy thief, but his reaction to Mallory Hunt was as extreme as ever. Apparently his reaction wasn't about being caught up in the excitement of a dangerous situation. His reaction had to do with the woman herself.

Hmm. Looked like a reassessment of his position was in order. Especially since he meant to stick very close to her while she worked to troubleshoot his system.

If she accepted the job after she heard his unusual terms.

He'd convince her to accept.

She owed him.

When she retrieved a wireless remote from her purse to disable what he imagined was a top-of-the-line home-security unit, she distracted him with purely professional interest. What sort of system did a security specialist with Mallory Hunt's credentials use to protect her inner sanctum?

He presumed a woman who knew all the industry tricks would secure her place tighter than Fort Knox. Especially a home she obviously took great pride in. And one glance inside her spacious town house revealed that she lived in the same classy style she drove. Jake didn't know much about interior design, but he did know style and upscale elegance when he saw it. It stared him full in the face right now.

Mallory Hunt struck him as the epitome of a contemporary woman, a woman who boldly managed life on her own terms. While the luxury of her home didn't surprise him, the coziness did. With its tall windows, sunny yellow walls and sleek marble floor, Mallory Hunt's inner sanctum possessed a charming, welcoming feel that struck him as almost…*homey.*

Moving past her into the foyer, he glanced at the books lying open on a coffee table in front of the sofa, more on the end table. Sheet music covered the music desk of the white baby grand piano positioned between two floor-to-ceiling windows in the room's far corner. A latte mug with a red lipstick circle rested on the mantel of a hall tree, as though she'd gulped down a last swallow of coffee before running out the door.

Jake wasn't exactly sure what he'd expected from a former thief gone legit, but homey wasn't it.

After locking her front door, she tossed her keys down and shrugged off her purse with a move that drew his gaze to the way filmy white cotton stretched across firm breasts. Hanging her purse over the banister, she turned to him and narrowed her gaze.

"Listen, Jake Trinity. I've got someplace to be right after we're through here. Do you mind if I get ready while we talk?"

He shook his head, not surprised she didn't conduct business in any ordinary manner. In his limited dealings with Mallory Hunt, he hadn't found anything ordinary about her. And he really didn't care how they conducted business as long as he got what he wanted.

"Hang on a second. Let me grab your proposal…." Her

voice trailed off as she headed through the living room and disappeared from sight. "I've written down some questions I want to ask you."

"I think we can come up with an arrangement that will be advantageous to us both."

"I think so, too," she said, reappearing in the living room, carrying a glossy folder with his company's logo.

She smiled. But this wasn't an impersonal smile of welcome. This was a full-fledged dazzling smile that nearly blinded him.

The effect was nothing short of devastating. The muscles gathered low in his gut in a purely physical response that was absurd in its intensity. He'd come today prepared to talk business, to convince this woman that she owed him so she'd agree to the unconventional terms of his job.

He hadn't come prepared for a full-scale sensual assault.

Unfortunately, he couldn't think of a damned thing to say that might reassert his control over the moment, so he simply followed her when she motioned him upstairs and led him into... "Your bedroom?"

She only nodded before pausing to flip open the folder casually and glance inside.

Okay. A business meeting in the bedroom. He'd come to this meeting today expecting the unexpected. No problem.

Her bedroom was certainly roomy enough to host a meeting. The second floor of her home boasted windows as large as those downstairs, only these windows weren't covered with sheer draperies. Through the lattice of magnolia trees outside, Jake could see the wide expanse of green city park across the street.

The furnishings were as upscale contemporary as downstairs, elegant and minimal, yet still creating a very comfortable feel. And her bed...

He skimmed his gaze over the neatly made pewter-frame bed, not at all amused by how the sight of the silk comforter and plush pillows knocked loose a few more of his brain cells.

"You brought the specs for your system, didn't you?" she asked, not bothering to glance at him as she moved to an open doorway and flipped on a light.

"Yes." He could always spread out the prints on the bed.

But no sooner had he formed the thought than Mallory disappeared inside an adjoining room.

A bathroom?

Jake glanced inside, watched her set the folder down on the vanity and tug the band from her ponytail. Shaking her head, she loosed a sheet of straight black hair that fell nearly to her waist, glinting like glass beneath the track lighting.

His breath caught hard. He was beginning to get an idea of her definition of "getting ready." And he knew right then she was testing his mettle, maybe even trying to shock him. He wanted to know why.

"You want to have our business meeting in the bathroom?"

She glanced back over her shoulder, lips pursed thoughtfully. "Can you handle it?"

Ten years ago, he should have restrained this woman and sounded the alarm. For a long time he'd regretted not doing that. He'd resented that meeting her—however unintentionally on both their parts—had screwed with his whole life.

But as he met her gaze now, recognized the challenge there, he found himself responding exactly as he had back then.

He wanted to see how far she would go.

"I'll enjoy it."

She smiled, silently acknowledging that he'd picked up the gauntlet. Then she disappeared from sight.

Jake drew a deep breath, mentally warned his body to behave and followed.

Her bathroom was as tastefully decorated as the rest of her home, with a double vanity and a corner shower with wall jets.

He almost asked if she expected them to talk while she showered, but as she was removing fresh towels from the linen closet, he figured he had his answer.

Setting his briefcase on the floor, he leaned back against the vanity, steeling himself for her next move.

It would be a good one, no doubt.

He only hoped he could think clearly beneath an assault of this magnitude. He was barely hanging on already.

No twenty-six-year-old woman of his acquaintance had ever oozed confidence like this one. He'd recognized her boldness ten years ago and he saw it again now. Understanding the unusual circumstances of her life explained a little, but Jake didn't think circumstances had everything to do with Mallory Hunt.

Then she dropped the towels onto the toilet lid and raised her arms to pull the T-shirt over her head and he didn't think again. He was reduced to folding his arms across his chest and trying to look completely unfazed by the sight of pale breasts swelling above a white cotton bra.

"I read your proposal, Jake," she said calmly, as though stripping in front of a man she'd only met once before—under very dubious circumstances—was a commonplace event. "It was pretty straightforward. You want me to troubleshoot your newest system. The…what was it called?"

"The Sentex 2000."

Her wadded-up T-shirt sailed inches past his face to land on the nearby hamper before she propped a foot onto the toilet lid to untie her boot.

"Right. The Sentex 2000. You're testing your prototype locally?"

"I have several in place with different clients of mine. I'm exposing it to a variety of scenarios."

"Good idea."

He was glad she thought so because he wasn't convinced that standing here while she stripped qualified as one of his better ideas. Not with her breasts jiggling as she toed off a boot then stripped her sock away to reveal a slim white foot with neatly polished red toenails.

Then she lifted the other and began the process all over again.

"I assume you know how I operate, Jake."

By stripping for potential clients until they're horny idiots who'll agree to anything?

"You try to infiltrate the system," he said, managing to sound reasonably composed as she unbuttoned her fly and started rocking back and forth while pushing the khaki shorts over her hips. Down, down, down....

"There's no try."

"Excuse me?"

Bending over to drag the shorts away, she slanted him a glance from beneath her hair. "There's no *try* to it. I infiltrate your system. Then I tell you where the holes are."

"Always?"

She straightened, giving him a view of her in profile, and no matter how much he wanted to keep his gaze on her face, there was simply no way he could resist glancing down at the sleek expanse of her pale curves. Firm breasts were clad in white cotton, her trim waist playing peekaboo

with all that shiny hair, her smooth stomach and gently
rounded hips barely holding up a teeny white thong.

He swallowed hard.

He was getting hard.

No matter how deeply he breathed to dispel the tightness
in his chest. No matter how much he reminded himself
that he'd acquired restraint in the years since their last
encounter. His reminders were nothing more than desperate, self-delusional bullshit while he stood staring at the
tight curve of her bottom and those long, long legs.

"Do you believe in a fail-safe system, Jake?"

Her tone made it sound as if a fail-safe system was
something out of a fairy tale. "As a matter of fact, I
don't."

"Good. I hate to disappoint my clients."

"I don't see much chance of that if you conduct all your
consultations in your bathroom, Ms. Hunt. In fact, it would
explain your impeccable references. You have a lot of
happy former clients out there."

"Call me Mallory, please." She chuckled, a low, silky
sound that purred through their close quarters as if it were
alive. "That's because I'm good at what I do."

Damned straight. This was a strip show of the highest
caliber.

She gifted him with a full shot of her back, the fall of
shiny hair, her heart-shaped bottom with that silky little
strap disappearing between her cheeks. Leaning into the
shower to turn on the water, she bent just enough to taunt
him with a glimpse of exactly where that little strap was
hiding.

Unfolding his arms, Jake braced his hands on the vanity,
every drop of blood in his body rushing south so fast he
actually felt dizzy.

For a man who hadn't had sex in…he dredged his memory for the last time he'd been involved. Damn, had it been *that* long? No wonder he was crumbling under this assault.

Although he didn't think anything could have prepared him for Mallory Hunt. No doubt she'd planned it that way.

Which led back to his original question…why?

"Shall we talk details?" She straightened and turned to him, dipping her head in a sexy motion, flinging her hair over her shoulder as she reached around her back….

Her bra sprang open and full breasts spilled out, pale, perfect, the deep-rose nipples aiming at him and proving that he wasn't the only one affected by her well-aimed assault.

Jake supposed he should have felt some consolation. He didn't. He found himself gripping the vanity instead, when she arched back to slide the straps down her arms.

The bra went whizzing by his face toward the hamper. It landed on the T-shirt and hung for a suspended moment before falling to the floor.

"I have some conditions that will have to be met before we can come to an agreement," he said, amazed that he actually got the words out. "But please, ladies first."

She inclined her head graciously and then fired the next volley…she bent over again.

This time she leaned forward as she slipped off her thong. She pushed the scrap of fabric down her thighs, along shapely calves. Her breasts plumped forward and her hair swept in front of her in a heavy fall of black silk, shielding his view for a tantalizing instant…until she retrieved her panties and stood up, unselfconsciously and quite breathtakingly naked.

Jake sucked in a breath of humid air.

Unfortunately, it didn't help. Not when Mallory Hunt was a vision from a fantasy with the steam curling around her, airbrushing her slender curves with mist.

His heart pounded. His blood thundered in his ears so loudly that he almost missed hearing her when she said, "I'll talk loudly so you can hear me above the water."

No problem, as long as *she* did the talking. His voice was trapped somewhere below the breath that had solidified in his throat. It had been way too long since he'd had sex, and Jake made a note to pencil in a reminder on his schedule.

Find a date.

He'd been a fool to ignore his needs for so long that he could barely breathe when faced with a naked beauty who was bent on taunting him. While this wasn't the first time he'd been forced to admit that he ignored his needs too often, it was the first time he'd ever found his control so seriously threatened.

He considered challenging her to see if there was an offer beneath her boldness. But Mallory Hunt clearly had an agenda and he wasn't taking one step in her direction until he understood what it was.

This woman was fire, and he'd been burned before.

"Okay, Jake. Here's the deal in a nutshell. You pick what you think is your most secure property. I'll research your system, determine where the weaknesses are, prove my position by infiltrating your system and then submit a summary so you can address the problems."

She slid the shower door open as he realized exactly what it was about her tone that he found so very intriguing.

There was no doubt in her voice. None. Mallory was completely confident in her abilities, just as she'd been while confronting him that dark night long ago.

He waited until she stepped inside and closed the sliding glass door before he played his hand. "I'll pick my most secure property, you get inside and take me with you to show me how you do it."

He saw her pause and experienced a surge of satisfaction that he'd surprised her. A definite first in their limited acquaintance.

She recovered quickly, though, and he heard her bubbling laughter over the running water as she stepped into the spray, tipping her head to wet that magnificent hair.

Until she responded, Jake had absolutely nothing to counter or debate, so he stood there and enjoyed the show.

Steam billowed around her, misted the glass and showcased her beautiful curves. The beige tile cast her pale body and dark hair in soft relief, drawing his attention to the graceful way she lifted her arms, reached for a bottle from a shelf.

He'd tried to anticipate every eventuality for today's meeting. But of all the unexpected things he'd expected, playing spectator while this slim beauty showered hadn't even made the list.

"I operate alone, Jake," she finally said.

"You didn't ten years ago."

"True, but I'm in a different line of work now."

Their encounter that night had sent both their lives spiraling off into entirely new directions. It had taken him a long time to make peace with the changes to his career plan. How had she felt about her own?

He didn't ask, just said, "I insist."

"Really." No question mark.

"Really."

"Why?"

A simple question, but one that surprised him. "I don't trust you."

He thought he heard her chuckle over the running water.

"But *you* contacted me, Jake Trinity."

"Yes, I did. I researched your references and looked into your business dealings. I understand you operate a legitimate business now and your services come highly recommended. But I also discovered that most of your clients don't realize how you honed your skills."

"I've never kept my background a secret."

He didn't doubt her. This woman impressed him as someone skilled in turning disadvantage to advantage. She was manipulating the situation to her advantage right now and he didn't know why. But she had a reason for putting on this show, for lathering her long hair with slow, sinuous motions, arms raised, body displayed through sheets of water and steamy mist.

She definitely had a reason for challenging him to combine business with the pleasure of watching her. His body was on red alert, and the conversation was the only thing helping him maintain control, forcing his focus on something other than the tumble of dark hair and lather playing over her sleek skin.

"Mallory, I'll be hiring you to infiltrate a prototype of the Sentex 2000 that's in place on one of my client's properties. They'll be allowing you to break in at my request. My reputation is on the line here. You must understand my need for caution."

"I do. But I'm guessing you don't have a clear idea of what it takes to infiltrate a security system. Trust me when I say it requires a skill that doesn't lend itself to spectators."

Here it was, and Jake went for it. "I don't want to be a spectator. I want to assist. Show me what to do and I'll do it."

"You want a course in thievery 101." Still no question mark.

"Yes."

She only reached for a bath sponge and started a whole new show by working lather over her neck and shoulders.

Jake followed her motions, the continued level of excitement wearing at his restraint. He found it increasingly difficult to concentrate when the memory of how she'd felt pressed up against him collided with the sight of all that bare skin. He struggled to stay sharp, because staying sharp was crucial to dealing with this woman.

"If I agree to your conditions, what exactly do you think you'll gain?"

"A couple of things," he said, shifting his position to ease up the seam that was biting into his crotch. "First is that I'll be with you when you infiltrate my client's property. I can offer them my personal assurance that their interests will be protected because I'll be overseeing you personally."

"And?"

"I want to see how you operate. You offer a unique perspective on security. I want to benefit from your experience and bring that knowledge with me when I design my systems."

The soapy bath sponge continued a leisurely path down her arms, graceful swirls of motion that drew his gaze to the way her back arched slightly, thrusting those incredible breasts forward, the rosebud nipples spearing through the lather.

He shifted position again, trying to ease the pressure of a tight seam.

"Are you willing to pay my fee?"

"I am—even though you quoted me a number that starts forty percent above what you charged my competitors."

She turned to face him, aiming another salvo with a full-frontal shot of all that soapy skin, that smooth stomach and the barely-there dark curls peeking out between her thighs. "Inflation."

Right. Even if he hadn't heard the amusement in her

voice, Jake knew better. Unfortunately, he was still no closer to understanding her agenda. With the dramatic decrease in both his willpower and IQ beneath her sexy assault, he wouldn't be satisfying his curiosity any time soon.

"Does this mean you'll take the job?" he asked out of sheer desperation to distract himself as that bath sponge wound a path between her thighs.

"Why should I? You've already told me you don't trust me. Think about all the extra work training you will mean for me."

He'd thought about it—long and hard, in fact. Her extra work meant his, too. He also thought about just telling her outright that she owed him, tipping his hand and letting the cards fall where they may.

But Mallory Hunt couldn't know that she'd cost him his job on that long-ago night. Jake should have tripped the silent alarm. He hadn't. He'd been too bowled over by her kiss. He'd been stumped as to why such a sexy young woman—and the instant their lips had met he'd known she was young—would participate in a burglary. Any logical explanation had been so far beyond the comprehension of his upper-middle-class value system that he'd been shell-shocked into indecision.

The rational side of his brain had insisted he report the break-in. The more impulsive side hadn't been able to get past the fact that sounding the alarm would have meant such a sexy young woman would likely end up in prison.

While the two sides of his brain had warred, fate had intervened and made the decision for him. Someone, he assumed the security guard, had sounded the alarm and the police had shown up and arrested one of the burglars—not her, he'd found out later.

The company president hadn't wanted explanations.

He'd wanted an employee who would put the company's best interests first. Jake didn't blame him.

As a result of meeting Mallory Hunt, he'd lost his job, his internship, his scholarship, a decent reference and any hope of a future with Innovative Engineering.

As his father had been golfing buddies with the company president, the real reason for his dismissal hadn't become part of his permanent record. Mallory Hunt couldn't know the details, and now didn't seem like the best time to tip his hand. Erection aside, the rational half of his brain had brought him here today. He needed this woman's expertise, felt she owed him a favor, but he didn't want to show a soft underbelly by letting her think he held a grudge.

"You should take my job because working together will be mutually beneficial. TSS will be a strong reference. My business is well respected in the industry."

She exhaled a laugh that was more exasperation than amusement. "What is it with you men?"

Jake didn't know what other man she was referring to and he didn't care. He wasn't finished yet. "I was going to say that your endorsement of my new security system will be good for the Sentex 2000. See, mutually beneficial."

Not the strongest of arguments, but the most logical to his way of thinking. Jake braced himself to counter her objections, mentally sifted through rebuttals that might establish his case.

What he didn't expect was Mallory to say, "Okay. It's a deal. You pay my exorbitant fee and I'll infiltrate the system of your choice and take you with me as my assistant."

She slid open the shower door, heedless of the drizzle spraying out from the wall jets as she extended her hand.

Jake had the wild thought that the last thing in the world he needed to do right now was touch this woman, but reason wasn't priority here—sealing the deal was.

Pushing away from the vanity, he swallowed hard when the seam of his slacks bit hard into his crotch. He schooled his expression and closed the distance between them.

But Jake knew before his fingers slid around hers that this was nothing more than a ploy. Mallory was testing his limits again, pushing him. To see if she could shock him? Or to get him close enough to...*what?*

He didn't know. He only knew that with her hair slicked back he could see her features more clearly than ever before. He stared down into her face, the perfect forehead, the elegant slash of her brows, the creamy skin, the high cheekbones, and knew a hunger for this woman more intense than anything he'd ever known before.

Then she lifted her gaze to his. Despite the water droplets clinging to her lashes and the lush landscape of moist skin between them, the challenge in those clear green eyes was so reminiscent of ten years ago...

Only this time *he* kissed her.

3

JAKE TRINITY had known how to kiss ten years ago, but the past decade had honed his skill to the point where Mallory forgot to breathe. His mouth possessed hers with a serious deliberation that made her knees grow weak, made an eager tenderness fill her breasts and draw her nipples into peaks.

She'd intended to taunt the man until he'd lost control and couldn't keep his hands off her. Well, his hands were on her now, but there was nothing about the fingers he angled beneath her jaw that suggested a loss of anything.

Jake Trinity's kiss was all about hunger, all about resolve, all about taking what he wanted. Deliberate. Thorough. As though he'd spent ten long years deciding how he might kiss her if the opportunity had presented itself. As though he'd meant to make the most of the moment if it did.

Mission accomplished.

He'd scattered her thoughts so completely that it took him driving his tongue into her mouth for Mallory finally to pull her thoughts together enough to react.

The best she could come up with was a sigh, one of those lips-parting-in-abandon, open-mouthed numbers that always made her laugh when she saw them portrayed in movies.

She hadn't believed women *really* felt that way.

Well, women like *her*, anyway. Confident, assertive

women who didn't have a problem taking what they wanted from life.

Or from a man.

But she felt that way right now. Boy, oh boy, did she.

She remembered exactly why she'd kissed Jake Trinity ten years ago instead of following the egress plan. Yes, she'd wanted to buy her dad time, but she couldn't deny that she'd also noticed how gorgeous her unexpected intruder had been, which had inspired her particular method of stalling.

He'd reminded her of a lion with his dark-blond hair, tanned skin and brawny body. He'd been tall—but not too tall, about six feet she'd guessed—but that sense of power about his strong shoulders and wide chest had made him seem...*solid.* Yet he'd moved easily, gracefully, as though he had his size thoroughly under control.

Jake Trinity all grown up wasn't what Mallory had been expecting. Nor was her reaction to him.

Water dripped from her face to flavor their kiss, bathing their tongues in liquid warmth that tasted of their mouths combined. A taste that had lingered in her memory barely remembered—until now when she tasted it again and realized just how firmly embedded he'd been in her consciousness.

Pressing her hands against his chest, she slipped her fingers beneath his jacket. She explored the feel of hard muscle through his shirt and traced the sculpted hollows as though she wanted to learn him by heart, uncaring that her wet hands and the shower spray were trashing his pristine dry-cleaning job.

And when she came across his tie, an accessory she'd thought conservative at first glance, she recognized the anchor it offered. Slipping her fingers around the expensive silk, she drew it down, down…forcing him to lean forward and his mouth to slant across hers even harder.

He explored the curve of her jaw with strong fingers, trailed them down her throat, and for a heart-stopping instant she thought he would continue moving downward, touch her aching breasts to feed this growing need inside her.

But ever the gentleman, he explored the pulse beating at the base of her throat, the sensitive hollow where neck met shoulder while awareness coursed through her with an intensity that made her burn.

No, Jake Trinity wasn't what she'd expected at all.

He didn't seem to mind that she held him trapped with his tie and met his tongue, stroke for devouring stroke, breath for clashing breath.

Her reaction to him wasn't what she'd expected, either.

Mallory had a plan to bring this man to his knees. She'd get him out of her system then leave him before he even knew what had hit him. But right now, with the water crashing on her back, the steam caressing her body until she felt every inch of her naked skin so achy beneath his strong fingers, her plan seemed less about satisfying vengeance than desire.

"Join me." She whispered the words against his open mouth, surprised by the husky intensity of her voice. Running her tongue over his lower lip, she chased the words with a bold stroke that reestablished some of her control.

But Jake didn't break their kiss, either. He nibbled his way along her upper lip, his hot velvet mouth nipping greedily, sending the most exquisite tingles shooting through her, and making a total lie out of her control.

"I thought you had some place to be shortly."

"I lied."

To her surprise, he chuckled, a burst of warm sound

against her mouth. He broke their kiss and she eased up on his tie, letting him lift his head. But she didn't relinquish her grip entirely. She liked knowing she could drag his mouth back down to hers when she chose.

"Why?"

"So I could get naked in front of you."

She wanted to put a dent in his composure, but he only inclined his tawny head in acknowledgment and slipped his wire-rimmed glasses from his nose. She watched as he snapped the arms into place and dropped them into his jacket pocket, seemingly unconcerned with the condition of his clothes, which showed the effects of her exploration in a big way.

Then he met her gaze, and she was surprised to find that staring into his brown eyes without the shield of clear plastic lenses and wire frames was an entirely different experience.

He had warm steady eyes, the rich brown shade an extension of his tawny hair and tanned skin, a color that added to her impression that he glowed golden from the inside out.

He eyed her, as though carefully considering her offer. His calm deliberation threw her. He shouldn't be so in control after the hot kiss they'd shared. He should be a little raw around the edges right now.

Like she was.

Mallory had no doubt he wanted her. One glimpse at the erection spoiling the tailored line of his slacks proved that beyond question, but he was far too in control of himself for her liking.

"You're testing me," he said.

She felt foolishly fluttery beneath his gaze. And standing here naked before his fully clothed self, she felt very much like an errant child who'd been caught with her hand in the cookie jar.

"Does that bother you, Jake?" she injected a level of calm she wasn't feeling into her voice. "I want to see what you're made of."

"You want to see how far you can push me."

"Are you hoping to call my bluff?"

He shook his head, sending thick tawny hair across his brow. "No."

"No?"

"I don't think you're bluffing."

Before she realized what he was about, his hand surrounded her breast, lightly abrading her skin with callused fingertips. Her nipple puckered and her breath hitched, an audible gasp that echoed above the running water and made him smile.

Pressing his advantage, he squeezed her nipple between his thumb and forefinger. A ribbon of heat shot straight to that sensitive place between her thighs. She sucked in another gulp of air that made his smile grow even wider.

"I'm not the only one here discovering my limits, am I?" he asked, his voice as sultry and sure as deep silk.

She didn't answer, was too busy breathing through that grasping pulse between her thighs. But she found that she liked the way he wasn't mowed down by her invitation. She might be standing here naked, and he might want her, but Jake Trinity was still thinking on his feet, questioning her motives, not willing to jump in until he satisfied his curiosity.

She found that rather…*stimulating*.

"Am I, Mallory?"

He pinched her nipple again, making her grow wet in a way that had nothing to do with the eight shower jets behind her.

"No." She sounded just the tiniest bit resentful and that seemed to amuse him, too.

"Do you always mix business with pleasure?"

"No," she replied honestly. "Only when it suits me."

"And I suit you?"

She laughed, an attempt to regain her equilibrium. "I'm surprised you have to ask me that question. I kissed you ten years ago, remember?"

"I thought you were trying to stall me, or distract me."

"I was." She took another deep breath against the way he was thumbing her nipple, raising her body temperature with each idle stroke. "But I'd never have come up with the idea if I hadn't found you attractive."

"So which was it, stall or distract?"

Each lazy stroke made that need sizzle low in her belly and her knees grow a little weaker. "Both."

"You succeeded."

She also liked that he admitted it openly. No pretenses. No delicate male ego needing to be propped up with lies. "Am I distracting you now?"

"Yes."

"Good."

"Am I stalling you?" he asked.

"Yes, but I don't understand why. You want me."

He inclined his head in a gesture she found almost regal in its certainty. "I do."

"Then why resist?"

"I'm not. I just haven't decided to take you up on your offer yet. I want to understand what you hope to accomplish."

With her fingers wrapped around his tie, she forced him to lower his head until she could whisper in his ear. "Orgasm."

The effect of that word was visible. His expensive suit

didn't conceal the way his chest rose and fell with a ragged breath, didn't hide the shudder that rocked his body and brought to mind an image of a big cat purring.

She wanted to press against him, feel the contrast of fine silk and hard muscle against her naked skin. She wanted to feel the vibration when his breath rumbled deep in his chest. She wanted to become intimately acquainted with the erection that kept drawing her gaze, fascinating her with its sheer proportions.

She wanted this man a little too much.

Loosening her grip on his tie, she let him retreat, put some much-needed distance between them.

"How about following your impulse, Jake? Let's finish what we started ten years ago."

"Do you think you can combine business with pleasure and not sacrifice one for the other?"

"There's no *think* about it."

He arched a tawny brow and those warm eyes regarded her steadily. "You don't expect me to be much of a challenge."

"Why should you be? We're attracted to each other. We have chemistry. Unlike the last time we met, we're both of consenting ages and uninvolved. Do you have something against having fun? I think we'll be good together."

"You know for a fact I'm uninvolved?"

He was still trying to gauge her, and she saw no reason to withhold what he wanted. He'd been equally forthcoming. "It's standard procedure for me to research potential clients."

"Do you usually find out about their personal lives?"

"Not usually. I wanted to know about you. I was surprised when you contacted me. I wanted to figure out if you knew I was the woman inside the warehouse that night.''

''The *thief* inside the warehouse, you mean.''

She conceded with a nod. ''The thief.''

Mallory recognized his pleasure in the way he schooled his expression to conceal it, in the way he steeled those wide shoulders as if defending himself from the effect she had on him. He liked that she didn't shy from the truth, and that she'd made the effort to learn about him, whether he admitted it aloud or not.

''Do you know what I found out about you, Jake?'' When he didn't reply, she continued. ''I found out that you're on the fast track to a heart attack.''

''You think so?''

''I do.''

She'd also learned that he'd dated quite a number of very beautiful and eligible women, but none of his relationships ever lasted long. ''I want to know if all work and no play makes Jake a dull boy.''

Jake frowned and Mallory would have bet the top-end fee she'd quoted him that he'd heard this accusation before.

And hadn't liked it one bit.

She pressed her advantage. ''I also found out you vote in every election, even the primaries, and volunteer at the polls. You always buy from the neighborhood kids to support their school fund-raisers, and TSS sponsors an impressive roster of Little League teams. You're a perfectly upstanding moral citizen.''

Self-righteous was more like it, as Mallory had learned firsthand ten years ago, but she kept that thought to herself. She didn't want even to hint that she might hold a grudge and interject that sort of baggage into their relationship.

''Climbing into the shower with a woman of my moral

fiber will be a whole new experience for you. An adventure."

To her surprise his frown faded and he laughed, a sound of such genuine amusement that *she* frowned. "Why do you need me to prove myself? Is it because you're trying to convince yourself I'm worthy?"

He squeezed her nipple again. Her sex clenched in response and she trembled.

"Why does it bother you that you want me, Mallory?"

There was no denying his assertion. Her breasts had grown heavy and tight. Her nipples speared toward his hand, begging for attention. Her knees were so weak she'd be swaying like a drunk if not for his hand on her, a point of contact every nerve in her body seemed wired to.

But how could he know about her conflict? Did he sense it? Or was she not nearly so composed as she'd hoped to be?

"I kissed you, remember?" She sounded defensive but hadn't meant to, which argued strongly that she was revealing a good bit more than she'd intended. This man was blowing all her intentions straight to hell. Not good.

"I've been remembering your kiss for ten years."

His admission was a whole lot more than a taunting declaration. There was substance to those words, an emotional context that seemed to come easily to him, but made her question exactly what he meant.

When had he remembered? In the light of day, when he could feel smug for catching a thief? Or at night in the dark, where they'd first encountered each other and kissed? Or did he think about her at any odd hour, as she often thought about him?

Stepping back, Mallory removed herself from his line of fire, her breast sliding from his grasp. Uncomfortable with the direction her thoughts were taking, she needed to figure out why she was getting contemplative. She needed to regroup.

Leaning into the spray, she shut off the water and considered how to refocus and regain control of this seduction. She didn't want to be distracted by her conflicting feelings for him right now. She wanted to savor the sensations he coaxed from her body, wanted to carry out her sexy revenge and work this man out of her system once and for all.

But the thought had no sooner crossed her mind than he grabbed her, his big powerful arms lashing around her as he dragged her out of the shower before she had a chance to react.

Suddenly he swung her up into his arms, anchoring her against his chest, heedless of the water sluicing all over him.

"I'll take you up on your offer."

Mallory didn't have a chance to respond before they were in motion. She slipped her arms around his neck to steady herself as he maneuvered her out of the bathroom.

The man knew exactly where he was heading. Without another word he strode across her suite, deposited her in a wet bundle in the middle of her bed. But he didn't join her. He stood there, staring down at her with those serious eyes.

"Got condoms?" he asked.

Mallory rolled to the opposite side of the bed, not caring that her hair dripped all over the silk comforter. She pulled open the night table drawer to reveal the variety of condoms she'd stored there with the specific intention of inviting him to visit. Not that she'd admit that aloud. Let him think she needed to keep a bulk supply handy, which seemed particularly significant since he apparently didn't have one on him.

"A buffet of protection." She'd heard the line in a movie once and it seemed to satisfy him. He nodded and shrugged off his jacket with a casual roll of those broad shoulders.

Grabbing a few of the foil packets, she tossed them onto her pillows before scooting back down on the bed. His gaze never left her, and Mallory found herself feeling very naked, a physical sensation that made every inch of her bare skin tingle in the air, made each drip from her wet hair glide down her back in slow motion.

"Let me help." She preferred participation to playing the spectator.

Some flicker in his gaze made her guess that her request pleased him. He took a step toward the bed, occupying himself with the buttons on his cuffs, while she tackled his tie.

She rose to her knees, and they were suddenly so close she could feel the heat radiating from his skin, even through his shirt. A hint of some sexy aftershave mingled with the scent that was all him—masculine, scrumptious male—an ambrosia that penetrated her senses and added to the experience of this man.

Even kneeling on the bed, the top of her head only reached his chin and she had to tip her head back to look into his face. He had a striking face, all strong planes and angles, a face saved from true ruggedness by the sculpted lines of his mouth and those soulful brown eyes.

His body, however, wasn't spared the same fate. After his shirt and tie had been relegated to a heap on the floor, Mallory was treated to the sight of that chest in all its glory as he dragged the undershirt over his head, a breathtaking display of shifting muscle and masculine brawn.

There was nothing small about this man. Not his broad,

broad shoulders. Not his powerful arms. Not even his hands, which were long and square-fingered and strong.

He was rugged in a way that was all grace, as if all his coarse edges had been buffed away. Or maybe it was simply that his golden skin and hair made him seem that way.

But something about the sight of his naked chest made her feel her own nakedness more keenly than ever. Perhaps it was anticipation that heightened her senses. She wanted to feel that hot tanned skin close, the crisp blond hairs brushing her nipples, that lean waist beneath her curious fingers.

Her hands trembled as she reached for his belt.

He assisted by unfastening his button and zipper and then he was shoving his slacks down. His hands tangled with hers as they maneuvered his erection from its soft cotton prison, both of them stunned into a speechlessness so silent it was reverent.

Ten years of waiting had been long enough to build the expectation to the breaking point. And she certainly felt close to the edge as he dragged his underwear and socks away, treating her to an up close and personal view of the whole package.

Wow. Her heart did this crazy sort of flip-flopping thing, missing a beat entirely. Jake Trinity was almost too gorgeous to be real and suddenly the impressive roster of women he'd dated made sense. Women would be attracted to this man. Just as she'd been. He was nearly too gorgeous, too masculine, too larger-than-life, but his calm, almost serious demeanor made him seem unaware of his looks and the effect they had on the opposite sex in a way that was just too appealing.

When he shed his glasses, his clothes and his professional persona, the real man emerged, a man who'd been blessed with a body that had been designed for sex. She paused with her hands hovering over his chest, his body heat spanning the distance to sink into her skin like a laser.

"May I?" she asked, although she didn't expect him to deny her. But there was something polite, necessary even, about the formality of gaining his permission before she went on a research expedition of his body.

He inclined his head, a studied motion that suggested he'd been waiting ten years for her to ask.

She'd been waiting, too. For ten years she'd wondered who this man really was, who he was growing up to be, had been alternately fascinated and repelled by him, and by herself because she'd so badly wanted to know.

Now finally, *finally*...

Threading her fingertips through the dark-gold hairs on his chest, she explored the terrain of muscle beneath warm skin. She splayed her hands upward over hard pecs, along the expanse of broad shoulders, down sculpted, powerful arms. The simple act of touching was an unusually potent experience given the years behind the need, given the sheer beauty of the man she touched.

Silky hairs trickled to a V beneath his belly button, a golden arrow pointing downward to the breathtaking region below his waist...lean hips, muscular thighs, *incredible* erection.

He was so...*solid.* Not just his equipment, but the whole deal. He was a man who could protect a woman from the world with his powerful body.

If a woman wanted to be protected.

Mallory wasn't the need-to-be-protected kind, but rather the live-for-the-moment, savor-his-gorgeous-body variety. She was a woman with a healthy sexual appetite and she hadn't made time for a lover in quite a while.

Jake Trinity was a feast.

Her own breathing grew shallow, echoing in the quiet

as she smoothed her hands down his waist, then ventured around to explore the feel of his muscular, perfectly shaped butt.

She almost wished he would say something to drown out the sounds of their excited breaths. But he only stood before her, legs braced apart, tolerantly allowing her to indulge her curiosity, which made her wonder what he would want in return for his patience.

Brushing her fingers down his thighs, she circled around to the front of him, lightly grazing the underside of his scrotum, then stroking the hard length of an erection that was no less impressive than the rest of him.

A huge shiver made him sway before her and his erection jumped in her hand, but he demonstrated an imposing willpower because he still didn't say a word or try to touch her.

The moment stretched with promise, a breathless moment where anything might be possible, where thoughts of sex and surrender and satisfaction all jumbled together in an almost visceral way.

Her heartbeat fluttered wildly again at the thought of him wedging that hard body between her thighs, at this magnificent length pressing deep inside her, filling emptiness with heat.

Her nipples beaded and her sex grew creamy wet. She wanted to lean forward and press herself against all this hot male bounty, feel her curves mesh with his, feel that erection brand the moist skin between her thighs.

She wanted to look into his face, to see if he was similarly affected, but she resisted, unwilling to let him glimpse the raw need she wasn't quite sure she successfully hid.

Sweeping the mass of wet hair behind her shoulder, she

leaned forward to press an open-mouthed kiss to the pulse beating low in his throat instead.

The contact of her mouth against his skin was the fuse that detonated his restraint. All of a sudden he seemed to explode. His strong arms lashed around her like whipcords. He scooped her beneath him with a violence of motion that took her off guard.

By the time she realized what was happening, she was lying on her back with his knee across her thighs, his heavy leg anchoring her to the mattress.

He'd done it again—totally taken her by surprise with that scoop-her-up-when-she-least-expected-it thing. A function of their disparate sizes, she supposed. A unique sensation and one she found stimulating. There was something so unfamiliar, so tantalizing about his power to assume control.

He brushed his palm across her nipples, a slow, very sensual motion, as if he wanted to draw out the moment, to savor every second of the way they speared toward his touch.

Then Mallory got her wish. With her cheek pressed to his chest, she could hear the rumble start deep inside, a purring that nearly drowned out the steady thud of his heart. She couldn't resist tipping her head back to look into his face, see if his expression mirrored that rumbling sound of contentment.

And the look on Jake Trinity's face, the reckless hunger, the yearning, just might have gone a long way toward satisfying her need for vengeance—if she hadn't been feeling a similar reckless hunger and yearning for him.

4

JAKE STILL didn't have a clue about Mallory's agenda but he'd reached his limit for her teasing. Denying her, and himself, wasn't going to yield anything more than frustration. He'd play her game and fight fire with fire to see if he couldn't shake loose the truth that way.

Orgasm. Her breathy whisper resonated in his memory. Had she meant it? He intended to find out.

Stretching out on her bed, Jake hauled her toward him, appreciating her size that gave him the advantage of maneuverability. He liked hearing her gasp in surprise as every inch of her slick wet skin unfolded against him. Her breasts pressed against his side. Her thighs parted around his hip, cradling him in lush warmth and acquainting him with her most private places.

She arched her hips, a movement so slight Jake thought he might have imagined it—until silky hairs abraded his skin. Until her moist folds separated to brand him with her heat.

Until she sighed aloud.

He chased that velvet sound with his thumb, traced her full bottom lip. Dazzling white teeth suddenly appeared between her kiss-swollen lips, and she caught his thumb soundly and nipped hard, a challenge flashing in her clear green eyes.

"So here we are, Jake Trinity. In bed. *Naked.*"

She exhaled the word, a sound that whispered through

him alive with promise. So here they were. Skimming a hand along the curve of her shoulder, down the sweep of her arm, he tested the reality of her, explored her shape, her texture.

"Definitely naked."

She fluttered a pale hand over his chest as though she meant to explore, too. He inhaled deeply, taking in the fresh scent of her damp hair, aware of her on so many levels that he experienced a strange sense of unreality to be lying in this woman's bed, with her draped naked around him.

Ten years was a long time to fantasize about what lay hidden beneath a ski mask.

This woman had been worth every second of the wait.

She stretched out before him, a lush terrain of creamy skin and slim curves, her red mouth pursed for his kisses, her rosy nipples pouting for his touch.

The sunlight from the huge windows slanted across their bodies, reflected by the long framed mirror behind the bed, a trick of light that highlighted the swaying of Mallory's sleek body, the way she rode his thigh with the slightest motion, warmed his skin with her heat.

Her hand continued a path over his stomach and Jake smiled at the way his muscles quavered at her light touches.

"Mmm, who do we have here?"

Her fingers zeroed right in on his erection, which jumped toward her hand, eager to make her acquaintance. A smile curved her lips and she brushed her palm along his shaft, a delicate touch that made his chest heave to release a trapped breath, a ragged sound that echoed in the sun-soaked quiet.

"Does he have a name?"

"No," Jake ground out.

"But he deserves one, I think." She circled a fingertip around the head and blood surged so hard that his erection visibly swelled beneath her attention.

"A big pretty boy like this deserves a good name. A *really* good name."

Her voice was a husky sound in the quiet, a sound that filtered through his senses and mocked his every reaction. She swirled her fingertips down his length to brush his balls, eliciting another pendulous swing that made her smile widen.

"How about Goliath?"

Jake wouldn't even dignify that with a response. Not that he could've managed a reply anyway with his heartbeat thundering in his ears.

Before he realized what she was about, Mallory sat up, one sinuous cat-like motion that sent her wet hair swinging forward to blanket her pale body as she arched above him, an inky black cocoon that sequestered her with his aching erection.

Sure enough…her hot velvet tongue dragged along his balls, ripping another groan past his constricted throat.

Jake had the vague thought that Mallory had assumed the control again in a big way, but he couldn't reason well enough to figure out what he wanted to do about it. Nothing. At least for the moment. Her breath burst softly against that wet spot, and her hands were skimming between his thighs, examining every inch of him with a thoroughness that made him quake.

"I'll bet women always compliment you on being so beautiful, Jake Trinity."

He took a stab at a coherence. "Beautiful?"

"Mmm-hmm."

"Ah, no," he said, a pretense at control when his voice

sounded strangely as though it belonged to someone else. "I don't recall any woman ever calling me that before."

She lifted her head, gazed up at him from beneath the fall of her hair. "An oversight then, because you most definitely are. Very beautiful."

She reinforced her statement with another touch, this time scooping her body low until he could feel the tight tips of her breasts along his thighs.

"You make me want to touch you. Do you mind?"

He intended to tell her to have at it, but before he found his voice again he realized her question had been rhetorical. She didn't need his permission. She was already kneading her fingers into his thigh, massaging his muscles with strokes that were equally skilled and erotic.

With a knowing smile quirking around her mouth, she poised above him like a pagan love goddess. The wild tangle of black hair tumbled around her naked body. Her rosy nipples played peekaboo through the shiny strands. And she proceeded to explore him as if she'd waited a long time for the privilege.

That thought undermined a little more of his control. When he'd been gearing up to handle the unexpected, he hadn't counted on the effect of Mallory wanting *him*. But she did. He could feel it in her almost reverent touch. In each languorous stroke of her fingers between his thighs, over his knees, down his calves. She wanted to explore him. He wanted to let her.

Man, did he want to let her.

Ten years of fantasies all boiled down to the feel of her soft hands on his skin. Sending both sides of his brain into battle. The impulsive side wanted to indulge all his plea-sure centers, wanted to surrender to her eager caresses, wanted to start up some exploration of his own. The rational side knew there was a point to this encounter and it wasn't all about pleasure. It was a power play.

The pleasure centers were taking control. Rationality was arguing that he should be able to exercise the restraint to mix business with pleasure.

And then Mallory hooked one long leg over him, straddled his hips, rode her woman's heat along the length of his erection and Jake lost this battle.

His hands fitted perfectly into her waist. She felt lightweight and sexy as he guided her bottom along for another wet stroke. And she was wet. Not shower wet, but creamy hot wet. Her lush folds enveloped him as if they were two interlocking puzzle pieces, aligned with breathtaking precision.

The image of plunging himself inside her made it almost impossible to breathe. And she must have known, because she was going out of her way to put on a show.

She arched backward, her hair tumbling behind her, wisping across his thighs with a brush of cool air. Her breasts thrust forward above her slim waist. Without thought, his hands began an ascent, dragging upward over her ribs, thumbing her satiny smooth skin.

The rational side of his brain was working just enough to want a response, so he caught her nipples and squeezed.

Her reaction didn't disappoint. A sultry moan slid from her lips and then she was leaning forward, pressing her nipples into his palms, skimming her hands along his chest and leaving arousal everywhere their bodies touched.

He thrust his tongue inside her mouth, mimicking the motion his body yearned to mirror. He caught the sound of her sigh with his lips, speared his hands into her hair to slant her head so he could deepen their connection.

This was no ordinary kiss, but making love with their mouths. Their tongues tangled, their breaths clashed, their needs came together as if ten years and a minimal acquaintance didn't matter. Need mattered. Desire mattered. Their bodies knew each other on some level.

It was a stunning realization, awesome in its simplicity.

Too awesome for Mallory apparently, because she broke their kiss and rose above him. Though nothing about her narrowed gaze and parted lips suggested she was rattled, Jake sensed she was. He sensed it in the distance she placed between them, in the way she backed off and said in a voice without its usual conviction, "Roll over."

He tried to make sense of her retreat, but his own brain was barely recovering from the intensity of their kiss and he couldn't pull all the pieces together. So he did as she asked, grateful for the chance to regain control of his runaway senses.

Unfortunately he didn't get much of a chance to recover, because she got the jump on him again.

Straddling him, she worked the muscles in his neck and shoulders with skillful fingers, dazing him with the languor of relaxation. She worked her way down his back, slowly, steadily.

"Do you like trivia, Jake?"

"Depends on what it's about." His voice sounded thick, drugged with arousal.

"About me."

"I'm interested."

She chuckled throatily as though she knew he was falling under her spell.

"I'm a bun girl." She sank her fingers into his butt, kneading the muscle so hard that he sucked in a breath that went a long way toward dispelling the clouds in his head.

"Really?"

"Really. And I'm pleased to report that you have a first-class ass."

"Glad you approve."

"Oh, I do. I approve completely." Her hard kneading yielded to the touch of a fingertip that trailed along the cleft, a leisurely stroke that left fire in its wake.

"There's just something about good-looking buns that does it for me. Mmm-mm, how do you keep yourself so tan? Do you lie out in the sun naked? I'd like to see that."

"Good genes."

She slipped her finger in just enough to separate his skin and make him shiver, one of those full-bodied jobs that she couldn't have missed.

"Like that, do you, Jake? Are you a bun man?"

Another grunt, which she could interpret to mean whatever she wanted. He didn't care, because he was too busy fighting the urge to grind his erection into the mattress to ease this ache that was testing his restraint in a big way.

Fortunately, she provided a distraction by shimmying down his body, her nipples glancing lightly over him as she resettled herself full length along his legs, pinning him beneath her.

He wondered what she was up to now—there was no doubt in his mind that she was up to something—when he felt a wet stroke of her tongue along his cleft. One moist stroke that caused him a moment of complete panic. He wasn't sure if his reaction was because of what else she might try while she was down there or because he was so close to losing control. Either way, Jake knew he was being tested.

He wasn't sure who Mallory was used to playing with, but she was in for a surprise if she thought she could toy with him.

The thought rallied his senses. Let her enjoy the upper

hand. Let her think she had him by the balls. She'd find out soon enough that Jake was no longer a nineteen-year-old with a hard-on. He'd been waiting ten years to solve the mystery of his sexy thief. He was a patient man. A *very* patient man.

And his patience had just reached its end.

"Nervous, Jake?" she asked.

He twisted in a wrestling move he could have accomplished easily with an opponent three times her size.

She came off him gracefully, recovering her balance with an economy of speed and motion. But Jake was ready. He caught her wrist and dragged her hand toward his crotch and the erection there that was swiftly reaching impossible proportions.

He didn't need to say anything more than "Grab a condom" before she was scooting toward the pillows with a smile.

As soon as she got there…he pounced.

"Jake!"

Mallory wanted to know why he'd suddenly fisted his hand into her hair, and he answered that question when he coaxed her head back so she could see their reflection in the large mirror that filled the wall above the bed's headboard.

He knelt behind her, his body behind hers, chin resting on the top of her head, his broad body framing her pale form with golden muscle. His erection pressed hotly against her backside. His strong thighs anchored her in place.

Their gazes met in the mirror, no less potent as reflections. His melting dark eyes caressed her face knowingly, challenged her to give up her control, promised she wouldn't be sorry. But he didn't say a word. He didn't have to. His expression said everything.

He wanted her.

Their sex was supposed to be about satisfying needs—her fascination with this man and her need for vengeance. But Jake kept stealing the control, kept shifting the balance of power, proving he was as in command of his responses as ever and unraveling her in a way she'd never been unraveled before.

She felt exposed, needy. She liked his big arms around her, the promise of that magnificent erection pressed against her. And staring into that mirror at their reflection meant facing just how much.

Her eyes were heavy with desire. Her lips were ripe from his kisses. She wanted this man with an urgency that she'd never known before, so she let her eyes flutter closed, blocked out the sight. Inhaling a cleansing breath, she tried to dispel this unfamiliar sensation, to regain control of her own responses so she could regain control of the moment.

But blindness only enhanced her other senses. The lingering taste of his mouth on hers, his rough-velvet tongue. The clash of their excited breaths through the quiet. The feel of his big warm body molding hers. The scent of his skin.

Mallory almost laughed, a knee-jerk reaction to the potency of the moment. She was the thief, but Jake Trinity was the one stealing…her calm, her control. She wanted to turn around and square off face-to-face, dispel this power he had over her, but she refused to give him the satisfaction. She'd started this game, and she'd play it until the end.

She could handle unexpected turns. She liked a good challenge.

And this man was proving to be one. Especially when

his body brushed hers as he knelt behind her, down, down....

He directed her to spread her knees wide, and she clung to the headboard as he pressed his face between her thighs, his hair brushing her skin, his faintly stubbled cheeks abrading her most sensitive places. His hot tongue dragged back along her folds, one hot stroke that she felt from the inside out.

She bucked hard. A half gasp, half moan spilled from her lips, echoing just how on edge she felt. That one hot stroke of his tongue and she turned into a puddle.

"I am a bun man, Mallory. And I'm pleased to report that you're first class in that department." He tossed her own words back at her, and the best she could do was exhale a trapped breath, a sound that skittered out in ridiculous bursts.

Oh, this man was just too good.

She'd expected a challenge, but she hadn't been expecting *this*. For the first time, Mallory questioned whether this man could be mastered at all.

A question that sweetened the bite of the challenge.

Suddenly Mallory couldn't stop herself from arching back against him, encouraging his devilish tongue to feed this need that was making her tremble.

But Jake had control now, and he was changing the rules.

He rose up behind her, and she heard the sound of foil tearing, resisted the urge to turn around. She clung to the headboard instead, waiting, playing this game his way, sighing when he positioned his erection between her thighs, a hot presence that caressed her damp folds and made her shiver.

"Open your eyes, Mallory," he said huskily. "Watch the way you melt when I push inside."

She wouldn't. She didn't want to acknowledge that he was right. That she was melting at the feel of him pressing inside, overwhelmed by each thick inch stretching her, filling her.

He moved slowly, generously allowing her time to acclimate to his size, to *melt* around him in supple degrees, to yield until she was so full she felt breathless. But before she could manage the sensation, he snaked his hand around her hip, over her stomach and between her thighs. He zeroed right in on that knot of nerve endings and sent fire bursting through her.

"Open your eyes, Mallory."

Still she resisted. She anchored herself against the bed frame and rode out the sensation, only vaguely aware of the way the cold metal contrasted sharply with the heat of her skin. Pressing back down on his erection again, she needed to feed this ache inside, wanted to feel him thrust inside her.

But Jake didn't move, just kept that hand wedged between her thighs, his finger lazily circling her aching flesh.

She recognized the power play for what it was, disliked that he could be so in control of himself when he was inside her. She almost gave in and opened her eyes, wanting to see some evidence of a struggle on his handsome face.

But she didn't want to find out that his struggle didn't match her own.

And he didn't ask again. He picked up his rhythm, pressing that huge erection inside just enough to make her squirm, making her arch back to encourage him to thrust harder. But he kept his own pace with those barely-there strokes, ruthlessly controlling her need. And his own?

Mallory didn't know. She just knew when he slipped

his hands between them, kneaded her backside to part her cheeks so his erection went impossibly deeper.

And Jake got his wish because her eyes shot open wide and she met his satisfied gaze, a gaze that saw things she didn't want him to see…like just how much she could feel him.

"Oh." The sound tumbled from her lips, and suddenly she couldn't stop her hips from swaying against him to feed the tension building inside.

"Look at yourself, Mallory. You're beautiful when you want."

With his command echoing in her ears and her tension mounting with his thrusts, she faced her reflection, found her expression mirrored exactly how she felt—she was coming apart at the seams, whether she'd intended to or not.

And she hadn't intended to. Their sex was supposed to have been about taking *Jake* apart at the seams. Yet her eyes were heavy with desire. Her nostrils flared on gasping breaths. As he rode her from behind, each sweet motion reflected in her expression for both of them to see.

And he liked watching. His gaze never left her reflection as he pulled out almost completely, a blinding move that robbed her of all thought as he sank back inside, the feeling of him driving deep, the fullness so overwhelming she cried out.

Her orgasm began, a huge rolling sensation that gathered and swelled until it brought her right to the edge. Her only consolation was that he seemed to be caught up in the phenomenon, too. He thrust again, and she recognized the hunger sharpening his features as he drove into her again, and again, and again.

Then Mallory simply exploded, a gut-wrenching collision of every nerve in her body. Sensation crashed in on her, consumed her from the top of her tingling scalp to the feet she'd wrapped around his muscular calves, and something that sounded suspiciously like a scream burst from her lips.

Her orgasm detonated his, and the rumbling began low in his chest, rising until it emitted as a throaty growl from his lips, a sound that echoed against her ear and quivered through her. She could only watch in the mirror, shell-shocked as she felt his muscles tighten against her as he came.

Pleasure overtook his expression, and she experienced a profound, almost absurd sense of relief when she saw the amazement flickering in the molten depths of his eyes.

She wasn't the only one bowled over here—she'd *screamed*. She couldn't believe she'd actually screamed.

It wasn't that she hadn't had good orgasms before. She'd had good ones, incredible ones, even. She'd just never had one like this. She would have collapsed into a boneless heap if he hadn't held her so tightly. "What is it about you, Jake Trinity?"

Their gazes met in the mirror. "It's not me. It's *us* together."

She couldn't contemplate that statement, didn't have the energy or the brain cells left to even try. "There is no *us*."

He arched a tawny brow, his gaze dragging over her reflection, his arm locked around her waist, his skin a dark slash against her paleness. He held her as if he didn't intend to let her go. "You don't think so?"

"No." The word came out much too fast to be taken seriously and the smile twitching around his lips suggested Jake didn't.

"Then what do you think just happened?"

"We had really good sex."

His steady gaze seemed again to be reaching deep inside her, searching for something, making her respond with that ridiculous, fluttery feeling again....

This afterglow was *not* going to work for her.

5

"LET ME GO," Mallory said, and if she expected Jake to comply, she'd seriously misjudged this man. He did withdraw his still impressively hard erection, but he most certainly did not let her go.

Dragging her back against him, he lifted her right off the bed before swinging her up into his arms in a move reminiscent of the one he'd used earlier to get her into the bed.

Slipping her arms around his neck, she hung on as he marched toward the bathroom. "Jake, what are you—"

"I'm ready to shower with you now."

"Like things on your terms, do you?"

He flashed a very roguish grin. "Always."

"Amazing how much we have in common, don't you think?" she shot back. "Because I do, too."

Neither one pointed out the obvious—that two people wanting control in any relationship, whether a work relationship or a personal one, spelled trouble.

On the positive side, Mallory definitely had the upper hand with work. He wanted a service that only she could provide—troubleshooting and training him as an assistant. But she suspected that Jake might have the edge in bed.

Her legs were still trembling from the strength of that orgasm. She felt tender and achy and strangely vulnerable, her emotions wildly on edge. While he, on the other hand, still sported a serene smile and just as much control over his reactions to her as ever.

Not good. She hadn't counted on this man being the bloody Rock of Gibraltar. He'd thrown her a curve by withstanding her best attempts to make him lose control. He'd completely turned the tables on her, and she needed to reevaluate how best to turn those tables back again.

Unfortunately, thinking clearly was a problem when he lowered her to her feet in a sleek motion that pitted her sensitive body full-length against hard brawny male. His fading erection dragged intimately along her tummy in a reminder of how well their bodies had gotten to know each other.

Without a word, Mallory stepped into the shower and turned the water on, not bothered in the least when the spray shot out icy cold. Icy cold felt good over her flushed skin and with a little luck her head might clear so she could get back on track with this man.

Jake joined her, and she said, more casually than she felt, "Welcome to my shower, Jake Trinity. I was beginning to think I'd never get you in here."

That smile still quirked around his mouth. "I'm here."

"Yes, you are."

And funny how his big tanned body seemed to fill up what had been a spacious shower stall a short time ago. He hadn't seemed to take up quite so much room when he'd been standing halfway across the bath.

Exhaling a sigh at her breathless reaction to this man, she reached for the shampoo, only to have him pluck the bottle out of her hand.

"I've got to shampoo my hair again," she said. "Or I'll never get a comb through it."

"Allow me."

There was something so gallant in his offer that Mallory

just dipped her head beneath the spray, not quite sure how to respond but knowing a refusal would sound childish.

He squeezed a dollop into his palm, returned the bottle to the shelf and proceeded to occupy himself by working up a healthy lather in her long hair.

His hands weren't the only things he occupied.

Dragging her back against him, he shielded her from the spray with his broad shoulders and back, nestling his softening erection against her backside. His fingers massaged her scalp, then he worked his way down the long strands with a thoroughness that proved he was very comfortable with women's grooming habits. The impression was reinforced when he directed her under the spray to rinse before he repeated the process with conditioner without her saying a word.

"So why don't women hang around you for long, Jake Trinity?" she asked, glancing around to catch his expression in her periphery. "Apparently they line up for a piece of the action, but they never seem to make the cut. Is the choice usually yours or theirs? I'm curious."

Something about that frown drawing his tawny brows together suggested he'd been asked this question before, but the fact he didn't have a ready answer implied he hadn't cared enough to figure out the answer.

"You're so sure they don't make the cut?"

"I'm a very thorough researcher. No ex-wives, no child-support payments and no former live-in girlfriends. Just a *whole bunch* of women flitting in and out of your life. Do you have a problem with commitment?"

That frown faded. "No. I just haven't met the right woman."

The *right* woman?

That answer was so prosaic and so completely unexpected that Mallory almost laughed. *Almost*. There was also something in his expression that suggested he was dead serious, which for some strange reason made her uneasy.

"So you're looking for Ms. Right?"

"I'll know her when she shows up."

Now Mallory did laugh. "So the knight in shining armor is waiting for his fair lady."

"You don't believe in soul mates, do you?" he asked.

"Or fairy tales."

"Why?"

A simple question that Mallory should have had a handy answer for. She didn't. "I've never really thought about it before," she said honestly. "I guess I'm too entrenched in reality to appreciate all those silly romantic concepts."

"Tell me about your reality. I researched you before I sent my proposal, but I didn't find out nearly as much about your personal life as you did about mine."

"I have *really* good contacts."

Now it was Jake's turn to laugh. "I'll bet you do."

After working the conditioner through her hair, he passed the slick length over her shoulders to move it out of the spray. Grabbing a bath sponge, he dispensed liquid soap and worked a lather over her shoulders.

"Determined to pamper me, are you?"

"Yes."

"Why?" Her turn for a simple question. She'd tested this man, led their business consultation straight past business and into personal, despite the fact that he hadn't fallen into bed as easily as she'd expected. That he seemed so determined to see to her needs now…she needed to understand his reasoning, try to determine his agenda.

"You pleased me." An equally simple answer.

He worked that bath sponge over her shoulders in slow spirals, lathered the soap over her skin, each stroke contributing to the lazy pleasure snaking its way through her senses. His every slow stroke drew attention to her achy bottom and the memory of the way his body had filled her so completely.

"You pleased me, too."

She glanced over her shoulder again and found him watching her with a golden brow arched dubiously. Clearly he'd already known and hadn't needed her to tell him.

"So tell me about your reality, Mallory. I do know you've never been married, and since I don't see any evidence of toys or babysitters around, I assume you don't have any children. Am I intruding on another man's turf?"

"Worried he might show up at an inopportune moment?"

Something about the way he shrugged those broad shoulders suggested he'd be up to handling another man if one did show up. But he seemed to think she entertained more than one man in her bed at a time. This annoyed her for some reason, which wasn't entirely rational since she'd gone out of her way to foster exactly that impression with her drawer filled with condoms.

"I don't like to share," he said. "So as long as we—"

"There is no *we*." The words popped out of her mouth without warning, suggesting a defensiveness she was unfamiliar with.

"So you've said."

There was no missing his amusement, and surprised, Mallory glanced back over her shoulder. His warm gaze was there to catch hers, and damned if a tingle didn't shoot right down to the tips of her toes.

He must have recognized how flustered she was, because he pressed his advantage, leaning close to work that sponge between her thighs. Her fluttery reaction to each intimate stroke contradicted her denial.

"Since there's no *we* happening here," she said firmly, "why don't we establish exactly what is happening so we're both clear on the details?"

"You want to delineate the terms for our relationship?"

"Makes sense to me. We're combining business with pleasure here and throwing in some unfinished business into the mix."

"Unfinished business?"

"The kiss." She arched back against him, was rewarded when his soft erection swelled to life. "I'd say we finally got around to finishing that particular business, wouldn't you?"

The sponge hit the shower floor with a wet plop. Reaching around her, he caught her breasts in his soapy hands. "So you're all done with me? Does this mean I can go home now?"

Her breasts grew heavy. Her nipples tightened. "Are you telling me you want to go home, Jake?"

"Not by a long shot." He tugged at her nipples, a lingering pull that made her sex give a low squeeze of anticipation.

He tugged again.

Another squeeze.

Suddenly he was bending low, his chin resting in the crook of her neck and shoulder. "Why don't we forget all about me going home?" Each word gusted against her ear and arrowed along every nerve ending from her head to her toes. "I'd planned to clear my schedule so I'm at your disposal."

"How…*considerate*."

"What does your schedule look like?"

"I'm all yours."

He ran his tongue over her ear, such a sexy move that she shivered. "Is that a promise?"

Mallory had certainly meant it as one, but something about his tone made her question whether he wanted more than she'd offered. "Yes."

"Good." Straightening up, he slinked those soapy hands down her middle. "You've assured me that mixing business with pleasure won't adversely impact your job performance, and I'm willing to take your word. So when and where and how will the work fit in?"

"The when is now—twenty-four seven."

He simply bent down to retrieve the bath sponge, poured out more soap and then went to work on her again, his expression suddenly all business. "The where?"

"In my workshop for the most part."

He snaked that sponge between her thighs, so she splayed her hands on the tile, leaned forward and provided him easier access to her backside.

If her pose was reminiscent of their bout in front of her mirror, well...she wouldn't mind roughing up his composure just a little.

Nothing.

"How about the sex?" he asked.

"We can fit that in anytime and anywhere."

Jake only inclined his head in agreement of her terms and Mallory found herself strangely disappointed that he hadn't responded to the innuendo in her challenge at all.

He knelt down before her, working that sponge down one leg and back up the other, his strokes so attentive and gentle. It struck her as a very intentional gesture, and one she could have been way off base about.

Admittedly, she didn't have a lot of experience with men who possessed noble streaks. And that's exactly what this was. Her gut was telling her, and her gut didn't lie.

Jake Trinity did things by the book.

He'd encountered a thief breaking into his employer's warehouse so he'd sounded the alarm.

He'd made love to a woman, so he made sure she knew he appreciated the favor.

It was really so knight in shining armor.

She had a fleeting thought to steer out of these uncharted waters. She wasn't recovering from their sex nearly as fast as she should have, and with all this delicious attention…she was feeling dreamy and sated. She would have liked nothing better than to curl up in bed beside him and lounge the afternoon away getting to know each other.

This man was distracting her from her purpose, and Mallory didn't like being distracted.

But she should have expected as much. Jake Trinity had been having this effect on her since their accidental meeting long ago. He'd preoccupied her with a curious blend of self-righteous anger and hurt betrayal. Although why she should feel hurt and betrayed was a mystery, because one chance meeting with the man didn't obligate him to her.

Perhaps the memory of their kiss had only muddied up the way she felt, which was also totally ridiculous because it had only been *one kiss*.

But the only thing clear right now was that what she felt for him wasn't rational. She needed to let him play his game, because resisting him would only reveal that he was getting to her.

The absolute last thing she needed was to give Jake Trinity more ammunition to use against her. They had an intense few weeks ahead. She intended to get him out of her system once and for all—her fascination with him and her need to pay him back for all the trouble he'd caused.

If he threw her a curve along the way, well…she liked challenges.

JAKE STEPPED OUT of the shower and exhaled in relief to put some distance between him and Mallory. She might be convinced there was no *us*, but he wasn't so sure. What was happening between them felt like a lot more than unfinished business. He'd barely managed to escape his second orgasm of the day despite her best efforts. And her efforts had been the best.

She'd insisted on scrubbing him with the same attentiveness he'd shown her, and she'd tried every trick in the book from shimmying her luscious body all over his to giving him an impromptu hand job that had nearly pitched him over the edge.

He'd only managed not to lose it because he realized that survival with this woman depended solely on his ability not to show weakness. Letting her assume control would be perceived as a weakness. He needed to survive until he understood exactly what game she was playing with him.

So far he was holding his own, a fact for which he was incredibly grateful when he heard a male voice call from the foyer, "Hey babe, you upstairs or down?"

One glimpse at Mallory's face, and Jake knew this guest was unexpected. Had she lied about being involved? As he raked his gaze up her wet curves, he had to ask himself honestly if he cared. Maybe he wouldn't find sharing so offensive if it meant being with this woman.

But the flash of surprise in Mallory's expression made him wary. She shot her gaze his way, exhaled a heavy breath and handed him a bath towel.

"Upstairs," she called out and there was no missing the resignation in her voice.

"Who's with you?" the voice asked.

"Jake Trinity."

There was a beat of silence before, "Great. I want to meet him. You kids decent?"

"Yeah."

"Mallory," Jake said. "Who's—"

"Please don't mention the Innovative job," she whispered, hastily dragging a towel over her curves. "He doesn't know you were the one there, and I'd like to keep it that way."

Turning away, she grabbed a robe from the back of the bathroom door and shrugged it on.

The Innovative job?

Jake stared at the back of her retreating form before his sex-dulled wits put two and two together.

Surely she couldn't be talking about—

"Hi, Dad," he heard her say. "What brings you by?"

"I wanted to see if you'd decided to take the job for TSS. Where's Jake?"

"In the bathroom."

Several thoughts struck Jake simultaneously.

The first was that the man currently standing inside Mallory's bedroom was a convicted felon who'd done hard time.

The second was that Jake's clothes were in that bedroom, in a conspicuous pile on the floor, which meant his new status as Mallory's lover wouldn't go unnoticed.

The third was that the convicted felon father of the woman he'd just made love to obviously knew his name but not that he'd been a part of the break-in resulting in his incarceration.

All of which left Jake facing an interesting dilemma.

Concealing that he'd been a rogue factor on the Innovative job didn't sit right. Mallory's request to keep that information a secret made him feel as if he was hiding something when he didn't have anything to hide.

While Jake hadn't tripped the alarm, the fact remained that this man had gone to prison that night, and Jake didn't have any prior experience with convicted felons to know if simply being on the property during a burglary invited retribution.

Kissing the man's underage daughter likely would.

In all fairness, Mallory had initiated that kiss, and while Jake had known she'd been young, he couldn't have known that she'd been only sixteen. Not with her ski mask on.

But according to Mallory, her father didn't know Jake had kissed her, which seemed like the lesser of two evils when his clothes currently resided on her bedroom floor.

He decided to honor Mallory's request until she had a chance to explain her reasons for wanting secrecy. He had enough to deal with at the moment—specifically, his lack of clothing.

Of course, she wouldn't bring his clothes into the bathroom so he could dress for this meeting. No, he had a clear enough sense of her game by now—if not the reasons behind it—to recognize another opportunity to test his mettle.

Jake could only inhale deeply while wrapping a towel around his waist. Then he headed out the door to meet his fate.

Through the years, when he'd envisioned what a man who burglarized businesses for a living might look like, he'd always imagined the hard-core, burnt-out type of criminal featured on crime shows. But Duke Hunt, just like his daughter, wasn't what Jake had expected.

The man was aggressively physical despite middle age, and Mallory resembled him a great deal. She possessed the same shiny dark hair, sans the silver streaks, the same confident demeanor, the same athletic mannerisms and poise.

Her striking eyes and delicate size must be gifts from

her mother, he decided, because her father had an inky-black gaze that met Jake's levelly, and he stood six feet in his bare feet. They were bare right now.

Duke Hunt was a cross between the Sean Connery and Gene Hackman types of felons glamorized by the movie industry. He was so far from a drugged-out criminal as to be laughable.

But Jake didn't feel like laughing. Not when he was standing here half-naked, extending his hand in greeting to this particular convicted felon.

Mallory performed the introductions. "Daddy, this is Jake Trinity. I know you've heard all about him. Jake, this is my dad, Duke Hunt."

That ink-black gaze assessed him in a glance, never showing even a flicker of surprise at Jake's attire. In fact, he had the distinct impression that both father and daughter were waiting for *him* to show some sign of his discomfort.

Jake was determined not to show any. He wasn't sure why the Hunt family discussed business and greeted guests in bathrooms and bedrooms instead of in offices and living rooms like normal folks, but he gripped the man's hand as if meeting people in a towel was an everyday occurrence. "A pleasure, sir."

He figured it couldn't hurt to be polite.

"Good to meet you, Jake," Duke Hunt said, his face splitting into a broad smile. "Mallory's right. I have heard all about you. You're well-regarded in our industry."

"What line of work are you in?"

"I'm a security specialist like Mallory."

"You're in business together?" This tidbit hadn't come up in his research.

"Dad and I cater to different clientele." She headed to her dresser where she unwrapped her hair from the towel and picked up a comb.

"Now there's an understatement." Duke gave a hearty laugh. "As different as the law from the outlaw."

Jake hadn't realized his attention had shifted to Mallory and the way the robe slid down her slender arms when she reached up to untangle her hair. But it took a moment for the significance of Duke's statement to hit him.

Law from the outlaw.

Although it struck him that confronting this man in his daughter's bedroom, given the logistics of the situation, probably wasn't the most intelligent move he could make, he had no choice but to ask. "Will there be any conflict of interest for TSS because of your *different* clientele?"

Duke arched a dark brow in a gesture of such studied skepticism that Jake recognized another mannerism he'd passed along to his daughter. "Is this your diplomatic way of asking if Mallory's going to share what she learns about your system so I can advise my clients how to circumvent it?"

"Yes."

The one word seemed to throb in the suddenly heavy silence. Or maybe that throbbing was Jake's heartbeat in his ears. As near as he could tell without his glasses, Duke Hunt looked stoic, and he reasoned that his glasses, or his clothing for that matter, would make no difference whatsoever if the man had a weapon. His glasses wouldn't help him dodge a bullet and his suit wasn't bulletproof. And if he wound up dead, at least he'd save the medical examiner the effort of having to undress his corpse.

"Of course there's no conflict of interest," Mallory said, bristling. "That would be unethical."

There was no missing her indignation, the way she abandoned the comb in her hair, squared her shoulders and scowled at him as if mortally offended he'd even asked the question.

Duke's gaze shifted from his daughter back to Jake. "There's honor among thieves."

"We run legitimate businesses," Mallory said.

"Despite our clientele," Duke added, and Jake thought he saw a hint of a smile.

"You researched what I do, Jake, you should know that. And I sign a statement of confidentiality that's binding."

There was something so earnest about her, so genuinely offended that he inclined his head, willing to accept her word for the moment. His research hadn't yielded any hint of suspicious activity that might connect Mallory's business with any break-ins. And Jake supposed the fact that Duke had shown up to present himself in person only reinforced that they kept things on the up and up.

He would put his people to work researching Hunt Security Specialists even harder, and maybe, just maybe, Jake would find he had to re-evaluate his interpretation of work ethics to include honor among thieves.

"The man's within his right to ask, babe," Duke said, frowning as Mallory impatiently tried to free the comb from her hair. "Here let me." Moving close, he brushed her hands away.

After untangling the comb, he began to work it through the long wet strands. Mallory tipped her head back to make the job easier, an automatic response that convinced Jake this scene was routine. There was something so tender in a father helping his child that he felt like an intruder.

"So you kids are square now on this issue?" Duke asked, his gaze journeying from Mallory's wet hair to the bed to the pile of clothing on the floor beside it. "Looks like you were getting along okay until I showed up."

Their gazes met above Mallory's head, and for the life of him, Jake couldn't read the man's expression. He could only assume that a poker face was another tool of the trade and it took an effort of will not to wince beneath that stoic gaze.

Especially when he caught a glimpse of a foil square protruding from beneath the edge of a pillow. "I've made Mallory an offer, sir."

"Which I've accepted," she said. "We just haven't worked out all the details yet. Jake had a few...*conditions.*"

"What sort of conditions?" Duke lowered his attention back to the comb, which Jake took as an encouraging sign.

"We're dealing with some trust issues," she explained. "He isn't comfortable with me infiltrating a client's property so he wants to come with me."

"Really?" Duke sounded surprised. "You've agreed to this?"

She nodded.

Jake wasn't sure what surprised the man more—that he'd asked to accompany Mallory or that she'd agreed. He wouldn't pursue the answer now, though. Not when Duke chose that exact moment to direct Mallory back toward her dresser, which left him with a clear path to his clothing.

"Understanding how Mallory works will help me when I design my systems," he said.

"Sounds like a match made in heaven." Still holding a length of Mallory's hair, Duke stepped around her so he could meet her gaze. "Exactly how are you planning to work this?"

Jake took the opportunity to ease toward the bed.

"He'll have to be trained enough not to get in my way on the job," she said. "I'll start him on the basics in my workshop."

"He'll need more than basics. You're not going to have him tackle his system cold, are you?"

"No, of course not. But I haven't figured out the details yet, Dad. He just sprang this on me."

"And you agreed." Duke shook his head and gave a laugh. "Talk to Eddie."

"Good idea."

Jake wondered who Eddie was and what Mallory thought was a good idea, but as he'd just reached his clothes and had the perfect opportunity to escape...

6

DUKE HUNT wheeled his Mercedes onto the neatly lined drive of Peachtree Financial and maneuvered his way around the building to a parking space in the rear. The name of the place always gave him a chuckle. Peachtree Financial sounded like a Deep South bank that had been serving the financial needs of Atlanta's old money since before the Civil War.

In fact, Peachtree Financial had only been serving the financial needs of Atlanta's old money for the past ten years and not in any conventional banking sense. The place was an upscale pawnshop that catered to wealthy folks who needed to hock their luxury goodies in comfort and confidentiality.

Ten years ago, when Duke and his crew had been forced into retirement after the Innovative job, Eddie Gibb had invested his share of the spoils into growing a niche market into an empire.

Duke smiled as he let himself in through the back door with his key, then de-activated the security alarm for this quadrant. He walked past the storeroom, where Eddie housed his expensive stock inside a clever two-vault system that would deter most burglars from bothering to make an attempt.

The system that protected Peachtree Financial had been designed by a former burglary crew with eighty-plus years of experience between them and was as damn near perfect as a system could get. Numerous engineers in the area had unknowingly contributed to its creation by being contracted to provide various components that Duke and his crew assembled and put into operation. They included TSS—because Jake Trinity was good—and Innovative Engineering, because Duke thought the company's distinction as his last official job would bring luck.

Glancing into Eddie's office, he discovered it empty and continued into the showroom, where he found Eddie and Opal toasting each other with crystal flutes. A bottle of Dom Perignon sat open nearby in a silver ice bucket. He greeted the scene with a smile.

While Opal wasn't a natural beauty in any sense, she was a work of art, from her skillfully made-up features, the lined cat eyes and flawless skin to her impressively maintained body. Her hair was a shade of platinum blond that Duke knew required regular visits to her hairdresser. As far as he was concerned, the result was well worth the effort and money spent.

Eddie, who made his living nowadays dealing in rare items of value, would have agreed that Opal was one of the rarest items of value to be found on two legs. He was fond of saying he'd never settle down until he met a woman of Opal's character, and had been telling Duke as much during their thirty-year acquaintance—along with calling him a fool for not staking claim to a gem like Opal.

Duke should have listened to Eddie a long time ago. A skinny black man with a mind quicker than a round of shots from an automatic, Eddie liked custom-made suits and had been part of Duke's team since he'd started training with alarm systems at the tender young age of seventeen.

He glanced at his watch. ''You've got no customers in

the middle of a business day, and it's not exactly cocktail hour. What are you two celebrating?''

"Life, boss man.'' Eddie flashed a fast grin that made his numerous gold teeth glint in the overhead track lighting. "We just unloaded Mrs. McGillivray's aigrette.''

Duke envisioned the piece of jewelry in mention, a plume-like spray of enormous sapphires, emeralds and rubies that had been as hideous in design as it had been hideously expensive.

But as Mrs. McGillivray had fondly fashioned the piece herself back when her investment banker husband had been flush, Duke respectfully tempered his response. "I would have bet the only person to pick up that ticket was Mrs. McGillivray herself.''

"Broke her heart to sell it for a pittance of its worth,'' Eddie said. "Broke my heart to buy it because I didn't think I'd ever unload it, but as she's such a good customer…''

Opal couldn't stop smiling. "Apparently that dear old lady isn't the only one in Atlanta with extremely bad taste, Duke. I'll be sure she knows it went to a good home.'' She raised her glass in salute. "To the merry tune of six figures.''

"Merry tune? That's a damn symphony.'' Duke leaned against the counter, shaking his head. "Pour me a glass, Opal, would you? This news does deserve a toast.''

Opal obliged, and the three of them clinked rims together.

"Good job, team,'' he said. "As always.''

Opal smiled, Eddie laughed and Duke thought that life was gracious to continue serving up such pleasant surprises. That every one of his crew had made good with their lives after retirement didn't surprise him, though. His crew was made up of intelligent people he'd handpicked himself. They'd only needed an opportunity to succeed in the world of legitimate business, and Duke had provided that opportunity.

Throughout the years of their affiliation, he'd invested a percentage of their earnings toward the day of their inevitable retirement—his version of a pension plan. This had turned out to be one of his better decisions, and he was proud of the choices his crew had made in the years since.

Even if he was getting more gray hair worrying about the up-and-coming younger generation. While Polish Paul's son Lance had been giving them all headaches for some time, Mallory was usually on the ball. *Usually.* He'd been reflecting on some of her choices lately, but after coming across Jake Trinity in her bedroom today, he needed to be doing more than reflecting.

"Opal, did Mallory ever mention to you that she knew Jake Trinity?"

"She doesn't know him. She was so surprised when TSS's proposal arrived that she specifically asked the man how he'd heard of her. I know because I worked up her preliminary quote."

Duke frowned, though he'd expected as much. Mallory hadn't mentioned any previous affiliation with TSS, and he'd gotten the impression she'd be meeting Trinity for the first time today herself. This situation was not adding up in his head, and he disliked question marks where his daughter was concerned.

"Mallory had an appointment with Jake Trinity this morning," Opal said. "Was there a problem?"

"I'm not sure," he admitted.

Eddie grabbed the champagne and topped his glass. "Well, that doesn't sound good, boss man."

"It's not." He glanced at Opal. "Did they spend a lot of time on the telephone together?"

"None at all to my knowledge. They set up everything by fax."

"Did their interactions seem like business as usual?"

She nodded. "Except for the obscene amount of money Mallory quoted him as her base fee."

"How obscene?"

"Filthy."

"Why was she quoting him so much?"

Opal gave an elegant shrug. "She didn't say anything except that if the man wanted to contract her services, he'd have to pay through the nose."

"Do you think she wanted to scare him off?" Eddie asked.

"If she did, it wasn't one of her better schemes," Opal said. "Jake Trinity reviewed her terms and faxed back the agreement to consult in less than five minutes."

"Really?" Duke considered this piece of information. "I wonder why he'd be so quick to let her gouge him?"

"She does provide a unique service," Opal suggested, but Duke thought it was more than that. He could feel it.

"What's up, boss man?"

He wasn't surprised his questions had piqued Eddie's interest. Both Eddie and Opal knew he didn't ask questions without reasons. He decided to come clean and ask for help. "Mallory's involved with the man."

"You don't mean *involved* involved, do you?" Opal frowned, an expression she usually avoided at all costs to spare the wear and tear on her flawless skin.

He nodded.

"Are you sure, Duke? Maybe you've been misinformed. I'd bet money that she'd never met the man before this morning."

Tightening his grip on the counter, Duke braced himself for the memory of the scene that had greeted him in his daughter's bedroom earlier. "I'm not misinformed. Trust me."

"Well, that doesn't sound like Mallory. She doesn't jump into relationships indiscriminately."

Duke heard Opal's concern and appreciated it. She'd always been there for him in every way that counted. She'd stepped in when his late wife had decided family life wasn't her thing, had helped him get on his feet with rearing his infant daughter.

Opal had simply never stopped helping. She'd become a part of his and Mallory's lives…without ever asking for any thanks, or any kind of commitment either. And as he gazed at her now, her beautiful face set in a careful expression, Duke wondered how he could have possibly been so stupid not to recognize the treasure he'd found in this woman.

She'd been young and wild when he'd first met her, a budding thief with a gift for role-playing and routing security guards. Sparks had flown from the minute he'd set eyes on her, and they'd become lovers. They were *still* lovers, on-again, off-again after thirty years.

Committing to Opal had simply never occurred to him. He'd never have married at all had he not needed to give his child a name when one of his lovers had turned up pregnant. And his so-called marriage had been such a disaster from the day he'd said, "I do" that he hadn't considered trying his hand at it again.

In true Opal fashion, she hadn't cried, bitched or nagged. She hadn't left him, either, which he found downright amazing upon reflection. No, she'd simply decided that two could play his game and enjoyed her life much in the same fashion that he enjoyed his. She treated herself to a healthy dose of him whenever time in their dating schedules permitted, and in the process, proved she was more than a match for him.

Duke supposed that the fact that he always wound up back in Opal's bed should have told him something. But it hadn't—until recently.

As Eddie had always said…*a fool*.

"My daughter is discriminating," he said. "Or she usually is. But she hasn't even been dating lately according to my calculations."

"Which is unhealthy," Opal pointed out. "She's young and beautiful and should be out having fun."

"I want grandchildren."

Eddie gave a low whistle. "Don't get old on us, boss man."

"What is old about wanting my daughter to find someone who loves her?"

"You love her, boss man."

"I'm her father, and I won't be around forever."

Opal looked thoughtful. "But you're here now, Duke."

True enough. But he didn't want Mallory to wind up the way he was—lonely. He had a great life filled with great people but that didn't make up for the nights when he woke up alone, thinking about the woman he wanted beside him. Opal. And he had no one to blame but himself for taking her for granted.

For too many years they'd flitted in and out of their relationship, always trusting the other would be there when something better didn't happen along. What Duke had come to understand these past few years was that the times they spent together were the something better.

The best.

Opal didn't know it yet, but he was about to help her come to the same understanding, too. And Mallory. He didn't want her waiting until she was as old as he and Opal to realize that allowing someone to love her was far better than shutting everyone out.

Of course, Mallory was only living what she'd learned from him. Live for the moment and don't dwell too much on the future. Just like the way he'd led her into a life of crime.

But Duke had helped his daughter change directions once he'd recognized their career for the potential problem it was. He would help her fix this problem, too. He just needed to be craftier about it, because Mallory was older and savvier now.

After draining his glass, he set it on the counter. "I need to pull my thoughts together. Why don't you two meet me at Polish Paul's tonight?"

"Are we meeting with a client, boss man?"

"In a manner of speaking. I have a job for us. Something's up with Mallory and Trinity. I want to know what."

Opal shook her head, sending platinum waves tumbling sexily around her face. "Stop worrying, Duke. Let her enjoy herself."

"You're playing with fire," Eddie said. "Mallory will take you out if you start messing in her business."

Duke nodded his head in agreement. Mallory definitely wouldn't appreciate his interference. "I got a feeling about this. Something's off with these two. I want to know what, and I need your help to find out."

That was all he had to say. Both Opal and Eddie nodded. Duke's *feelings* were gospel. His feelings had kept them all out of prison more times than he could count.

Except for him, of course, but there was a story there.

JAKE BLINKED when Mallory flipped on the light. Stepping off the last riser, he gave his eyesight a chance to adjust to the bright track lighting before peering around the basement that she'd transformed into a workshop.

"So this is where you work your magic."

"I work my magic in the bedroom." She tossed a bold gaze back over her shoulder. "This is where I work."

Under normal circumstances Jake would appreciate the distinction. As it was, he still hadn't recuperated from the shock of being caught in a compromising situation by Mallory's father. Nor had he recovered from his surprise that after a lengthy get-acquainted conversation, the man had actually said good-bye and left with Jake still in one piece. Then to top matters off, the lust that had died a swift death upon the man's arrival was back in force after watching Mallory dress in a casual sweat suit that hugged her curves in clingy white jersey.

She'd left her hair free to air-dry down her back, and it shone like obsidian. The memory of those cool strands between his fingers assaulted his senses, and, as an admittedly desperate attempt at distraction, Jake surveyed the room around him, taking comfort in the calming familiarity of business.

Mallory's workshop quickly revealed itself to be a high-tech world of bright lights and expensive power tools, large drafting tables and cutting-edge electronic gadgetry that brought to mind a small-scale version of his own labs at TSS.

"You studied business and engineering," he said. Both were reflected in her workspace.

"You did your homework." It wasn't a question.

"Public records, client references. The usual stuff."

He didn't add that the usual stuff had been the extent of his research. He wouldn't offer up his limits on a platter, and she didn't need to know that he didn't have the kind of connections that she had. *If* she didn't already know.

"Even with my impeccable references, you still don't trust me?"

He would have answered her in the affirmative, but he didn't, realizing his feelings weren't as clear-cut as they'd been earlier. "I want to get to know you."

She didn't miss the significance of that statement. "You didn't trust me before we slept together."

"No, I didn't."

"And yet you're willing to consider it now." She flipped her hair behind her shoulder and smiled wryly. "Does sex always affect you this way?"

"Not always."

The honest answer was *never,* but once again he wouldn't give honesty to Mallory. He'd never actually slept with a woman he didn't trust. If he were equally honest with himself, he'd have to admit to never actually sleeping with a woman that he'd wanted to get to know this much, either.

Jake couldn't be sure there wasn't an *us*. Something was going on between them, something that had started ten years ago when they'd been nothing more than accidental strangers. He wanted a chance to find out what that something was. In order to do that he needed to understand Mallory, to know how she worked, how she played, how she lived and how she reasoned.

"You brought the specs," she said, suddenly all business.

Striding to a worktable, he snapped open his briefcase. She helped herself to the contents, and he retreated, glancing at a wall that housed an assortment of gear hanging from hooks and metal shelving.

He recognized rappel lines and harnesses and an image

filtered through his memory of his first glimpse of Mallory. The sight of her sinuously descending a rope, the slim lines of her body softened by darkness.

He'd been shell-shocked by the sight of her then, a reaction he'd always attributed to youth. As the only child of upper-middle-class parents, Jake had been focused on his accomplishments from a very young age. He'd planned for his future, been fortunate enough and privileged enough to be able to realize his dreams.

Hindsight told him that he'd had life too easy. When he'd been thrown a curve in her shapely form that night, he simply hadn't had any frame of reference for someone like Mallory Hunt. He'd experienced an unfamiliar indecision that he'd paid for dearly, and it had taken considerable time and effort to develop the skills he'd needed to deal effectively with having all his careful plans derailed.

But Jake had grown from the experience and was content with his accomplishments and the path his life had taken. So he found it a little surprising now that youth hadn't been solely responsible for his intense reaction to this woman. He'd been shell-shocked by her ten years ago; the woman who pored over the blueprints for the Sentex 2000, seemingly unaware of his presence, fascinated him.

Jake watched as she reached for a table light, bent it forward on a retractable arm to closely view the specs. Her hair swept in front of her shoulders as she leaned over, concealing all but her profile, the silky dark brows, the lush lashes, the straight nose, the kissable mouth.

He cocked his hip against the table and folded his arms across his chest and almost smiled. Almost.

No, youth had nothing to do with his reaction to Mallory. Nothing at all.

"You're operating with utility and environmental systems controlled at the source," she said.

"For my full-service clients."

"You're one point of service for the U.S., Canada and Puerto Rico? Instantaneous signals to the central alarm monitoring station and police dispatch. You've got that kind of satellite coverage?"

Jake nodded, satisfied that she sounded surprised. Looked like his resources weren't the only ones with limits. "I've just negotiated a deal to expand my coverage so I can accommodate clients with multi-site businesses."

She nodded approvingly, flipped the page and reached for a large magnifier attached to the worktable to position it over the electrical schematics of the alarm.

From the power specifications, Mallory would find that his circuitry ensured the integrity of the microprocessor under any conditions. And when she flipped the next page, he knew she would recognize that his central monitoring stations were the most up-to-date on the market.

His gaze drifted across the room to the corner desk that housed her office equipment, which, while small by comparison to the space allotted the rest of her workshop, was clearly a cutting-edge set-up that included a computer with flat-screen monitor, fax machine, telephone system and free-standing copier.

"So, Jake," she said. "TSS's monitoring stations are utilizing uninterruptible power supplies, power generators and redundant systems that allow each facility to be backed up by other locations during emergencies."

"You sound like the blurb in my promotional brochure."

When she didn't reply, he turned around and found her holding a copy of TSS's promotional brochure. He smiled.

She smiled back.

"You're providing some serious closed circuit TV and video surveillance capabilities with the Sentex 2000. Indoor, outdoor and covert cameras. Twenty-twenty lenses with pan, tilt and zoom. Interactive video to monitor critical systems. Is all this really cost-effective?''

''It will be. I plan to customize each system personally to suit my clients' needs.''

She leveled that crystal gaze at him. ''Oh, now I see. The real reason you want to work with me. You need my expertise so you can compete in my field.''

''Only for my clients.''

''Your clients could be my clients. They won't be though, if you can offer my troubleshooting services.''

Jake laughed. ''I think it's fair to say I'll never compete with your level of expertise. That's why I'm considering creating a position for you in my organization.''

''Oh, you are, are you?''

''I have big plans for TSS's future. Someone of your particular talents would only strengthen my position in the market. Especially if you're not assisting my competition.''

Mirroring his position, she folded her arms across her chest and stared up at him. ''But you decided to contract with me for only one job and pick my brain about the way I work. You've piqued my curiosity, Jake. Why?''

''Aside from the trust issue, I couldn't come up with a package I felt was lucrative enough to attract your attention.''

''Were you worried I'd laugh in your face?''

''There was that, too.''

She laughed, a silvery sound that underscored their closeness, the space of mere inches that separated their folded arms, their hips that rested against the edge of the worktable. ''Well, you read me right on that score. Money talks, but it's not the end-all and be-all of my existence.''

He'd gotten that part loud and clear. Being challenged

was clearly a motivating factor, and he was obviously providing her with a big challenge right now. "For the time being, what I learn from you will help me target my clients' needs. I'll be satisfied with that."

"For the time being?"

"I told you, I have plans for the future of my company. I'll eventually need to create your position."

"And here I thought I was offering a unique service."

Unable to resist the urge, Jake brushed his thumb along her full lower lip. "You are, which is why I'm willing to pay your fee."

She darted her tongue out and Jake's blood heated in the wake of the moist path she traced along his skin. "I hope you won't be sorry."

He couldn't be entirely sure that she was referring to their new status as lovers when the memory of her father's security consulting business was still fresh in his head. "Is that a warning?"

"Still worried about my dad, are you?"

Jake found it a little unsettling how easily she'd read his thoughts. Lowering his hand from her mouth, he met her gaze evenly. "I'm willing to take you at your word."

"My contract legally binds me to confidentiality."

"I know. My attorneys went through it."

"Passing along information to my dad would be a bit obvious, don't you think?"

"Only if a court could prove complicity between your father and a burglary ring."

She arched a dark brow. "You have given this some thought."

He nodded.

"Well, Jake. I suppose it all boils down to your willingness to make a leap of faith until you know me better and believe I'm trustworthy. Are you willing to make it?"

"I wouldn't have made love to you if I hadn't been."

Something flashed in her clear gaze, some emotion he couldn't nail down, but when she said, "You're very noble and romantic aren't you? A regular knight in shining armor." He knew she wasn't complimenting him.

"Just someone who considers all the angles."

"How wonderfully…*thorough*. So we're all set then. Papers are signed and we understand each other."

He nodded.

"Good, because your Sentex 2000 is very impressive on paper. I'm looking forward to seeing it in action."

She was suddenly all business, and he had no doubt that her statement translated to mean she was looking forward to proving there were imperfections. "You're not seeing any red flags at first glance?"

Jake honestly didn't expect her to say yes. He was confident in his work and the engineers on his staff, successful in his field only because he put forth the extra effort it took to cover all the bases. The introduction of the Sentex 2000 onto the market would elevate TSS into the big leagues of commercial security, and he'd carefully planned for that event.

"Not at first glance. You're utilizing traditional system components in some innovative ways," she said generously. "There are two things here that I question, but I won't be able to target my concerns until I see your system in action and the kind of coverage it provides."

"No problem. I've chosen a property for us to burglarize."

She inclined her head, but that slight smile playing around the corners of her mouth suggested that his liberal use of the term *us* amused her. "You understood everything in my introductory packet then? Have you made the arrangements with your client yet?"

"We've discussed the situation."

"Good. And he's okay with *us* breaking into his property?" she asked, closing the folder and rummaging through the stack of papers in his briefcase. "Did you bring the signed releases?"

Jake pulled his briefcase across the worktable toward him. Withdrawing a stack of documents, he handed them to her. "All the paperwork you need to cover your ass legally. I had my attorneys check these over, too, and re-create a set for me."

"They're essential, I'm sure you'll agree."

Jake inclined his head, but before he had a chance to answer she said, "You were that sure I'd agree to your terms?"

"I didn't intend to take no for an answer."

"Not only romantic and noble, but determined, too."

Leaning toward her, he inhaled deeply of the freshly showered scent wafting from that mass of still-damp hair and whispered close to her ear, "Very."

He was rewarded by the shiver that rippled full length along her body. She lifted her gaze to his, a slight smile playing around her mouth. She was clearly comfortable with her sensuality, and he decided he liked that about her.

"Then we're all set," she said. "All I need to know is the name of the business and what you want me to steal."

All thoughts of shivers and sensuality flew out of Jake's head, and he frowned.

"Forgot that part, did you?" Tracing the arm of his glasses with a fingertip, she raised up on tiptoe to whisper in his ear, "It's no fun if there isn't anything to steal."

Now it was his turn to shiver as every drop of blood in his veins plummeted, and he was sporting a promising erection before he'd managed to suck in another breath.

"Why don't you go get me something to steal, and then I'll start walking you through the process of how I plan a burglary."

Somehow she made that sound like a promise.

7

THE SKY was melting into the golden shades of sunset when Mallory settled onto her sofa with a cup of freshly brewed espresso. She sipped appreciatively, admiring the view through her living-room windows before reaching for the contracts bearing Jake's signatures.

He hadn't said specifically when he'd return, but she figured his arrangements would carry him through the end of the business day. If she read him right, Mr. Noble and Romantic would show up on her doorstep at the crack of dawn tomorrow morning, raring to begin his first day of burglary training.

The thought made her smile.

Mallory took another fortifying sip and watched the golden glow of sunset fade over the trees in the park across the street. Jake Trinity was providing her a challenge she hadn't expected, and after her initial surprise had passed, she couldn't say she was sorry. Her sex life hadn't been serving up any challenges lately—so few in fact, she hadn't even bothered making the effort to meet anyone in quite a while.

Maybe Jake was exactly what she needed. Not only could she exorcise the man and their baggage from her system, but she could jump-start her lethargic libido in the process. She really hadn't needed to brew this espresso to wake her up right now. The memory of their awesome sex still radiated through her. She wanted to stretch and purr, and jump Jake's bones again.

She had needed to brew the espresso to figure out what she was going to do about her dad, though. While he often expressed interest and opinions about her work, he was too curious about Jake for her peace of mind. She certainly hadn't expected him to show up during their consultation today.

For a moment, she'd worried that she'd been wrong and her dad did know that Jake had been the informant on the Innovative job. But after seeing them together—especially given the logistics of the situation—she didn't think so. Her dad hadn't been picking Jake's brain to play cat and mouse. He'd been...*visiting* with a man whose work he admired.

Now her dad thought she was involved with Jake, which was exactly the occurrence she'd hoped to avoid. She'd intended their working relationship to cover up their sexual one. But that plan was bust now. Bust in a big way, too, if she read her dad's approval rating correctly. Mallory had no doubt he'd tell all the crew, if only to enlist their aid in supporting his position, which would lead to awkward questions and lies for everyone when she ended her relationship with Jake.

Her dad was well-intentioned, Mallory knew. He wanted to see her have the security of a conventional future, which did absolutely nothing to change the fact that she had no interest in settling down to a house with a white picket fence.

When the telephone rang, she automatically reached for the handset she'd placed on the end table earlier and glanced down at the lighted display. Her heart gave a hard throb of relief. "Lance, where have you—"

"Whoa, hot mama," a voice drawled over the receiver, slurred and fuzzy. "Slow down."

Mallory recognized the voice as Lance's closest friend from a short list of undesirables. "Call me hot mama again, Kyle, and I promise to rip that stud right out of your tongue the next time we're face-to-face."

"Yes, ma'am."

"Much better. Where's Lance?"

"Behind Big Jim's. Figured I'd call before Big Jim finds him and calls the cops."

Swinging her legs around, Mallory scooted to the edge of the sofa and set the mug on the coffee table. "*Behind Big Jim's?* Is he all right?"

"He's breathing."

"What happened?"

"Partied too hearty." And from the sound of Kyle's voice the same was equally true of him.

"You've been drinking? Anything else?"

"Oh yeah, *every*thing else."

His garbled laughter provoked a chill that made Mallory breathe deeply to dispel the sensation. "All right, Kyle. Listen to me. Do not get in the car. Tell Big Jim if he comes outside that I'm on my way—"

"Uh-uh. I'm outta here."

She exploded off the sofa and headed into the foyer to find her shoes. "It'll take me fifteen minutes to get there. I'll give you a ride."

"Uh-uh. I ain't hanging around. I'll cover him up…with this…" A rustling on the other end of the line sounded like Kyle dragging something—a box maybe?—over the ground. "He'll wait."

"Will he be all right?"

"Don't see why not."

Of course not. Damn kid. He didn't see anything wrong

with climbing behind the wheel of a car in his condition, either. "Listen, Kyle. If he has anything on him, take it with you."

Another muddled laugh. "All right, hot mama. But *you* tell Lance you gave me his shit."

In I'm-high-speak, that statement translated to mean that Lance had drugs on him that promised to continue the party a while longer. But this boy getting busted wasn't an issue for Mallory if it saved Lance from a potential problem. And Big Jim calling the law only to find Lance in possession was potentially a big one. "I'll tell Lance—"

The line disconnected.

Mallory pulled on her climbing boots, didn't bother to tie the laces. Grabbing her purse and keys, she disabled her alarm system, pulled open her front door…

And found Jake Trinity walking up her stairs.

She stopped short in the doorway. "What are you doing here?"

He inclined his head to the garment bag he held slung over his shoulder. "You said twenty-four seven. I picked up some things to last me a few days."

Well, she'd said twenty-four even if she hadn't expected around the clock to start right away. One glimpse into Jake's eyes made her suspect he'd known it, too. This was a game, one that under normal circumstances she would enjoy playing. Unfortunately, right now she didn't have time to pick up the gauntlet and make the next move.

"Come on in, Jake." She motioned him inside. "I'm on my way out, but you can wait here until I get back. I won't be long."

Jake might have agreed, but something raw was roughing up Mallory's usual composure. "Hop in and I'll drive you," he said.

Her acquiescence was his first clue to trouble. Tossing his garment bag into her foyer, he escorted her down the stairs and held the door while she climbed into the passenger side. His second clue came when she said, "Head toward the Main Mall."

Hitching her knee up on the seat, she stared through the windshield, as if willing the distance to pass in the blink of an eye. There was no missing her agitation, but he didn't ask for an explanation. He did as she asked.

The Main Mall was a collection of older shops in the seedy fringes padding the business district. He also knew that after the close of the workday, the only people to inhabit that part of town were there for no good reason.

When Mallory didn't stop him at the Main Mall but directed him into a rough neighborhood beyond, he was very glad he'd offered to drive her.

"Make a left here and pull around back," she said, shoving her purse and keys under his front seat.

Jake pulled into the parking lot of a low-slung building tucked back from the street and obscured from the wash of the street lamps. An air conditioner unit was propped inside the only window with a two-by-four, and music blared through the open front door beneath a large hand-painted sign that read Big Jim's Elbow Bender.

Circling the building, he bit back yet another question and came to a stop behind the back door where a bald light bulb burned weakly.

She cast him a sidelong glance as she opened the door and slid out. "Just hang on, I'll be right back."

Jake took one look around the parking lot where he could see about ten feet in any direction and got out behind her.

She glanced around in indecision then took off toward a concrete stall that contained a full Dumpster and stacks of flattened boxes beside it. He was a step behind her, but she didn't seem to notice as she began flinging aside sheets of cardboard.

"Mallory, let me—" He cut off when he saw what she'd been looking for—a kid in his teens huddled against the wall.

In an instant, Mallory was on her knees beside him, pressing her fingers to his throat to check his pulse.

"Talk to me, Lance," she said sharply, gripping him by the chin and shifting his face back and forth. "Come on, wake up."

The kid was out.

The night eclipsed his features but Jake could see the faint stubble around his mouth, the glint of a silver stud through his eyebrow. His hair could have been blond or brown or any color in between for as much as the filthy dew rag revealed of the greasy strands below. His shirt and too-large hoodlum jeans weren't in much better shape.

"Who is he?" Jake asked.

"A friend," she said without glancing up.

Jake let her ambiguity pass. Now wasn't the time to play twenty questions. She shook the boy's shoulders, her frustration revealing itself in each impatient shake. A breeze lifted strands of hair away from her face and off her shoulders, revealing the tight lines of her expression and that she wasn't just a little worried.

Kneeling beside her, he slid a hand behind the boy— Lance—and propped him upright. The muscles beneath his hands contained the wiry tension of a boy who was close to but hadn't yet reached manhood.

Lance gave a grunt and tried to shrug him off.

Jake dragged him up so he was leaning against the brick enclosure, his head lolling onto his chest, before Mallory forced it up, peeled back an eyelid and inspected the bloodshot eye below. "Talk to me, Lance. I need to know what you're on."

Another grunt.

With a heavy sigh, Mallory patted down the pockets on his shirt, then moved on to his pants. She appeared to have found something because she was suddenly fumbling deep into a pocket before withdrawing a small glass tube.

"Crack. Nice. I suppose that answers my question."

"He's been drinking too."

She nodded. Using her shirt, she wiped off the handle with impatient swipes and tossed it into the garbage. Disposing of the evidence, he guessed.

Grabbing Lance by the chin, she said sharply, "You talk to me right now or I toss your butt in the back seat and take you straight to the emergency room. Then I'm calling your dad."

Her threat produced more life signs than Jake had seen so far. Lance exhaled heavily and looked as though he was trying to shake off the effects of whatever he was on.

"Mal," he managed to grind out.

"Are you all right? Are you going to sleep this off or do I need to get you help?"

He shook his head with a little more energy and mumbled something that sounded like "Drank too much."

Mallory sat back on her haunches and frowned.

"You going to take his word?" Jake asked, more than a little surprised. The kid looked wasted in his estimation, but as he had no idea whether or not this was a frequent occurrence, he refrained from further comment.

"I don't know yet. I want to see if I can get him up and talking some more."

Jake stood, dragging the kid to his feet. "Come on, Lance. We're taking a walk."

Mallory caught the kid beneath his other arm and together they managed to get him moving, a stumbling, weak-kneed effort that seemed to be helping him shake off his stupor.

"How'd you know he was here?" Jake asked.

"His friend called me."

He glanced around, in case he'd missed signs of someone else in the dark.

"Let me rephrase that," she said dryly. "His *friend* called me before he took off."

"Got it."

Even through the darkness he could see worry clouding her features, though he sensed from her tough-guy tone that she was doing her level best not let him see how affected she was.

"Come on. Let's get him to the car, Mallory. I think he's coming around. If not, I'll just drive to the hospital."

She nodded.

Lance roused enough to assist their efforts to get him situated in the back seat. Jake fastened the seat belt while Mallory stepped back, shaking her head.

"Have you got a bag or something?" she asked. "He doesn't look so good. You might be sorry you offered to give me a ride."

"Don't worry about it. Get in. There are napkins in the glove compartment if you need some."

She leaned over the seat, dragged the Dew-Rag from Lance's head and started up a steady stream of conversation that began as one-sided, but eventually included monosyllabic replies from Lance. She seemed satisfied.

"Let's take him home." She gave him directions to a nearby street that hosted a variety of nighttime businesses—a liquor store, a nightclub and several strip clubs.

Jake only nodded, following her lead and observing her closely, interested in how she handled the situation and unsure if he was reading her tough act right. She hadn't shared a thing with him except this boy's name and his status as her friend. Not much, given the circumstances. She'd retreated into herself to cope alone and privately. He had no doubt she would have handled Lance whether he'd accompanied her or not.

But she was worried. Her actions proved that louder than words could. Here was another piece of the puzzle to Mallory, a piece that hinted at a vulnerable woman beneath the tough exterior, a piece that proved how little he knew about her.

And how much he wanted to know more.

"Head around back of that tattoo parlor," she said, and Jake wheeled around to the back of the two-story building to find the lot crowded with several very expensive vehicles.

Lance struggled to keep his head up in the back seat. "Shit," he said, barely decipherable but clearly unhappy. "Damn crew. Don't…leave."

He wasn't the only one frowning, and Jake recognized the war waging in Mallory's expression. She avoided looking his way. "No can do, Lance, but I'll make you a deal. Promise me you'll stay put, and we'll bypass the shop and get you upstairs. I'll call your dad. That's the best I can do."

Her tone left no room for argument, and Lance was apparently coherent enough to recognize it. Again, Jake questioned if accepting this kid at his word was the smartest choice.

"Who owns this place?" he asked, pulling beside a Mercedes sedan and shifting into Park.

"Lance's father." Mallory slipped out of the passenger's door before he could ask another question. "Let's be fast."

Together they helped the unsteady teen up the stairs leading to the second-story apartment. Another piece to the puzzle of his mystery woman came when she pulled out her own set of keys to unlock the door.

Obviously Lance and his father were *very close* friends.

While she settled the boy into his bed, Jake took a look around what turned out to be a surprisingly comfortable home. The building was in a commercial district that catered to a rougher element, but the inside of the spacious apartment might have been a home in an upscale suburb.

"I need to call his dad, so let's go," Mallory said when she reappeared in the living room. "Lance's all set, but I don't want him alone for long."

She hurried Jake out the door and locked up quickly, casting a sidelong glance at the cars parked in the lot.

The crew. Jake added another question to his growing list of questions about this woman that he wanted answers to.

Only when he'd backed into the street did Mallory pull a cell phone from her purse and dialed. "Hi, Polish Paul," she said with a cheeriness that was shy of being reflected in her expression. "Guess who I just tucked into his bed upstairs."

Jake could hear the man's booming voice through the receiver even if he couldn't distinguish the words.

Mallory slanted the phone away from her ear as she relayed the course of events that had led her to the back of Big Jim's Elbow Bender. "He's trashed, but he was alert enough so I was okay with bringing him home. You need to keep your eyes on him."

Jake braked for a light and shifted his gaze to Mallory, who'd brought a hand up to massage her temples.

"I know," she said in response to the man on the other

end. "I saw you all there. Tell Daddy I figured you were meeting with a client so I didn't stop."

Another piece of the puzzle fitted neatly into place as Jake accelerated with the light and made a right turn onto the Interstate on-ramp. Now he understood who owned one of the high-ticket cars in the lot—Mallory's father. He couldn't say for sure whether she was telling the truth about not wanting to interrupt a possible meeting, but he found it very significant that she hadn't once mentioned his name.

From what her father had said earlier about his current clientele, a business meeting in a tattoo parlor at night fit neatly with Jake's impression of a consultant who advised thieves on how to circumvent security systems.

Mallory completed her call and deposited the phone back in her purse. "Thanks for your help, Jake. Getting Lance settled would have been difficult without you." She hiked her knee up on the seat and faced him. "And thank you for not grilling me."

"You noticed."

"I did."

"Lance is obviously a close friend. And his father, too."

He didn't ask, just stated the obvious as he saw it, introducing the conversation so she knew he was interested. The choice to continue talking was hers.

She stared at him thoughtfully before saying, "I lived with Lance and his dad once upon a time."

"Really." Jake merged into traffic, taking a second to decide how best to phrase his reply and deciding up-front would be best. "While your father was in prison?"

"Yes."

"So this...*Polish Paul* and his family were the ones who took you in. After I learned you were underage, I'd wondered what happened to you."

"Did you, Jake?" He heard no emotion whatsoever in her voice. "So you followed the trial. Did you want to make sure all the loose ends were tied up?"

Although he never shifted his gaze from the road, he could feel the intensity of her stare, sensed an undercurrent of resentment between them.

Another piece of the puzzle clicked into place.

"I wasn't interested in loose ends. I was interested in you. I had no frame of reference for why you'd be in that situation taking those sorts of risks. I needed to understand."

"And do you?"

"Not really. I'd like to."

She didn't reply, but there was something about the silence, something about the way she watched him that told Jake he'd surprised her with his frankness.

"Polish Paul was my dad's inside man. He was the first member of the crew. Signed on long before I was even born."

A *very close* family friend. "The crew?"

"My dad's coworkers," she said, and he glanced over at her to find that her pale face might have been carved from ivory for as much emotion as he could see in her expression. "Polish Paul was the inside man. Opal was the surveillance specialist and Eddie handled the alarms."

"And your father?"

"He cracked the safes and stole the goods."

She might have been discussing careers as mundane as medicine or law so easily and openly did she referred to these people's expertise. "Exactly when did they all retire?"

"After the Innovative job."

When their ringleader had gone to prison.

"Only your father served time. Wouldn't the state have reduced his sentence if he turned in his accomplices?"

She shrugged. "He would never have turned them in. They're his crew. It was his job to protect them."

More honor among thieves.

"So now the crew is back together, assisting your father in his consulting business. Is this business legal?"

Mallory shrugged. "I'd say it's not prosecutable."

Fair enough. Jake was beginning to grasp that in her world there was a huge distinction between the two.

"So you went to live with Polish Paul after your dad was arrested."

"Eventually. I went into foster care first."

Jake hadn't known that. He glanced at her, found her watching him with such a poker face that he was reminded of her father. "For how long?"

"Six months. Until Polish Paul and Opal could get married and prove to the courts they could provide a suitable home."

"Polish Paul and Opal are married, but Lance isn't her son?"

"Polish Paul and Opal only married to spring me from foster care. They dissolved the marriage as soon as I turned eighteen. Lance's mother had died of cancer a few years before."

Jake stared out at the highway unfolding before him, a stretch of dark road punctuated by the glow of passing red taillights. The scene struck him as lonely. Vehicles shooting past each other, the occupants concealed by blackened windows.

Duke Hunt's loyalty to his crew and the crew's loyalty to their boss struck him as both moving and extreme. Here was another place where Jake had no frame of reference.

The people in his life had always been there for him unconditionally, and would be, Jake knew, no matter what.

Sure, he'd gotten into his fair share of trouble, most particularly with Innovative Engineering, but his family's loyalty had never really been tested in this type of foundation-shaking situation. When a father's arrest left a minor daughter in the state's custody…*that* qualified as foundation-shaking—a situation Jake couldn't relate to at all.

Which explained a great deal about how Mallory had chosen to handle Lance tonight. Loyalty had guided her. He was her friend, and she would help him. Despite the fact that the kid was clearly out of control, she'd involved him in her decision-making process, expected him to be accountable for his actions and to have a say-so in the consequences.

Whether or not Lance was up to that accountability, Jake couldn't say. He certainly hadn't seen anything to give him the impression the kid was making rational choices. From where Jake stood it looked as if the kid had needed more help than just a friend taking him home to sleep it off.

But the loyalty was beginning to make sense.

"Why did you ask me not to mention the Innovative job to your father today?"

She seemed surprised by his question. Not that she did anything overt to give him that impression. No, Mallory was skilled at controlling her emotions and right now she wasn't sharing. But something about the way she cocked her head to the side and looked at him from beneath those lushly fringed lashes suggested she hadn't expected him to switch gears.

"I would have thought that was obvious."

"If it should have been, I missed it."

She rolled her eyes. "How could you miss my dad's

approval rating? I didn't think we'd ever get him out of my bedroom.''

Maybe Jake was slow tonight. Maybe the intensity of their sex and the constant challenge of trying to stay a step ahead of her had killed off more brain cells than he'd thought, but he still had no clue what she was talking about. ''Your father's approval rating for what?''

''For you. You've been cleared.''

For what specifically? He didn't ask. ''I still don't understand why you didn't want me to bring up Innovative Engineering.''

She exhaled in exasperation that he recognized wasn't feigned and felt stupid because he was missing something she considered very obvious.

''Honestly, Jake. Do you think my dad would approve of you and stand there making chitchat if he knew you were the informant from the Innovative job?''

Time seemed to stop with the same abruptness as if he'd pressed the pause button on a remote control. A freeze-frame. Mallory's scowl. Her words, which filtered into his brain in slow motion…

Informant?

Then it clicked. Mallory thought he'd tripped the alarm.

Jake's first impulse was to laugh, but he just gripped the steering wheel tighter, forcing his gaze back to the road, which was exactly where it should be when he was cruising along with the traffic at eighty miles per hour.

His whole life had taken a left turn because of his indecision that night, yet Mallory thought he'd pressed the button that had sent her father to prison.

''There's a very good reason why your father doesn't know I was the informant,'' he said, amazed and a little impressed by how collected he sounded.

''Really?'' She arched a brow dubiously. ''And why is that?''

''Because I wasn't.''

8

OVER THE PAST ten years Polish Paul's Tattoo Studio had grown to be an institution in Atlanta based solely on Polish Paul's artistic talent. The man had a gift for creating images much in the same way he had a gift for conceptualizing the components to get Duke's crew in and out of a secured facility.

Through thirty-plus years of friendship, Paul Ruffin, known to everyone as Polish Paul, had wielded his gift whether he was sketching egress routes or pinch-hitting between jobs with an airbrush or tattoo needles.

Duke hadn't been surprised when Polish Paul had opened his own studio upon retirement, and he liked the simplicity of the place, which didn't come to life until the sun went down. There was no forced elegance, only bright lights, hydraulic chairs and lots of mirrors.

And Polish Paul's pride and joy—a pool table that took up a chunk of his workspace.

Duke also knew his friend would have knocked out a wall and laid the slab for additional square footage himself before abandoning that pool table. Just as sporting one of his tattoos—or a ''Polish Paul'' as they'd become known—was considered an honor, an invitation to shoot a game of pool on this table was equally regarded by the underworld elite.

Polish Paul was gruff and partial to dark beers and fine Cuban cigars, one of which he kept clenched between his teeth at all times, even while he worked. Duke knew most people considered inhaling second-hand smoke at close range a small price to pay for an original Polish Paul.

"Bless that girl of yours." Polish Paul reappeared in the studio, circling the counter.

"How is Lance?" Opal sat up in a hydraulic chair and crossed her shapely legs.

Polish Paul dragged the stogie from his lips and set it in the ashtray by the cash register. "Sleeping it off upstairs."

Duke dragged his gaze from Opal's legs and asked, "Where did Mallory find him?"

"She swept him up off the ground behind Big Jim's."

"Big Jim let them onto his property?" Eddie folded his arms across his chest and gave a low whistle. "I'd have expected him to call the law. Think he's finally gotten over you stealing Connie out from under his big nose?"

Polish Paul shook his grizzled head. "Wouldn't bet on it. From what Mallory said, he didn't know Lance was there. That boy has the devil's own luck."

"Let's hope that luck doesn't run out any time soon." Opal didn't allow herself a frown, but Duke didn't need the corresponding facial expression to hear the worry in her voice.

"She's right, Paul," he said. "This has been going on too long. Lance doesn't seem to be coming around."

"Damned kid is making me nuts." He slammed a hand down on the counter, made the cigar in the ashtray jump.

Opal caught Duke's gaze in the mirror, gave him a look that revealed she saw an opportunity to speak her mind and was going for it. "You can't keep picking up the pieces for him, Paul. You're not doing him or yourself any good."

"What else can I do? Throw him out in the street?"

Duke cocked a hip against the pool table and said, "Get him some help."

Polish Paul scowled. "He won't go, and if I force him, I'm as good as throwing him out. He'll drop out of school and won't come home."

"He's barely coming home now." Opal pointed out.

"She's right, man," Eddie said. "He's got you hostage. He knows you won't force him to go see somebody, so he's just doing whatever the hell he wants."

"We're worried about him, and you." Duke hadn't been this worried about his friend since Paul had lost his wife. "None of us want to see Lance crash and burn."

"Of course not," Opal agreed. "We want to see him live up to his potential. He's a smart boy—"

"If Connie were alive, he might have stood a chance." Polish Paul thrust his fingers through his hair in frustration, making it stand on end.

"That's not true." Opal rose in a fluid burst of motion that drew Duke's gaze from the top of her sleek head down the length of her curvy body, beautifully displayed in dark blue silk.

She went to stand beside their friend and patted his hand. "You've done a wonderful job rearing Lance. You know as well as I do that Connie would never have had a child with you if she didn't trust you to raise him right."

What none of them said was that Connie hadn't expected to contract the ovarian cancer that had killed her. And ever since her death, Polish Paul had been trying to play the roles of both father and mother to their only son. A difficult enough job even for someone who'd had a stable upbringing. Polish Paul hadn't. Like the rest of them, life had knocked him around enough during his youth to make gaining his feet in adulthood a task of monumental proportions.

And like the rest of them, Paul stood tall. He'd always done his best by his son.

"Give it some thought," Duke said. "You've done all you can alone. The kid needs help. We're all here if you need us."

Polish Paul met his gaze and nodded. Retrieving his cigar, he shoved it in his mouth and bit down hard. "Looks like today's the day for kid grief, eh, Duke? Lance woke up enough to ask me who the guy with Mallory was."

"Who?" Now here was a curve he hadn't expected.

"Lance said she called him Jake. I'm guessing he's the same guy we've been talking about. He threw my son over his shoulder and got him home in one piece. You tell him thanks for me when you see him."

Duke nodded. "I'll take care of it. That would certainly explain why Mallory didn't drop in tonight. What the hell is she doing?"

"Kid grief sums it up adequately," Eddie said dryly. "And Opal and I get to live vicariously through you two. Thanks."

"The older they get the less control we have," Duke admitted, still considering Mallory bringing Trinity along to pick up Lance.

"Yeah, thanks," Polish Paul reached for his cigar.

"Buck up, gentlemen," Opal said. "You can't solve all the problems of the world in one night. But do what Duke says, Paul, and give professional help some thought. It wouldn't hurt for you to talk with someone yourself. Get a few new ideas about how to help Lance. It can't hurt."

"An excellent suggestion." Duke caught her gaze and nodded his approval.

"I'm glad you like my advice," she said. "Because I have some for you, too. Butt out of Mallory's life."

"You've been told, boss man." Eddie laughed, and even Paul managed a smile.

"No can do, gorgeous. Something isn't right between Mallory and Trinity. What's up with her dragging him along to pick up Lance? When was the last time you saw her bring any guy around?"

Several shrugs precluded the need to answer that question.

"I still fail to see the problem," Opal insisted. "You want Mallory to find someone she cares about. So what's the problem? Don't you like Jake Trinity?"

"Liking him isn't an issue. I don't know him." Although Duke couldn't help but chuckle when he thought about the man wrapped in that bath towel. "He's certainly no pushover. I'll give him that. He stood in the middle of my daughter's bedroom and asked me if I was colluding with her for information about his new security system."

"You didn't wipe the floor with him?" Polish Paul asked.

"The thought crossed my mind, believe me. But I kept getting the feeling I should know him."

"Why, boss man? Have you been working with TSS on something you haven't told us about?" Eddie asked. "When we were working on my system we went out of our way *not* to meet the guy."

"I've never met him personally. But he was familiar somehow. Like I've seen him somewhere. I've been racking my brain, but I can't remember where."

"How do you expect us to help you with that?" Polish Paul asked. "I wouldn't know Trinity if he walked up and kissed me on the cheek. What's bugging you?"

"Mallory gets involved with this guy and as far as we know she's never met him before. And…" He paused, more to muddle through this anomaly in her behavior than for dramatic effect. "She's letting him help her when she tests his system."

"You're kidding?" Eddie said.

Duke shook his head.

"Well, you're right about one thing," Polish Paul mouthed around his stogie. "Our gal sure is acting weird."

Opal met his gaze. "How good-looking is this Jake Trinity?"

"How the hell do I know how good-looking he is, Opal? What, is there some sort of yardstick for that?"

Her arched brows disappeared beneath her platinum bangs. "You do look in a mirror every day, don't you?"

Okay, that stopped him. "Well, then yeah. I suppose he's good-looking. If Mallory likes blond guys."

Opal smiled. "I'll bet Mallory would find a blond guy just scrumptious if he was good-looking and *sexy* enough."

"Shit, Duke. Tell me they don't have a yardstick for *that*." Polish Paul struck one of those flexing muscle, body-builder poses that lost a great deal of the effect with his beer gut and stogie. "You don't stand in front of the mirror checking yourself out to see if you make the cut, do you?"

"Argh, TMI." Eddie held a hand in front of his eyes and the gold rings on his fingers winked in the overhead light. "Too much information. The thought of seeing Duke in front of the mirror is turning my stomach." He shook his head as if clearing the image. "And didn't I just say I thought of Mallory as a daughter? She's still twelve as far as I'm concerned. She does not do *it*."

Duke wouldn't have minded hanging on to that delusion himself. Especially after walking in on her and Trinity with wet heads. "Damned straight. Too much information."

"She's a beautiful, healthy girl. Emphasis on the word

healthy.'' Opal tipped that regal nose in the air. "Leave her be. You're all a big bunch of babies."

Duke didn't want to hear it. He was entitled to being whatever he damn well pleased when it came to his daughter and her boyfriends. Another argument for getting her settled down with a worthy man who would treat her right.

"Enough of this, crew. Let's get back to business. I've got a plan and I need your help. I want all of you to start making appearances when Mallory and Trinity are working together. Keep your ears open. I want to know what the deal is between these two." Duke shot Opal what he hoped was a quelling glance. "And I don't want to hear about *it.''*

"What do you think is going on between them, boss man? Love at first sight?"

"Eddie, that is so sweet." Opal smiled a smile that proved his quelling glance hadn't bothered the romantic heart beating beneath her impressive bosom one bit.

"Nothing would make me happier. But I'm a realist, and that's not my daughter," Duke admitted. "Opal, you'll be easy. Mallory will be working with Trinity in her workshop for the next few days so you can pop in whenever you get a chance. Meet him for yourself and see if you can ferret anything out. And Eddie, I suggested that Mallory should call you to use your place to put Trinity through his paces."

"You got it, boss man. I'll do my thing."

"What about me, Duke?" Polish Paul asked.

Eddie winked at him. "Invite her to bring the guy in for a tattoo. Two little matching hearts on their butts."

"Right." Paul plucked the stogie from his mouth and stubbed it in the ashtray. "I'll tattoo a little heart on your ass, too."

"Paul, you got your hands full with Lance, so sit tight," Duke said.

He clearly wasn't happy with that answer, but didn't argue. He knew the rules as well as anyone—if his mind wasn't on a job… "All right. I'll sit back on this one. Unless an opportunity presents itself. I owe Mallory one for helping me out with Lance."

Duke nodded, accepting the compromise. He'd always called them like he saw them, and he didn't intend to conduct business any differently now. Even for an unusual job like this. The risk might not include a stint behind bars, but if Mallory found out they were spying on her…the attitude his daughter could sling around was nearly as daunting.

"Let's wrap it up," Duke said. "Do your thing, crew, and call me when you have something. Paul, need a hand upstairs?"

"No, but flip that Ring the Bell sign on the door since you're standing there."

"Call if you need anything," Duke told him before following everyone through the back door.

The crew said their good-byes and parted ways. Polish Paul headed back upstairs and Eddie hopped into his showy Porsche and gunned the engine. Duke motioned Opal to stay behind.

"What's up, Duke?" she asked.

"Leave your car here. I want to swing by Mallory's to see if Trinity's car is parked in her driveway. Then I'll take you home with me for the night."

She lifted those baby blues his way, her gaze glinting curiously beneath the starlight. "It's been a while."

"Too long."

She tipped her nose up at him, a look that told him she wasn't going to make this easy. "Well, that choice has been yours because there have been gaps in my schedule lately.''

"I know." The unfortunate truth, because Duke had no one to blame but himself.

He'd been doing a lot of soul-searching lately and realized that Opal had thrown him for a loop. When they'd met, he'd had to conduct a full-scale seduction to get her into bed. She hadn't been a pushover, and he'd been *too* challenged by her. He'd wanted her *too* much.

He'd fought the unfamiliar feeling with distance, contenting himself to share his work and bits and pieces of his life. He'd been the fool that Eddie had always accused him of being. Fortunately, he wasn't one to dwell on his mistakes, not when he saw a way to fix them....

Taking her slender hand, he brought it to his mouth for a kiss. "I've needed time to think, Opal, to decide what I want from you."

She twined her fingers through his, a perfect fit of warm skin and sensitive nerve endings. "You never had to think about what you wanted from me before."

"I've decided I want more."

"You want more than sex from me, and you want grandchildren from Mallory?"

Though her voice dripped with disdain, Duke thought he heard something else in there, too. Something promising.

"You're growing sentimental, old man."

"No, Opal, I'm just growing."

"YOU'RE TELLING ME that you never set off the panic alarm, Jake?" Mallory swept inside her foyer and tossed her keys on the hall tree, leaving him to lock up. She sidestepped the garment bag he'd left on the floor, a solid reminder that he'd shown up intending to spend the night.

"That's exactly what I'm telling you," he said. "Where did you get the idea that I had?"

She stared up into his face, the square jaw showing signs of nighttime stubble, the strong features set in granite, the warm eyes shielded from full potency behind wire frames and plastic lenses. Her impulse was to call him a liar because she'd known for ten years that he'd triggered the alarm. But Jake's surprise wasn't feigned. Neither was his curiosity. Mallory simply didn't believe that a man as by-the-book and *noble* as this one would stand here and lie to her face.

And even if he was lying, she'd see right through him. She didn't.

"We need to talk." And she'd never meant anything quite so seriously. "But my head is about to explode. I need to grab some acetaminophen. Do you want anything?"

"No."

She made her way to the kitchen, trying to sort through the jumble of her thoughts. Something was so not right here. Every nerve in her body was on red alert and her head was pounding so hard, each throb vibrated straight to her toes.

Her dad had said he'd tripped the alarm, and every brain cell rebelled at the thought.

She hadn't deluded herself into believing her dad was fail-safe, but tripping an alarm? That was a *stupid* mistake. Sure, Duke Hunt made mistakes, but not *stupid* ones. Never stupid ones.

Something strange had happened during the Innovative Engineering job, and she needed to find out what. Three gelcaps later she headed back to the living room to find Jake standing in front of the fireplace, looking as disturbed as she felt.

"What made you think I was the one who sounded the alarm?" he asked.

Sitting on her sofa, she glanced absently at the contracts and the mug of stone-cold espresso she'd brewed before Kyle's call. Back when she'd believed she'd understood the situation with Jake and had it under control. "Who else was there in the building that night, Jake?"

"The security guard. I thought he was the one who'd sounded the alarm. But if you're sure—"

"I'm sure. He was contained before my dad ever went into the vault and I met up with you. Opal and Eddie secured the monitoring station. The guard couldn't have tripped an alarm."

Jake nodded. "What exactly was your job that night?"

"Securing my dad's egress from the building." Her voice sounded flat and factual, but that night loomed inside her memory like a brewing storm, each image sharp, focused, as though illuminated by a strike of lightning. "I only needed to stall you for less than two minutes so he could complete the job and get out."

"You did stall me."

"Yes, and it should have been long enough. But we all got out and the law arrived before my dad cleared the building."

Along with the images came the familiar, crushing sense of guilt. Had she called Polish Paul for egress immediately, her dad would have gotten out in time. She'd already had his route cleared. Even if Jake had run straight to a panic button...

But Jake hadn't. Or so he claimed.

"The alarm didn't go off until after I left you," she said, squelching down emotions that had no place surfacing when she needed to think clearly, to sort out Jake's claim and reason through the events of that night. "There

was no one else inside the building, just you and the security guard.''

''I didn't sound the alarm, Mallory.''

His voice was low, alarming in its earnestness. Though
outwardly he appeared composed, standing with his strong
legs braced firmly apart, his hands casually by his sides,
he radiated such intensity he took her breath away. His
dark gaze held hers and she could only stare, enthralled
by the gravity she saw in his eyes, in his expression.

He didn't lie. He wouldn't.

And she didn't want to accept that. It was almost as if
she needed to believe he'd sounded that alarm so she
wouldn't have to face that she believed him, despite herself, despite the facts. She didn't want to face that this was
just one more example of how her feelings for this man
hadn't been rational since the night they'd met.

''Why should I believe you?'' she asked, though the
question was a lie, a knee-jerk reaction against unfamiliar
emotions. And even though she knew exactly what she was
doing and her need shamed her, she did it anyway. Attack
was her only defense against this powerful feeling, this
desperation.

''I don't lie.''

So simple, and, Mallory knew in her heart, so true.

''Right. And you expect me to believe that Mr. Fast-
Track-to-a-Heart-Attack passed up the opportunity to
prove his loyalty to the almighty corporation and miss the
chance at a big promotion or a raise.'' She couldn't stop
the words from pouring from her mouth. ''I'm sure upper
management appreciated your loyalty to the company.''

It was a verbal slap, but the man didn't flinch.

''Obviously you didn't dig deep enough while you were
researching me,'' he said, and the steel in his voice cut
clear across the room. ''If you had, you'd have found out

that I didn't work for Innovative Engineering after that night.''

His dark eyes pierced the distance between them, the silence so complete that she was almost sure he could hear her heart pounding. She was being relentless and totally unfair and Jake could have so easily responded in kind. He could have told her to find out for herself and walked out the door.

He didn't.

''Why?''

He gave her own words back to her. ''Upper management would have appreciated loyalty to the company.''

At least one of them had some control of his emotions.

''They let you go?''

He inclined his head.

It took a moment for the implications of his admission to register. For so long she'd believed that her life and the lives of everyone she loved had been thrown into upheaval because of her meeting with this man. She'd known her dad had lied to her, the whole crew knew he'd lied so she wouldn't feel responsible, and she'd just assumed that Jake had done the deed. That he'd gone on his merry, self-righteous way, satisfied he'd snagged a thief and brought justice to a bad guy.

She'd never once considered any other scenario.

Not once.

And then another thought struck her.

''Why didn't you sound the alarm, Jake?''

He faced her squarely, let her see everything in his face, his expression so brutally honest that she recognized ten years worth of conflicting emotions that rivaled her own.

''I might have, if I'd have had more time to think about it. I can't honestly say. But at first, right after you left, I couldn't seem to get past the fact that if I tripped the alarm a bold young woman with beautiful green eyes might wind up in prison.''

Mallory didn't know what to say. She had no reply to make, wasn't entirely sure she understood all the nuances of what he claimed or the impact his admission was having on her.

She needed to think. Couldn't. Her head pounded as though it was about to explode. The damn painkillers hadn't taken effect yet, and it didn't look like they were going to.

Massaging her temples, she brought herself a reprieve from his steady gaze. She was rattled. He knew it. And she didn't like being this way in front of him, had already been worn down by tonight's ordeal with Lance. Jake shouldn't have been here to witness that, either. Lance was her family, and her family was off limits to lovers.

But that was *her* rule, and she wasn't the only one making rules here. Jake clearly had his own agenda. He could have done so many things in that moment. He could have lorded his position over her. If everything he said was true, then he'd lost his job because he hadn't sounded the alarm. And she'd convicted him of a crime he hadn't committed. Had never questioned his guilt. Not once in ten years.

She half expected him to toss her own stupidity in her face. He could have walked out the door and left her stewing in her own self-righteousness.

But he simply strode across the room and sat down on the opposite end of the sofa. ''Come here.''

Before she even thought to resist, he'd pulled her back against him, was guiding her head against his chest and lightly running his fingers along her brow. ''How does that feel?''

She sighed, the only answer she could give him because her throat was suddenly tight.

He hadn't defended himself. He'd greeted her attack with caring and concern, each caress of his fingertips against her aching head making her feel more overwhelmed, and more humbled.

"Relax," he said softly. "We'll figure this out."

Together.

He didn't say the word aloud. He didn't need to. It was there in his touch, in the way his body enveloped hers in a strong embrace. She could feel the hard muscles of his chest against her back, feel the heat of hard thighs that anchored her between his legs. Every sweep of his fingers against her temples made the ache recede, leaving in its wake an awareness of this man that was unlike anything she'd ever known before.

Because *he* was unlike any man she'd ever known before.

The events and revelations of the night had sparked urgency in her, but not Jake. She wanted to take action, to find out what was going on, to deal with the problem so she could feel back in control.

But not Jake.

He trusted that he'd figure everything out on his own schedule. The problem would be waiting when he was ready to deal with it. This wasn't a crisis unless he chose to make it one and he didn't. He'd chosen to make her the priority.

He was a man in command of himself and his emotions. And of her.

She melted beneath his concern. She melted beneath his touch. Her thoughts scattered. Her skin tingled with awareness of their closeness, his body heat radiated through his jeans and cotton shirt, so her nerve endings kindled with the glow of it. His touch was gentle and concerned. Intimate.

"If you didn't sound the alarm, Jake, then who did?" she asked, needing to hear the sound of a voice, *any* voice that would distract her from this vulnerability that made a total lie out of her composure.

"You're sure the alarm didn't go off in the monitoring station?"

"No, I'm not sure. I assume it didn't because Opal and Eddie were in there." She couldn't bring herself to admit that her father had claimed responsibility. This was a family situation, and no matter how confused she was about her feelings for Jake at the moment, he wasn't privy to family situations.

Even if he had helped with Lance.

"We need to see the reports from the Golden Hawk central monitoring station," he said. "They're the security company that Innovative Engineering used at the time."

"They went out of business years ago."

"Wouldn't their reports have been admitted as evidence in your father's trial?"

"I don't know the statute of limitations."

"I can have my attorneys inquire—"

"No, thanks. I've got a friend in the department who'll be able to find out and keep it quiet." The absolute last thing she needed was for her dad to somehow get wind of her interest.

"Then give your friend a call in the morning. There, all fixed. Don't worry anymore. We'll figure it out."

The *together* was in there again, but Mallory ignored it because she'd found solace in their conversation, a distraction from her troubled thoughts.

But that solace proved to be short-lived when he asked, "Answer something for me. Have you held me responsible for what happened that night?"

She wondered why he bothered to ask the question.

Surely every move she'd made since he'd walked through her door this morning was painfully transparent. He must have guessed the answer, or at least part of it.

"Not entirely."

"No?"

"Getting caught is a risk that comes with the job. It's a given," was all she said, unwilling to explain the irrational hurt and betrayal she'd felt.

"Did you want to get even with me? Is that why you accepted my proposal?"

He'd been honest. He'd met her unprovoked attack on his honor with kindness, and Mallory found that she couldn't do anything less than meet his question with equal honesty.

She suddenly found herself grateful that she wasn't looking him in the face, that she had the safety of distance between them.

"Yes."

"What did you expect to do?"

She found his use of past tense interesting, as though somehow the situation had changed since they'd made love. "I wanted to screw with you."

The bluntness of her reply seemed heavy and crude in the ensuing silence.

"You're not talking about sex, I take it." She shook her head, and he asked, "What did you think you'd accomplish?"

Again the past tense. "I thought I would feel better."

"But you don't?"

He put the question mark at the end of his sentence as a courtesy. And how could she respond, really? Could she admit that she'd been obsessing for the past ten years, that she'd planned to have a fling with him to get him out of her system and then laugh in his face when he wanted more?

She wasn't laughing now, nor was she able to admit that making love with him today had changed everything.

"I don't know," she said, the ultimate cop-out, egress from the vulnerability that was hammering at her composure and fraying her around the edges. "But I do know that I can't talk about this anymore or my head will explode."

Jake could have laughed at her. He could have pointed out that she'd started this game and was now retreating like a coward.

He didn't. He showed amazing insight into handling her when she was so close to the edge by letting her back out gracefully.

"Come to bed, Mallory," was all he said.

He clearly assumed he'd been invited to install himself in her bed. A few hours ago she would have laughed in his face and proven that he should never assume with her. But now…

A part of her yearned simply to take his hand and let him lead her upstairs, to abandon herself to the oblivion she knew she would find in his arms. She was tempted. *Too* tempted.

"You go ahead, Jake. I need time to clear my head. I'll be up in a little while."

9

If Jake hadn't made the call, then who had? The question played over and over again in Mallory's head, a distraction from the more pressing problem at hand.

Controlling her reaction to this man.

A lost cause, if ever she saw one. She might choose not to open her veins and bleed in front of him, but she wouldn't be anything less than honest with herself. And the simple truth was that this man impacted her on a level where she was completely unfamiliar and very uncomfortable.

Mallory curled in the corner of her sofa, knees drawn beneath her chin, staring into the darkness illuminated only by street lamps and the full moon glowing through her living-room windows. Her head spun with questions—and an intense awareness of the man upstairs and how much she wanted to be with him.

Revenge for a crime Jake hadn't committed had ceased to be an issue. Getting a grip on her reaction to him and working him out of her system was now top priority. That and finding out what had really taken place on the Innovative job.

Forcing her thoughts back to the night in question, she struggled to concentrate when concentration felt beyond her reach. What had she missed that night? Who else could have been inside the building to make that call?

Mallory's mind drifted back, recreating the memory in

sharp detail, almost as if she dreamed in full color. Sitting in the back of the van while Polish Paul maneuvered through the late-night streets of Atlanta, grilling each of them in turn.

Reality check, he'd said, a familiar term that had thrown the crew instantly on alert.

Access through the security fence on the northwest corner of the property, her father said. *Eddie and I cross the lot when the surveillance camera sweeps north.*

Mallory and I follow when the camera sweeps back, Opal added.

Access through the roof to avoid the perimeter alarm. Then we'll have fifteen seconds once we make the monitoring station to subdue the guard so I can disable the alarm, Eddie said.

I'll monitor police communications on the scanner inside the van, Polish Paul said.

And so on and so on. They reviewed how much time they had to complete their individual jobs, the access and egress routes, procedure if anything went wrong. Each of them reciting their own job and the others' jobs with equal familiarity.

It was tense work where adrenaline kicked them into a state of such complete concentration there was simply no time for nerves or emotion. Just skill and focus. A team that worked together like the gears in a clock, each component of the job coming off with precise timing.

Mallory remembered lowering herself into the warehouse foyer that night, so intent upon reaching the keypad and disabling the door sensor that she hadn't sensed the presence of the young man watching her.

That had been her first mistake. The whole point of coming through the ceiling had been so she could surveil the room before entering. And she had. Jake hadn't been there when she'd started down the line, but he'd shown up during her descent.

Chalk that one up to inexperience.

She should have made for her line the instant she'd seen him. She'd had less than two minutes to secure her dad's egress route and manage her own. It would have taken her twenty-five seconds to get back through the ceiling where she should have radioed Polish Paul and told him she'd been made.

But there was just something about the way Jake had stood in that doorway watching her....

Chalk that one up to stupidity.

To this day Mallory couldn't say exactly what had drawn her to him, what had made her think of kissing him as a stall tactic. Yes, he'd been delicious-looking with his tawny brawny self, but even as a sixteen-year-old, possessed of all the raging hormones of youth, she hadn't made a habit of throwing herself at good-looking men. Especially when a good-looking man might have overpowered her and turned her over to the law.

Maybe she'd been fascinated because he could have come after her so easily. But he hadn't. He'd watched her from that doorway with something so much more than surprise on his face. He could have overpowered her, but he'd kissed her instead.

What was it about Jake that made her lose her head?

Mallory needed to think, knew she'd never be able to sort out her thoughts as agitated as she was. Not to mention that she needed to stay sharp until she figured out what had gone on at the Innovative job. She wouldn't be sharp if she didn't get some sleep tonight.

Forcing herself up, she made her way out of the living room. Then she did the only thing she could think of to help clear her head—she sat down at the piano to play.

She chose a classical composition she always enjoyed, a romantic piece she hoped would lighten her mood, and one she'd already made her own so she didn't need to read the sheet music. Depressing the pedal to soften the sound so as not to disturb Jake, she brought her fingers to the keys and began to play.

Music was Mallory's passion. Not the variety of genres that could be heard blaring around the clock on Atlanta's impressive bandwidth, but the black notes on yellowed staff paper that had been passed from generation to generation of gifted musicians.

At the piano she could lose herself in the one place in the world where success depended solely upon her performance and skill, a place where confusion didn't exist, only order and precision. When she played, her life scaled down to a world she could understand, a world where right and wrong, ethics and values became very black-and-white concepts to define.

Giving herself over to the first movement, she lost herself in the one place in the world where she could forget her conflicted emotions.

And the man upstairs in her bed.

When she finally noticed him, before the last of the music had faded to silence, she had no sense of how long he'd been standing there in the shadows beyond the arched doorway, watching her, listening.

"You're so talented." His throaty whisper seemed intimate in the sudden silence, almost a visceral force in the darkness.

She wasn't back yet from the place she went when she played and something deep inside her fluttered to awareness, something unfamiliar...pride maybe, or perhaps pleasure that he seemed so awed. She was struck by the thought that it would take a lot to impact this man. Perhaps she felt that way because she was so impacted by him.

He wore nothing but a robe belted around his waist, his hair and skin golden blurs in the shadow. He seemed too masculine in contrast to her neat home, a man out of place with the refined furnishings, yet curiously at one with them, as though his sheer maleness was exactly what had been missing.

This was a fanciful thought for a woman who wasn't disposed to fanciful thoughts, and Mallory had the urge to say something to interject reality into the moment.

But Jake didn't give her the chance. He crossed the room with purposeful strides and came to stand beside her, gazing down with an expression of such longing that he chased away her thoughts. She could only turn to him and stare up into his face, drawn by the sight of the hunger he didn't try to hide.

Lifting a hand, he brushed her cheek with warm fingers, traced the line of her brow before threading them into her hair, forcing her head back to expose her throat to his view.

Her hair spilled out behind her, over the keys, over her shoulders, a weight she shouldn't have noticed, but did, feeling it as another assault on her senses when she was already so sharply aware of this man.

His gaze never wavered as he outlined the curve of her throat, the hollow of her collarbone, a caress designed to explore, to stake a claim on her body. He dragged his thumb along her jaw, twined his fingers into the curve of her neck as though learning the feel of each curve, as if he was free to touch her by right, didn't need permission to coax this jumble of sensations inside her.

"Jake, I—"

He pressed a finger to her lips. "Don't talk," he said. "Don't think, just feel."

His command was a dusky whisper in the quiet, a sound that filtered through her in rich degrees, spurred her awareness of him impossibly higher. The tender scrape of callused fingertips along her skin. The way his gaze anchored her in place to emphasize his command.

A command she didn't want to fight. A command she couldn't fight without the safety of distance.

And there was no distance between them now, only need. Her need for this man. Her need to separate fantasy from reality, because some rational part of her brain knew she could never handle her runaway emotions until she did. But the night's revelations, the worry, the uncertainty and her unpredicted response to him had all worn down her will.

He seemed much more fantasy than reality right now, standing so tall and powerful above her, holding her captive with potent bedroom eyes that only lent to the fantasy of the moment without their usual shield of clear plastic lenses.

But he was reality, too, a man to guide her through this unfamiliar place where she was trapped between the real and the imagined. Solid, as he'd been by her side tonight while she'd dealt with Lance, never pressuring her with questions, only offering his help.

Despite her sense of unfamiliarity with this feeling, Mallory knew she wasn't imagining his longing. It was there in his expression. If nothing else about the moment was real, the connection between them was undeniable.

Then Jake bent down, lowered his face to hers, claimed a kiss with a simple possession that stole her breath. He tasted of hot male and hunger, invading her mouth with bold strokes of his tongue, inviting her to explore their attraction for each other, this unique chemistry they made together.

Mallory surrendered to the power of his mouth on hers, allowed her lips to melt beneath his, lured by the strength of his demand, and shamed by her need for it.

Once again the control had shifted to him and she was caught up in the wildness of their kiss and the way her body seemed to unfold in readiness for his touch. Her stomach tightened with anticipation. Moisture pooled between her thighs. Instinctively, she reached up for him, slipping her hands around his neck to drag him closer.

As she had earlier, she knew an overwhelming desire to explore this man. For ten years, she had obsessed, alternately been fascinated and angered and repelled by this man, and yes, had denied the connection they shared, a connection that had niggled deep into her subconscious.

His robe proved no obstacle. Her fingers slipped beneath the collar, traveled over shoulders stretching broad and wide and strong. His skin was warm to her touch, firmly muscled, solid.

The robe parted enough to let her trail her hands down that hard chest, her fingers sinking into the depressions of sleek muscle, abrading the silky hairs along the way. Earlier Jake had let her explore his body at her leisure, but now, his patience seemed limited. Slipping his hands around her waist, he lifted her up from the piano bench, forced her to her feet. He broke their kiss and to her surprise a sound of protest escaped her. She stood there with her mouth still wet and tingling, still wanting *him*.

From within the folds of thick cotton, she caught a glimpse of his erection bobbing wildly as he shoved the piano bench behind him. Then he sank to his knees, the robe pouring around him in a plush puddle. He bent his head low…. Seizing the waistband of her sweatpants, he dragged them down her legs in a thorough move that took her thong along with them.

Mallory assisted his efforts so he could pull her clothing away, and then he was forcing her ankles apart, widening her stance. She stood before him, the shirt she wore making her feel all the more bared from the waist down, more exposed to his appreciative gaze and to the sultry night air.

His warm hands ran down one leg, then back up the other, lingering strokes that traced her shape, her every curve. She shivered at the teasing lightness of his touch, goose bumps spraying along her skin while her stomach swooped in on itself in eager reply.

Then Jake slipped his hands on her hips and pressed her back against the piano. Her bare backside landed directly on the keyboard, sent a shriek of impossible notes through the quiet, making her cringe. Or maybe that was only her response to his fingers prying her thighs apart, his tawny head lowering…

The first stroke of his hot silk tongue along her sex made her jump, and she gasped a sound that was drowned out by another crash on the keys.

He licked her again. Only this time he drove his tongue a little deeper, separating her sensitive folds just enough to make her breath come in a series of shuddering gasps that echoed over the fading remnants of sound.

Her thighs quivered. Her chest rose and fell in a vain attempt to catch a breath. And when he unveiled the tiny bud of nerve endings from its hiding place, she could only arch backward and close her eyes and decide she didn't need to breathe after all.

What was breathing when Jake trapped her in a fantasy? The way she felt couldn't be real. Every muscle in her body was melting, a crazy liquefying sensation that contrasted curiously with the tension building inside her.

And when he sucked that sensitive little bud into his

mouth, a tight pull that made her entire body shudder, she let out a moan that sounded more like a whimper.

A *whimper*.

Before she could absorb the fact that he'd dragged such an undignified sound from her, he was curling his fingers into her wet heat, separating and stroking. His stubbled cheeks prickled her skin. His mouth drew on her with slow pulls until she couldn't resist rocking against him, a delicious motion that depressed the keys beneath her, strident blasts of sound she barely noticed as her insides mushroomed on a wave of sensation....

Over the edge she went, an orgasm so intense that a moan slid from her lips, increasing in volume like a crescendo.

Jake sat back and gazed up at her with those melting dark eyes, his mouth gleaming from her body's desire. She could only stare at him dazed, his golden features contrasting sharply with her pale thighs. The hem of her shirt had snagged on his hair, mussing the tawny waves and lending him a look of supreme satisfaction, a contentment that was so totally male.

And then he smiled. A smile that suggested kneeling before her, his fingers buried deep inside as her body clenched greedily around him was the only place in the world he wanted to be.

"Did you prove yourself?" she managed to ask.

"Depends on whether or not you can stand."

Arrogant man. She sniffed haughtily, refusing to admit that if not for her piano and the hand he still had wedged between her legs, she'd have dissolved into a puddle at his feet.

His thumb found that sensitive knot that sent need curling straight to her core, and she arched against him, riding his hand, unable to stop moving. He thrust deep until her moan made a total lie of her composure.

"Well, if I haven't made the cut yet…"

He let his statement trail off, but his golden brown eyes flashed. And then he was on his feet, rising in a move that was all compact motion and graceful male.

Flashes of tanned muscle peeped out from his robe, a strong calf, a hard thigh, rippled abs, and then he was crowding against her with his big body and his male heat.

This man definitely had something to prove, and she didn't move when he slipped his hand away, refused to let him know how much she felt the air caress the dampness clinging to her thighs. She braced herself on her hands and stared at him defiantly.

"What is it you're trying to prove, Jake?"

He unbelted his robe purposefully, left it to fall open and reveal the powerful lines of his body, and he stroked his erection, a slow pull that made him swell visibly. He stroked himself again and Mallory dragged her gaze from the sight to prove she wasn't affected.

A lie.

"I'm not trying to prove anything. I'm trying to make you forget everything except the way my hands feel on your body. I want you to accept the way you respond to me."

His throaty declaration shouldn't have sounded like a threat. But she took it as one. He wanted her to lose herself in him, and she didn't think he could possibly know how close he was to making her do just that.

"I came." A concession.

"You will again." A promise.

"We'll see." A dare.

He inclined his head. "Yes, we will."

Before she even registered his move, Jake had wedged

himself between her thighs. His big hands gripped her knees and brought them up around his waist, opening her wide as he forced her ankles behind him and caught them tight with one hand.

She could only go with the motion, secured as she was against the fallboard of her piano, her hair tangling around the music desk. Mallory did gasp this time, not only from the suddenness of his move, but from the appearance of that erection between her thighs.

His features grew stark with his hunger as he ground his hips to draw that hot length against her heat. She watched transfixed as his mouth set into a firm line, his jaw clenched tight while he took deliberate aim.

She was wet from her orgasm, ready, and he thrust inside with a sleek motion. Bracing herself against the piano, she tried to appear unaffected but there was no way a woman even as accomplished at concealing her emotions as she could pretend that making love to him wasn't out of the ordinary.

She was spread wide to receive him, their bodies joined at the hips. She couldn't catch her breath, could only grab on to his shoulders and hang on, her whole body aching to press full length against him, her breasts heavy and tight and yearning for his attention. She would have stripped her shirt over her head but he chose that moment to move. A smooth purposeful motion that rocked her against the keys to another crash of impossible notes that drowned out the sound of their broken breathing.

He began to ride her, hard, each stroke bringing him out almost all the way, before he plunged back, a well-planned assault that trapped her between the piano and him. She could only hang on, lifted higher with each thrust, totally dependent on his pace and his pleasure to feed her own growing ache.

He released her ankles and slipped his fingers around her neck, urging her to tip her head back, and she did. She met his gaze, was completely awed by how beautiful he was in his passion, how open and honest. He didn't hide his hunger, an expression on his face that revealed just how much he wanted her.

It was she who lifted her mouth to his, silently begged for a kiss. He lowered his face and his mouth came down on hers hard, possessive. He never slowed that incredible motion of his hips, and she mirrored each stroke with her tongue, the only way she could feed the intensity building inside her, lifting her higher than she'd ever known she could go.

Their hearts pounded together, breakneck. Her skin grew hot and sticky beneath her sweatshirt, her thighs encasing his hips were covered with a thin sheen of sweat.

Then his body began to vibrate, and she clung to him because she could do nothing else. She could only absorb each powerful thrust, marvel as he came with such force that he dragged her right along with him.

The last harsh notes from the piano lingered over their ragged breaths. He lowered his head until his brow rested against hers, his hands still locked around her neck as though he was too shell-shocked to move them.

The thought made panicked laughter rise inside, because this man had accomplished exactly what he'd set out to do. She'd forgotten everything but the feel of his hands on her. She'd abandoned herself to him in a way she'd never abandoned herself before. *She,* a woman who always controlled her actions and emotions because she couldn't control life, couldn't control herself around Jake.

Her heart raced in her chest and she couldn't catch her breath. Her body was weak with contentment. He'd leveled her with his demands and his orgasms.

And the way he held her told her he knew it.

Then without a word, he lifted her up into his arms and carried her toward the stairs. He didn't ask. He just assumed control, proving his earlier claim that he did indeed like things his way. And that he had the patience to outlast her no matter how determined she might be.

He wanted her to come to bed, and now she would.

IN THE DARKNESS of late night, Jake wrapped his arms around Mallory, nestled her warm body into the contours of his. He'd peeled away the last of her clothes and her every naked curve pressed against him, her long legs twined with his, her smooth stomach curled around his hip, her hand lightly resting on his chest, her cheek in the crook of his shoulder.

She was a natural fit and slept easily in his arms, shaping and reshaping her body to his throughout the night. He hadn't slept nearly as well, only dozing as he stared into the moon-soaked darkness, resting his chin on the top of her head and inhaling the scent of her hair.

His restlessness had nothing to do with exhaustion. His body was physically sated, more content than he'd ever been.

Which seemed to be the problem.

His mind played over every second since he'd pulled up in front of her brownstone at precisely ten fifty-seven yesterday morning.

Less than a day.

He wouldn't have believed so much could change in so short a time. But *everything* had changed. His thoughts raced with the day's events, with every word Mallory had spoken, every gesture she'd made, every challenge she'd issued.

This kind of psychological turmoil precluded sleep no

matter how content and exhausted his body was, and he tried to make some sense of what was taking place between them.

And more importantly, what he was going to do next.

Their every interaction was a power struggle that was becoming increasingly important as Jake realized how much he didn't want to lose.

A very ironic twist for a man who'd been called self-absorbed by more than a few women, accused of being so wrapped up in his work that he had no time or concentration left for anyone or anything else.

He'd always entertained that there was truth to the accusations. When he looked at his past history, he agreed that Mallory had been well within her rights to question him about the frequency with which women entered and left his life.

He enjoyed dating and casual entanglements, had known some very lovely ladies, but he'd never felt compelled to further any of those relationships, had been content to move on to the next woman rather than put forth effort to convince anyone to stay.

He believed what he'd told Mallory. He hadn't met the right woman yet. He never questioned that he would. Perhaps this was a direct result of being part of a solid family, of witnessing his parents' love for one another. They'd been together since high school, as content and close today as Jake could remember them during his youth, proof that soul mates existed. He'd always maintained he'd know the right woman when he met her.

And he had. Ten years ago in a dark warehouse.

He'd avoided commitment because he'd been waiting to catch up with this woman, and as he held her in his arms, Jake knew that he wanted to find out if there could be an *us*.

Which meant he now had a problem. A *big* one. Mallory had spent years believing him responsible for the events that had changed her life. While he'd believed the same of Mallory, Jake couldn't equate losing his job at Innovative Engineering to the way life had blown up in her face.

And he wasn't apologetic, either. Once he'd tracked her down to learn she'd given up crime and turned her life around, he'd discovered another good thing had come from their meeting.

But did Mallory feel that way? Once again he had no frame of reference for how she might digest tonight's truths, but he did feel certain she planned to hang around long enough to bust his chops some more and collect her hefty check.

She'd flat-out said she'd only accepted his job offer to exact some sort of sexy revenge. And while he was encouraged that she'd made love with him again tonight, he wasn't naive enough to think this was any concession.

Yeah, she'd wanted him, but that was because the sex was good. They had chemistry. But chemistry wasn't an indicator of her emotions.

But chemistry was all Jake had to work with at the moment. Chemistry meant more sex. More sex meant he had her attention. At least until they figured out who had tripped the alarm that night and she fulfilled the terms of their contract.

When she stirred in his arms, exhaling a deep sigh that burst across his skin, Jake felt a wave of heat through his body that underscored the enormity of the task he faced ahead. He tightened his arms around her, searched for ways to bridge the distance between them. He could see the problems more clearly than the solutions. Trouble was he knew next to nothing about Mallory's personal life.

He needed to know whether her aversion to *us* was an aversion to *him* specifically or to *commitment* in general before he could figure out how to encourage her to give him a chance.

One thing was for sure, Jake wouldn't tip his hand and let her know how interested he was. He'd either lose his edge or send her running. He didn't intend to do either, which meant he needed to take a page from her book and start playing hard ball.

Let the games begin.

10

—

"OKAY, JAKE." Mallory met his gaze over her coffee mug and Jake couldn't see a trace of the intimacies they'd shared last night in her cool green eyes. She was all business. "You want to observe this job from start to finish as if I were planning a real one."

Leaning back against the worktable, he sipped from his own mug and nodded. Business it would be, then. She obviously didn't want to deal with any of last night's revelations, and he found that significant. She operated with distance between her personal life and her career, keeping them separate even when they overlapped as they did now.

He filed this piece of the puzzle away for safekeeping. He'd already added some new information to his arsenal today by learning that Mallory was a morning person who liked to get a jump on her day.

Consequently, the sun was only just rising as they'd made their way downstairs to her workshop to begin their first day of work together and his first day of thief-assistant training.

"What about my system specs?" he asked. "Have we compromised anything because I've shown them to you?"

"Good question and the answer is no. I always work from the specs of whatever security system I intend to penetrate. You've only saved me a step in the process."

"Doesn't that give you an edge over a real burglar?"

A quicksilver grin flashed. "Real burglars work from

the specs, too.'' She glanced at a wall clock above the computer station. ''I'll walk you through the acquisition process, but we'll have to wait until the business day starts. Right now you need to brief me on the job. So, what am I going to steal and from whom?''

''The blueprints to a vault at the Atlanta Safe Exchange.''

She tipped her mug to him in salute. ''Clever. The premise being that a business already dealing in security will have a leg up on a business that doesn't, I assume.''

That and the fact that he was a close enough friend with the owner to feel comfortable asking for a favor of this magnitude. ''Something like that.''

Jake set his mug on the worktable and popped open his briefcase to extract the documents while Mallory made her way to her computer and booted the system to start their day in earnest.

The history of the Atlanta Safe Exchange, upper management, press releases, copyright patents and an abundance of other information was readily available online if one knew where to look. Mallory did. With lightning-fast motions of her manicured hands, she navigated around the Internet, explaining to Jake how each piece of information was important to understanding the safeguards in place around her target.

She kept a file open where she continually logged questions and things she needed to check out later. All the while Jake sat by her side, amazed by her intensity, by the way she reasoned quickly and logically, a gorgeous woman whose expression lit up with excitement.

''I want to show you how a burglar acquires the specs for a system, but I can't use the Sentex 2000 since it's not on the market yet. What's the name of another of your clients who's not testing your prototype? Something large and reputable.''

Jake cast around for a name and came up with Nu-Tech Electronics, one of his largest accounts and an established corporation that produced and marketed electrical components for a variety of industries.

She typed the name into a popular Internet search engine and within seconds the Nu-Tech Electronics Web site appeared on her screen. She navigated through several pages that detailed Nu-Tech's services and product lines before reaching for the telephone, activating the speakerphone function and saying, ''Just a note here, Jake. If this were a real job, I wouldn't be using my home phone because the telephone company would have a record of the call.''

She dialed the company's direct line. ''Good morning,'' she said in response to the greeting. ''Someone in sales, please.''

Rolling his chair back a few feet from the computer desk, Jake folded his arms across his chest and watched her work, liking her confident smile that warned him she was about to put on a show.

The call connected and a male voice shot out over the speaker, ''Good morning, Gordon here.''

''Hello, Mr. Gordon. My name is Gail Nelson, and I'm with Southeast Wireless. We're intending to switch providers in the next quarter, and I'm researching potential suppliers for electrical components on a line of our digital cell phones. I was wondering if you could answer a few questions for me?''

Jake noted that she chose the name of a real up-and-coming corporation, one that would be considered worthy of courting as a new account. Apparently this was the case because Mr. Gordon proved very helpful when Mallory began shooting off questions about the company's history, its years in service, its current rating on the stock exchange, much of which information was available right in front of her on the Web site.

She was pleasant, pausing often as though jotting down the information and thanking the man for his help, and Jake decided that a large part of becoming a successful criminal was based on natural acting ability. Mallory had it in spades and without the slightest change in her tone, she neatly began grilling the man.

"Obviously one of my company's key concerns is piracy of our cell components. Before I can make a recommendation to meet with you, I need to assess the potential for theft at the source. What can you tell me about the security of your production facility?"

That was all it took to launch Mr. Gordon into a pitch of Nu-Tech's affiliation with TSS and all the special features of the Apex 1200 and how satisfactorily the system operated. While Jake appreciated his client's confidence in his product and services, he recognized that the man was sharing all the information that Mallory, or any thief, would need to accurately assess the security in place around his property.

"All right, Mr. Gordon," she said pleasantly. "I have the information I need to write up a proposal for the next phase. My recommendations will go to committee on—" she glanced up at the wall calendar tacked to a bulletin board "—on the twenty-eighth, so I'll get back in touch with you sometime after the first to let you know if we'll progress to the interview phase. Thank you so much. You've been very helpful."

Damned straight. And it looked as though Jake needed to educate his clients about what information to provide over the phone. Not that Mallory couldn't have dressed in a suit and shown up in Mr. Gordon's office with the faked credentials of a Southeast Wireless employee, but at least acquiring the information wouldn't have been so embarrassingly easy.

She disconnected but didn't say a word as she turned her attention back to the computer and typed in a frenzy on the keyboard to bring his own company Web site onto her screen. She dialed the toll-free sales hotline and within five minutes his helpful staff provided the specs for the Apex 1200 via fax.

She smiled smugly while handing him each sheet as it rolled off the printer. The entire process had taken less than thirty minutes from start to finish and now she had a thorough understanding of the type of security measures she'd be up against if she'd really wanted to break into Nu-Tech.

"At least tell me that my systems present a little more of a challenge than most." A question prompted solely by ego.

"Don't worry, Jake. They will. That's why you hired me."

Not exactly the reassurance he was looking for, but it was all he got before she dialed the Atlanta Safe Exchange and conducted a similar conversation, only this time asking the salesperson more specific questions about the facility.

As Jake listened to the conversation, he decided that in addition to acting ability, successful criminals were also skilled at handling people. Mallory dangled a plum account like Southeast Wireless before this salesman's nose deftly, and in return, received forthcoming answers.

When she disconnected the call, Jake asked, "Why do you need to know the name of the architect who designed the facility and when it was built?"

"So I can look up the blueprints in county records." She rolled away from the computer, stood and went to her worktable. Grabbing her PDA, she inputted some information and as Jake watched, a thought occurred to him.

"Mallory, what happens after a company's burglarized? Isn't there a possibility a salesperson could remember your conversation and connect it to the robbery?"

"Excellent question and the answer is yes." She held up her PDA to present the calendar on the small screen. "This is where follow-through is important. I'll call back exactly when I promised to and give those salespeople some reason why we won't be progressing to the next phase. I keep it business as usual. That minimizes the risk of detection."

"And if the salesperson, or the police for that matter, put two and two together, they can't trace the call anyway."

"Exactly." She flashed him a bright smile, dropped the PDA into her purse and headed toward the stairs. "Come on, Jake, let's make a trip downtown."

As Mallory knew exactly what she was looking for, acquiring the blueprints became a simple matter of knowing what county offices to visit. By noon they sat in Starbucks, reviewing the blueprints of the Atlanta Safe Exchange over espresso. Having designed the Sentex 2000 to fit this property himself, Jake was familiar with the plans and watched with interest to see how closely Mallory assessed the precautions he'd put into play.

"Okay, the salesman told me the Atlanta Safe Exchange is using a video station, so I'm going to say it's located right here." She pointed to a small room but didn't wait for Jake to confirm before dragging a fingertip over the paper. "And this is obviously the vault. I'm guessing that you've implemented those innovative motion sensors of yours right here down these hallways and this floor."

She was exactly right, and Jake was again impressed

with her knowledge base, with her feel for a property based on so little information. He supposed he shouldn't be. He'd known Mallory was good, but somehow witnessing firsthand how efficiently her mind analyzed the situation made her even more impressive.

Then she peered up at him, clear eyes glinting. "Well, well, well, Jake, very nicely done. Unfortunately, this also presents my first problem with having you for an assistant."

"Why is that?"

"You've cut off my access to the vault from all sides."

"That was the point."

She smiled. "I gathered that, but it means we'll have to come in through the ceiling."

"If entry is that simple then what's the problem?"

"You are. Unless you're proficient at rappelling."

"Not in my repertoire."

"Didn't think so, which means, my handsome apprentice," she said in a drawl that made him smile. "You're going to need some practice before we go live."

Taking a hasty swallow, Mallory drained her cup and got to her feet. "Let's head out. We can drive by the property before swinging back to my place. I'll need to case the place at various times over a twenty-four-hour period to determine whether or not they're using armed guards or dogs."

Okay. Jake rolled up the blueprints and followed, admiring the sway of her hips as she stepped out of the coffee shop into the sunny afternoon. She'd dressed in business attire for their visit downtown and had advised him to do the same, but the black high-fashion sunglasses she slipped on now lent a decided hint of bad girl to her otherwise polished appearance.

Jake smiled as he reached for the door of her sporty

five-speed convertible. This bad girl was in for a big surprise if she thought he was going to be content to keep her in bed. He might not have figured out exactly what involved an *us* yet, but after working with her this morning, Jake knew he wouldn't be satisfied until Mallory signed on to his team.

His bad girl was one of a kind, and he intended to see that TSS benefited exclusively from her unique abilities, which meant he had his work cut out for him, figuring out how to make his offer attractive enough so she wouldn't laugh in his face.

HAVING THE upper hand in her business dealings with Jake helped Mallory regain some of her equilibrium after he'd brought the world down around her ears with his revelations and his sex. She was still trying to sort through the fallout. Step one had been to contact a friend in the police department to ask for help tracking down the reports they needed to start investigating the alarm transmissions on the Innovative job.

Getting the wheels into motion on a ten-year-old mystery had been a piece of cake compared to figuring out what to do about Jake. Work made an admirable hiding place, but it was only a temporary fix for what was becoming a real problem.

Not only did her dad think she was involved in a full-fledged fling with this man, but so, apparently, did Jake. And worse yet, her own emotions were so all over the place that she couldn't honestly say she wasn't. The only thing she did know for sure was that her sexy revenge idea had blown up in her face with the force of a two-ton blast.

And the way that Jake was handling himself wasn't helping matters one bit. So many men of her acquaintance would have had an impossible time playing the role of trainee to her mentor. She was a woman, and the typical male ego struggled with accepting direction from any female.

Jake clearly wasn't typical. His ego appeared to be quite intact. He'd bought a service and expected her to deliver. He obviously respected her knowledge. He cooperated easily, asked sharp questions, picked things up quickly and had thoroughly routed her plan to put him at a disadvantage.

Of course, he could afford to be generous. He'd balanced his own equilibrium often enough by proving his superiority in bed. Which constituted yet another problem because the memory of sex with Jake kept creeping into her thoughts. She was still brooding on how he'd rattled her cage when she pulled onto her street and came face-to-face with yet another problem—Opal's Jaguar parked in her driveway.

"You've got company," Jake said unnecessarily. "Your father?"

Mallory shook her head, debating whether or not to keep driving. But not only did she need her climbing gear, she knew she wouldn't sidestep the problem for long by avoiding her house. She had to come home eventually and her dad would keep sending people over until someone caught her and Jake home. He might even drop by himself again if he thought he could manage it without being too obvious. He'd clearly decided to stay apprised of her dealings with Jake, and Mallory wasn't surprised in the least.

When Duke Hunt wanted something, he did whatever it took to get it. He wanted Mallory married and settled down and now that he'd approved Jake, he'd be relentless. She just wished he would respect that she didn't want to settle down. It wasn't that she had anything against marriage per se, it just wasn't her thing. She liked her freedom. She liked being able to rise to life's challenges, and she wouldn't be able to do that with a white picket fence and a man around twenty-four seven.

The latest crisis with Lance had certainly proved that. Twenty-four seven with Jake meant sharing things about her personal life that she didn't particularly care to share.

Even if she did have to admit that he'd been decent about the whole thing. He hadn't pried. He hadn't tried to shove his opinion down her throat. He'd *helped*.

Chalk one up for Jake Trinity.

Which in no way, shape or form translated into wanting to keep the man around permanently. It was bad enough that he'd thrown her a curve and now she had her dad to deal with, too. If Mallory actually believed in luck, she might entertain that she was having a bad run of it.

"Today's your lucky day," she said dryly while pulling into the driveway. "You're going to meet Opal."

"Your former foster mother and the surveillance specialist."

"Very good. You remembered."

He shot her a grin that made her sex give a needy little clench with a reminder of what that mouth felt like between her thighs. Picket fence, indeed.

"Missing a trick around you might be fatal," he said.

"You seem to enjoy a good challenge."

"I do."

Now it was her turn to laugh. She reached for her door but, he said, "Hang on. I'll get it."

She let him do his knight-in-shining armor routine, still smiling. "Do you know you made *fatal* sound like a compliment?"

"I intended to. I was hoping you'd find it charming."

She met his gaze as she slid off the seat and found those warm brown eyes sparkling. "I do."

Then he shifted his gaze above her head. "Do you and all of your father's crew swap keys to each others' houses?"

Mallory glanced around to find Opal watching them from the glass cutout of her front door. She opened the door a moment later and said, "So this is the man of the hour. I've heard all about you, Jake Trinity."

Jake escorted Mallory up the stairs while his sharp gaze took in Opal, who was a sight even on the days when she wasn't showcased on the portico above her audience.

She looked especially together in a pale-blue silk pantsuit designed to make men drool over her assets. She was a glamorous woman, and to Jake's credit his gaze didn't snag on her chest, even when he was eye level as they climbed the stairs.

He was very gallant, in fact, when he took Opal's hand and brought it to his lips. "I've heard about you, too. You've been a very important part of Mallory's life."

Opal visibly melted and her platinum bob swung across her shoulders when she slanted her gaze toward Mallory. "Oh, honey, this one's a keeper. No wonder your daddy's all worked up."

Mallory rolled her eyes. Great. "He sent you?"

"Of course. He doesn't want to be obvious." Hooking her arm through Jake's, she escorted him inside, leaving Mallory to close the door. "Duke wants Mallory to settle down," she explained. "He's got his heart set on grandchildren. Getting old, I think. Don't you, honey?"

"Senile, definitely. And I'd appreciate a little help running interference, if you don't mind."

"I'm trying. I keep telling him that you're young and need to be having a good time. Don't you think so, Jake?"

"I wouldn't give a statement without your attorney." Mallory cautioned him. "It might come back to haunt you."

Jake just laughed. "I don't see that having a good time and commitment are exclusive."

Mallory scowled, refusing to dwell on the subtext of *that* statement, but Opal looked delighted.

"I'm getting a good idea why your daddy likes him so much."

"So what's up, Opal?" she tried to swerve the conversation onto a different course. "Are you only here because Daddy asked you to spy on me?"

"Actually no. It so happens that Eddie was feeling lonely today. He's been working the floor all morning to socialize with the customers and hear himself talk. I figured it was the perfect time to sneak away and wrap up your quarterly reports. I promised to bring him back sushi from Ichiban. *Your* treat."

As Mallory tried to figure out a way to suggest tactfully that Opal go pick up the brown rice and sesame balls right now, Jake asked, "Eddie, the friend who was also the alarm specialist?"

Opal grabbed the question. "Oh yes. He's been like an uncle to Mallory ever since she was born."

"And you work for him?"

"I'm his office manager and right-hand man. A stockholder in his company, too." She guided Jake through the foyer and into the living room, where she sat beside him on the sofa. "I do some work for Mallory, too. She's been so successful that she hasn't had a chance to keep up with her paperwork."

"Don't let her fool you, Jake," Mallory said from the doorway. "She's a spy."

Opal sniffed haughtily. "She doesn't like to admit that she needs help. Never has, even as a child."

"Mallory told me who you are," Jake said to Opal. "But she hasn't told me much else."

"What is it you want to know?"

"Everything."

Opal's grin revealed she'd be more than happy to fill in the blanks. "I've been a friend of the family since before Mallory was born. I was very young myself, of course. But I have the distinction of being her only constant female influence all her life. Her mother died tragically when she was only an infant, you know."

"Mallory hasn't been very forthcoming about her early life even though I've expressed an interest."

That was all it took to send Opal off and running on a biography lesson, and Mallory listened, knowing nothing short of a tornado would divert Opal from her course.

This didn't surprise her. She had, after all, known Opal all her life.

But Jake's determination to find out about her did surprise her, and Mallory couldn't quite figure out why. Perhaps she'd thought that a man who'd been involved with as many women as he'd been shouldn't be so focused on her. She was one woman in a long line of many, and he should have had a much better grasp on how to conduct a fling by now. Digging into personal histories was against all the fling rules.

It's not me, Mallory. It's us. *Together.*

His words echoed in her memory, a reminder that no matter how many flings this man had enjoyed in his past, he still liked to play the knight in shining armor.

Exactly what she didn't want to play with.

With a sigh, she said, "While you two get acquainted,

I'm going to work. I'll be in the workshop if you need me.''

If they heard her, neither acknowledged her when she left.

DUKE GLANCED at the number flashing on his cell phone display and depressed the power button to take the call. ''Well, how'd it go?''

''Hello to you, too,'' Opal shot back.

''Hello, gorgeous. Forgive me. I'm too damned excited about Mallory and her affair. I can't think straight.''

''*Too* excited?'' She issued a sultry laugh that made his pulse spike hard. ''That has definite promise.''

''So it does.'' Duke smiled, unwilling to resist this opportunity to further his own cause. He had so much lost time to make up for and had the nagging feeling that time was slipping away. He'd never been the most patient of men—especially when dealing with his own deficiencies. ''Spend the night with me again tonight, and I promise you won't be sorry.''

''Actually, you read my mind, Duke. I do want to see you tonight. We need to talk.''

''Then talk to me, gorgeous.''

''Not now. In person. The only reason I called is because Mallory asked me to run interference with you.''

''She wants me to lay off, I know. But I won't, so don't waste your breath.''

''Hmph.'' Opal sniffed over the line. ''If you're sure then, I'll just say good-bye right now.''

There was something in her voice…he knew this woman too well. She was stringing him along. ''Don't say good-bye yet. It's been hours since I've seen you. Too long.'' A nice recovery. Of course, Opal wouldn't buy it, but it should be good enough to get him back in the game.

''I wasn't telling you to lay off, obstinate man.'' She

was clearly undecided if he was worthy of a second chance.

"I'm listening, gorgeous. There's nothing I'd rather be doing than hearing the sound of your voice."

Overkill? Duke didn't think so. Not when he could practically hear Opal's smile when she said, "I thought you might want to know that Mallory and her man of the hour are heading for the Vertical Playground right now."

Duke blew a kiss over the receiver. "Have I told you lately how much I love you?"

And heard her sigh on the other end.

JAKE STEPPED into the shower spray of the gym locker room, closed his eyes and let the hot water wash away the last two hours of his life. Talented on a wrestling mat he was. Talented with rappel lines he wasn't.

Mallory had arranged for them to use a private room at a rock-climbing gym to practice his control while scaling down walls on a line. He hadn't had much. Despite her patient and proficient instruction, he'd slammed into her and the wall so many times that he wasn't sure what was worse—the bruises to his body or his pride.

Mallory had assured him he'd get better with practice, but Jake, painfully unused to being inept—especially in front of a woman he was trying to win—wasn't sure he could believe her.

"At this point I'm wondering if I'll ever see you dressed," a familiar voice jarred him from his waterlogged reverie.

Opening his eyes, Jake came face to face with Duke Hunt as the man stepped inside the gym's community shower and pulled off his towel. Sweaty, as if he'd been climbing, he raked a dark gaze over Jake then shot a grin that was pure Mallory bravado.

"I suppose it's some consolation to know you can service my daughter properly." He stepped beneath a showerhead, placed a bar of soap in a dish and turned the water on.

Jake stared, but to his credit, he did manage to keep his mouth from hanging open.

Duke must have noticed because he said, "I'm impressed. Did I stun you speechless or are you consciously choosing not to antagonize a convicted felon?"

"Actually sir, I was more concerned that you're the father of the woman I'm involved with."

"Not speechless then?"

"It factored." Jake had to be honest.

That seemed to please the man because he nodded approvingly and stepped beneath the shower spray. Soon he reemerged and reached for the bar of soap. "Tell me about your involvement with my daughter. I want to know what your intentions are."

Jake reached for his soap, buying himself time to consider his response. There were several ways to approach Duke Hunt, and dealing with Mallory gave him a definite leg up because she was a chip off the old block. Duke Hunt's attitude screamed *Challenge* with a capital C, so Jake would handle the man the same way he handled his daughter—honestly and with no glaring weaknesses.

"I'm not sure what I want from your daughter yet. I've been trying to figure that out. You'll be among the first to know when I do."

With a narrowed gaze, Duke considered him from beneath a headful of soapy lather, and Jake waited, amazed at how interminable the waiting seemed.

"Fair enough. Been there. But a word of caution. Don't tell me you're having a fling with her. That's not what I want to hear."

Inside information was good, Jake decided before soaping his hair, a reprieve from the unreadable gaze currently staring holes through him.

"And since I'm willing to wait for you to make up your mind," Duke said, crushing any hope that Jake was off the hook yet. "Satisfy my curiosity about something else."

"Shoot, sir."

"When and where did you first meet her?"

Great. The questions he couldn't answer without disregarding Mallory's wishes not to let her father know he'd been present at Innovative Engineering.

What was that old adage about everything going wrong that could? Jake knew he was out of his element here. Way out. Mallory and her father operated on a level that he was wholly unfamiliar with, one that made every word out of his mouth feel as if he was tossing the dice with a large bet riding on the roll.

"Honesty usually works for me, sir, but today it's placing me in an awkward situation with you."

"How awkward?"

"Very. I met Mallory a long time ago. Unfortunately, when you showed up at her place, she asked me not to mention the details. She wanted to explain herself. I agreed to respect her wishes. I'm guessing she hasn't had a chance to talk with you yet."

"You haven't let her out of your sight since you walked through her door. That might have something to do with it, don't you think?"

Not a casual statement. The man was clearly very well informed of his daughter's comings and goings, a fact Jake made a mental note to remember. "Most likely."

Duke stared through him with a look he could have used in prison to scare off fellow inmates. A hard-edged, inscrutable look that could have meant he was contemplating murder as easily as he considered changing a TV channel.

But Duke Hunt apparently recognized and respected the truth when he stared it in the face, and to Jake's surprise—and yes, relief—the man inclined his soapy head and said, "Well, I suppose it's also something that you're keeping your word to her. And I'm glad to know she isn't losing her mind and jumping into bed with a strange man."

Jake thought he was getting a bead on what the trouble was. "If it's any reassurance, I met Mallory a *very* long time ago. Unfortunately we had a miscommunication that prevented us from getting together again before now."

"Interesting. Is that why you pursued her through TSS?"

"Yes."

Jake might not have recognized it at the time, might have told himself that contacting her was about the job and her owing him a favor, but he now knew he'd been waiting to see her again. Waiting for a *very* long time.

He couldn't share that information with Duke Hunt, though, and the conversation obviously wasn't over yet. Duke followed him when he returned to the locker room and toweled off on a nearby bench.

"Let me give you some advice," he said. "My daughter doesn't let a lot of people into her life and on the off chance you make the cut, I want you to know I'm going to need some sort of guarantee you're worthy of her. She's very loyal to the people she loves, which is why there are so few of them."

Jake remembered her rushing out to help a young kid in trouble. "I do understand. May I ask you a question?"

"Shoot."

"What does Mallory have against soul mates?"

Duke tossed aside the towel and opened a locker. He

withdrew his clothing but didn't answer as he shrugged on his shirt.

"I don't know what Mallory would tell you, but since you're asking me, I'll give you my spin," he finally said, lifting his gaze and meeting Jake's head-on. "My daughter isn't white bread, and I don't think I need to tell you that our lives haven't exactly been mainstream. It takes an effort to help someone understand our circumstances. The same goes for her trying to fit into someone's quote-unquote *normal* lifestyle. I don't think she's met many people worth making the effort for."

The reasoning certainly fit the bill and again Jake was impressed by how well Duke Hunt knew his daughter. "I appreciate the opinion."

"So now that we understand each other, Trinity, tell me how the training's going."

"I'm getting a feel for why so many criminals prefer armed robbery to burglary."

Duke smiled. "Not too many people want to put forth the extra effort it takes to be good. Says something about our society, don't you think?"

"It does."

And the fact that Duke Hunt had put forth the extra effort to make sure Jake understood the parameters of dealing with his daughter meant Mallory had been right about his approval rating. And if the people who knew her best were on his side then he just might stand a chance.

They finished dressing in silence and as Jake was returning his soiled workout clothes to his duffel, Duke said, "Before you go, Jake, there's something else."

He lifted his gaze to find the man completely dressed and tossing his own bag over his shoulder.

"A friend of mine asked me to thank you for helping

Mallory get his son home.'' He extended his hand and Jake shook it.

"Glad I could help."

Couldn't hurt to have this man owe him one.

11

"WHERE HAVE you been?" Duke asked Opal when she walked through the door of his house a full two hours after leaving work at Eddie's place. "You couldn't call to let me know you were going to be late? Or at least keep your cell phone on so I could get through to you?"

Her strappy heels ringing out on the marble foyer, she sauntered right up to him, raised up on tiptoe and planted a kiss on his cheek. "Worried, were you? I'm flattered."

He scowled to conceal the fact that he was pleased. *Very* pleased. Opal apparently liked that he'd noticed her absence, that he'd made the effort to call and track her down.

Small wonder. She deserved to be treated as if she mattered, and it was his new quest in life to prove to her that she did. "You still haven't answered my question."

"That's it, Duke?" she asked, her mouth pursing in a deliciously pouty moue. "It hasn't been long since you professed your intention of wanting something more than sex with me, and already you're taking me for granted. No 'How was your day, dear?' Or 'Can I fix you a drink?'"

"Martinis have been waiting to be poured for over an hour." Slipping a hand on her elbow, he motioned to the lanai at the back of the house. He'd play her game. Not only had she earned his cooperation, but also he wanted to win her as the prize.

But playing meant walking a fine line. He wouldn't let

her push him around. Give Opal an inch, and she'd take the length of the Mason-Dixon Line. "Shall we?"

Together they passed through the wall of French doors to the lanai, where a waterfall bubbled into the pool which glowed in a profusion of calming blue and green lights.

Opal dropped her shoulder bag onto the table and sat down.

He poured the martinis, brought her a glass. "So, how was your day, dear?"

She sipped her drink, proceeded to stare out at the pool and ignore him. Obviously since she'd had to tell him to ask, his question wasn't enough to soothe her ruffled feathers.

He tried again. "Thanks for telling me about the Vertical Playground. I cornered Jake in the shower and we had a chat."

That got her attention. He could see a grin tickling the corners of her mouth. "The shower?"

"It was the only place I could catch him without Mallory. Those two are stuck together like barbed wire."

"That's the truth, so what did you chat about?"

"About the man's intentions toward my daughter. What else?" Duke set his glass on the table and sat down beside her. "He shows up out of nowhere and within hours he's showering in her bathroom? I was within my rights to ask."

"Of course. And what did he say?"

"That he hasn't figured out yet what he wants from her."

"Do you believe him?"

"No. He's got a lot more than a hard-on for her whether he's figured it out yet or not."

Duke wouldn't mention that he recognized the symptoms because he was suffering from them himself. Opal would have a party with that information.

"Of course you offered to help him figure it out."

"Of course." Duke smiled. "At least to help him sort out his priorities about what I find acceptable and unacceptable regarding his behavior."

She tipped her glass in salute. "And did you?"

"Absolutely. I also asked him how he knew her."

Something about that made Opal smile, a slow, secretive smile that made the hairs on the back of his neck prickle. "Really? And what did he say?"

"He *claims* he promised Mallory not to say anything. Apparently she wants to explain the situation to me herself."

"You believe him?"

Duke shrugged. "I don't know why he'd lie. He doesn't strike me as stupid, and I'll find out from her soon enough. He did admit to meeting her before."

Her smile widened, and Duke plucked the glass from her hand and set it back on the table. He knew this woman too well not to recognize when she was stringing him along. "What's up?"

Curiously, he watched her reach for her bag and flip open the leather flap to withdraw a videotape. It took a minute for him to place it.

A surveillance tape from the Innovative job.

By all rights that tape should have been destroyed ten years ago. Disposing of the evidence was normal procedure after every job. But the Innovative job had been different.

After his arrest, his crew had quickly stored his belongings to get them out of reach of the law. The surveillance tapes had been buried with his things and after his parole, Duke hadn't disposed of them because he'd been feeling sentimental about his last job. He hadn't thought about them in years.

Then the significance of that tape clicked.

"You're not telling me he's—"

"One and the same." Opal laughed, and with her eyes glittering beneath the lights, she looked more beautiful than ever before. "I recognized him the instant I saw him. I ran by the storage facility to pick up this tape. That's why I was late."

Duke couldn't contain a shot of adrenaline that launched him up out of the chair. "Clever woman. What would I do without you?" He dropped a kiss to the top of her head, pleased she preened beneath the attention. "Let's play it."

Within minutes he had the tape in the video player, and was turning the television to face them. Using the remote, he fast-forwarded through long spans of silent nothingness—the dimly lit interior of a business closed for the weekend.

The tape had degraded badly over the years, but Duke could still make out the entry to the warehouse where Mallory had been slated to disconnect the alarm sensor that would secure his egress from where he'd punched through the vault wall from his access point in the warehouse.

He almost fast-forwarded past her entrance and had to rewind to catch her rappelling down the line, dropping to the floor with an agility that the years had only honed.

His daughter moved with an economy of motion that still brought him a crazy feeling of pride, and he watched as she punched in the access code on the keypad to disable the sensors.

Despite the grainy quality of the tape, Duke recognized the instant she'd sensed something was wrong. Her whole body tensed, and she turned around fully to face the camera.

He stood beside Opal's chair, thigh brushing her shoulder as they watched this long-ago scene play out in silent slow motion. Mallory raised a finger to her lips and tugged up the bottom of her mask as she moved across the room toward the young man who'd suddenly appeared in the camera's range. She engaged the kid in a kiss that no warm-blooded male alive would have been able to resist.

Jake Trinity hadn't been able to resist. And there was no mistaking that this young man was Jake Trinity.

Duke had known about Mallory's run-in with this employee since the start. He'd never forget his first visit with her in the county lockup. She'd been hysterical, believing that her decision to stall the young man had been the deciding factor in getting him busted. That hadn't been the case, and he'd assured her all the error had been his. He'd activated the alarm.

He remembered wanting to wrap her in his arms, as he'd always done when she'd been upset as a little girl. He'd wanted to tell her how proud he'd been of her. She'd been training superbly, and her actions when dealing with that unexpected situation on the Innovative job only proved it.

Her stall tactic would have worked if not for the silent alarm, would have bought him the extra time to complete the job. Given the situation, she'd made the same call he or any of his crew would have made.

But Duke hadn't told her. He hadn't wanted to do or say anything that might encourage her to continue living the life he'd raised her in, a life that could all too easily land her exactly where he was—behind Plexiglas and unable to comfort his heartbroken daughter.

He'd needed to make a point—crime *doesn't* pay.

And it didn't. He'd learned too late that the price of their lifestyle was too high. Way too high.

He couldn't have foreseen that Mallory would run into

Jake Trinity, who shouldn't have been in the building during the break-in. He couldn't have known she'd assume the responsibility for his arrest. Duke also hadn't counted on the courts refusing to honor the documents he'd left with his attorney, which would have allowed Mallory to live with Opal.

All events which proved that he never should have involved his daughter in such a lifestyle in the first place.

Duke rewound the tape and played it again. "No wonder I had the feeling I'd seen him before."

"Amazing," Opal said softly. "I can even see it on this grainy old videotape."

"What?"

"Their chemistry. Do you see what they're like together? They practically glow."

There was no missing it, and Duke hadn't had to see them half-naked together to notice, either. "I always wondered what gave her the idea to kiss him."

"She obviously thought he was cute. He is. *Very* cute."

Duke frowned. "Her stall tactic worked. Trinity didn't trip the alarm."

"No surprises there. The promise of sex scatters most men's wits. Most men think with their penises, or haven't you heard?"

"*Most* being the operative term." Duke might have been offended except he was still reeling from the shock of Trinity's identity and the implications of him showing up again in Mallory's life. "So what the hell is going on between these two? They kiss once and then jump into bed the first time they see each other in ten years."

"It must have been quite a kiss."

"If my daughter had wanted this man that bad she'd have gone after him years ago."

"Which raises a very interesting question. How did Mallory know it was him?"

"She recognized him just like you did."

Opal shook her head. "I don't think so. The instant Jake's proposal came through on the fax, Mallory went on red alert. I told you about the astronomical fee she quoted him to take the job. I think she knew who Jake was when she saw his name."

"So how and when did she find out?"

Opal eyed him thoughtfully. "It wouldn't have been that hard to find out who he was. You know that. Jake wouldn't have been in the building unless he worked for Innovative or the security company. She could have tracked down the information through personnel records."

"Why would she care enough even to bother? And why would she ask Trinity not to tell me and then not tell me herself?"

Why seemed to be the operative question, and unfortunately, it was a question Duke thought he could answer.

Depressing the pause button, he stared at Mallory and Trinity's frozen forms on the television screen, recalling that first visit with her after he'd been busted.

I should have called Polish Paul and told him I'd been made, Daddy, she'd said. *Then you would have gotten out.*

He turned to find Opal watching him. "Mallory thought she was responsible for my getting arrested. She thought the kid she'd run into—Trinity—had tripped the alarm."

"I know she did. The poor thing was beside herself, but you explained what happened."

"I told her I tripped the alarm, but what if she didn't believe me? What if she thought I was lying so she wouldn't feel responsible?" Duke sank into a chair, the effort of standing suddenly too much. "I've always played it straight with her. Why would she think I'd lie?"

Scooting her chair around, Opal reached out to take his hands, and Duke held on, grateful she was here and he didn't have to sort through this mess alone. Maybe she was right. Maybe he was getting old. Or just tired of tackling life alone.

"Is it so hard to understand, Duke, really? Why would Mallory think you made a mistake? You were the best."

"Everyone makes mistakes."

"Mallory thinks you're as close to perfect as they come," she said simply. "So does your crew."

"Well, I've always had an exalted sense of my self-worth." He gave a brittle laugh. "You've told me so often enough."

"I'm just saying it's not so hard to understand why Mallory might not believe you tripped that alarm."

There was something in her voice…something that raised his hackles even more.

"Accidents happen to the best of us," he said. "If you put yourself in high-risk situations, you're bound to run into trouble sooner or later. I surrounded myself with the best people so trouble would happen later rather than sooner."

Her impeccably manicured fingers tightened around his. "I understand that, but Mallory was sixteen years old at the time. You're her father, and she loves you. Put yourself in her position. She should have called for egress, but she chose to stall instead. It was a good call and would have worked had you not triggered that alarm."

There was no missing that…*something* in her voice now, an intensity that threw his senses into high alert. "What's your point, Opal?"

"Come on, Duke. Think about it. You trained us all. Did you really think we'd just casually accept that you'd screwed up? We're better than that. You must have expected us to investigate and figure out exactly what happened.''

Duke sat back in the chair and stared hard. "But I did trip the alarm."

She met his gaze as pointedly. "Not by accident."

The silence hung between them, heavy with implication, with the weight of a decade's old truth. And as he absorbed the silence, Opal held his hands, gave him an anchor to cling to, her thoughtful expression revealing that she not only knew the truth, but understood.

"How long have you known?" he asked when he could get the words out.

"Since shortly after the job." She shrugged lightly, a gesture he knew she hoped would lessen the intensity of the moment, the intensity of knowing he hadn't fooled anyone—especially the one person he'd needed to fool. The most important person of all. "It took a bit, but we finally pieced it all together."

"Did you tell Mallory?"

"No. We understood why you did it. To protect all of us, of course, but to give her a shot at a better life. I can't speak for Eddie and Paul but I wasn't surprised. I'd seen it coming for a while. The minute Mallory started pushing you to let her join the team."

"Risking my ass was a lot different than risking hers."

"That's what makes you such a good father." She lifted his hands, bent low to press a kiss along his knuckles, a gesture he found so much comfort in that he couldn't help but feel humble.

"A good father would have gotten a real job and set a better example for his daughter."

Opal squeezed his hands tightly. "You were entrenched in the life long before Mallory was born. It was your shot out of the gutter and you took it. You've made good with your life. Don't regret that.''

"You're right, of course." He knew it, but he didn't feel it.

"If you don't mind me pointing out the obvious, Duke.'' She didn't bother hiding her exasperation. "It wasn't as if you'd actually planned to tackle family life. Normally, I'm not one to speak ill of the dead, but honestly, if it wasn't for that idiot you were sleeping with forgetting whether or not she'd taken her birth control pills from one day to the next…''

Shaking her head, she sent platinum waves fringing around her face, a face that even while frowning was still so beautiful. "And you did do the honorable thing by marrying her. You reared a wonderful daughter. This was your life when Mallory came into it. Would you have rather missed out on her because your life wasn't set up for a family?''

"Of course not." Although he could have argued that he'd been well acquainted with his late wife's flightiness and had made the choice to trust her enough to operate without a condom.

But he didn't. Not when he so enjoyed Opal fiercely coming to his defense.

"Ironic though, don't you think?" he said. "I was telling the truth about tripping the alarm and my own crew didn't believe me. The more I think about it the more convinced I am that Mallory didn't, either.''

"And I'm just as sure that if she didn't, she would have kept it to herself.''

"Maybe even decided to do something about it.''

Opal inclined her head. "You think she blames Jake?''

"Not entirely. Mallory isn't stupid, and she's not one to cast off her decisions onto someone else. But he did get in her way. If she hadn't run into him, she'd never have been forced to make a decision. There's some reason she went through the trouble of finding out who he was. And I don't care how much chemistry's between them, she wouldn't just jump in bed with this guy after ten years. If she wanted him that much she'd have found him a long time ago.''

Opal smiled thoughtfully. ''I think you're right.''

''This simply isn't acceptable. The whole point of going to prison was so that everyone would be safe and off the hook. Mallory can't feel responsible.''

She ran her thumb along his hand, didn't say anything.

''Not to mention that Mallory finally has met a man who might be worthy of her and she's going to run him off.''

''Back to that again, are we, Duke?'' Opal rolled her eyes in a look of profound tolerance. ''If it helps any, I don't think Jake will be easy to chase away.''

''Mallory's relentless.''

''Just like her father.''

''She won't let up.'' Which meant she'd probably take until the eve of her sixtieth birthday to recognize a good thing. He didn't admit that to Opal. ''I've got to fix this.''

''Tell her the truth.''

''Tell her that I got myself busted and forgot to mention it? Oh, I'm sure that'll go over big.''

Opal leaned forward until they were so close he could smell the faint scent of Chanel on her skin, see the glint of moisture in her eyes. ''You tell her that you cared enough about her and all of us to take the hit and break us out of the life.''

''Telling her undermines the point, don't you think?'' he asked dryly, finding those almost-tears disconcerting.

''Ten years ago maybe, but not now. We've all moved on. Your plan worked. You made sure we all had enough money to get fresh starts, and watching you sit in prison made sure we all wanted them.'' She blinked against her tears, shot him a look that was pure Opal bluster. ''Why are you frowning? You can't be worried that Mallory will go back to the life.''

''Not hardly. She's been having too much fun working for the law lately.''

''Actually, I think she's having more fun working for Jake,'' she said. ''Explain why you did it, Duke. She's all grown up. She'll understand.''

He didn't say anything, couldn't think of anything to say.

''Promise me,'' she persisted. ''You'll never get grand-babies if Mallory thinks Jake helped get you busted.''

He glanced at the television screen where his daughter and Trinity were frozen in time, arms wrapped around each other and… Well, Opal was right. They did sort of glow.

''I'll think about it.'' That was the best he could do.

Apparently it was enough because Opal slipped out of her chair and into his lap. ''And now that everything is out on the table, I want to talk about all this self-sacrifice. I really had no idea you had such a noble streak.''

The tears were gone, and he was back on familiar ground. Lifting her hand, he pressed a kiss to her smooth skin. ''You know, nobility happens to be a good quality in a husband.''

''A husband, Duke?''

''Yes, a husband.''

12

JAKE CONSIDERED HIMSELF one of the more knowledgeable people in the security industry, but Mallory's tutelage proved his knowledge base was nothing to hers. They'd been playing a very intense game with her unraveling the mysteries of his system and him savoring each obstacle he tossed in her path to easy infiltration. His triumphs were coming few and far between.

True to her word, she hadn't questioned him about the Sentex 2000. She could have cut her research time significantly with internal knowledge of his system, but he was paying to watch how a real burglar worked. So she worked while he watched and analyzed, discovering that the key to her thoroughness was the way she broke down the job into components that forced her to ask questions he'd never have asked when designing a system.

Addressing the ways to access the property meant a thorough understanding of the fencing, the best entry points, the structure and placing of the gates, the distance between the entry point and the building, the timing of the surveillance camera sweeps, the presence of armed guards or watchdogs.

When Jake designed a new system, he focused on all the ways of getting onto the property and into the building. Mallory however, spent as much time analyzing how to get onto the property and into the building as she spent on how to get back out again, which raised new questions that needed answers.

She made sure she found those answers no matter how long it took. They'd spent two days researching details about the property to determine how best to approach the building. Another two days studying the building plans for entry. She collected each piece of her research and formulated a theory, which she then presented to him for confirmation or denial.

Her accuracy rate had been nothing short of astounding. If Jake hadn't known better, he'd have thought she'd been inside his head when he'd conceived his design, and this had made him more determined than ever to make Mallory part of TSS.

Unfortunately, being together twenty-four seven hadn't shed any light on what would make an offer attractive to her.

Not money, surely. Even if he'd been in a position to pay her some ridiculous sum, she wouldn't be sufficiently motivated. She seemed to have enough money to live the way she wanted to and appeared content. Nor would the challenge of growing TSS be an incentive when she wasn't personally invested in the company.

If he could have moved past fling into a relationship, Jake might have stood a chance. But she'd been stonewalling him in the *us* department.

Her friend at the police department had run into trouble tracking down the ten-year-old information they needed. He'd had to launch a needle-in-a-haystack type of search that wasn't yielding results quickly.

This left a question mark between Jake and Mallory: although she claimed to accept that he hadn't sounded the alarm, he wasn't sure he believed her. Not when she refused to move their relationship one step beyond bed or work.

She wouldn't go near his place and had point-blank refused to meet his parents when he needed to drop off tickets for a cruise he was sending them on to celebrate their thirty-fifth wedding anniversary. She was keeping their relationship under control with firmly delineated boundaries.

Jake didn't want boundaries. He wanted her.

But the more time they spent together, the more he realized how important control was to her, and how insightful her father had been about her unwillingness to mesh their lives. She thrived on challenges, but she liked a neatly controlled life to come back to in between them.

Jake had been doing everything he could to prove himself worthy of standing by her side in those in-between times, but his efforts were yielding results about as fast as their police investigation. So he decided to kick-start the process, but he couldn't do this alone.

Luckily, he didn't have a problem admitting when he was outclassed and outgunned, so he went straight to people who could help him.

"Hey folks." Jake turned the corner of the flagstone path that led to the backyard of the suburban home he'd grown up in.

Though it was late on a Saturday, his parents were still involved in mulching the yard—a job Jake knew from personal experience would take the better part of the weekend. His dad wielded a shovel while his mom was on her knees in the flower bed. Her obsession with fresh air, sunshine and anything that bloomed had long ago infiltrated their lives, and Jake couldn't help but smile at the familiar scene.

"Hello, son," his father said, propping the shovel

against a trellis. "You must be busy lately. We haven't seen or heard from you in weeks."

"Too long, Jake," his mom admonished, extending a gloved hand for him to help her to her feet. "You could at least call once in a while to let us know you're alive."

There was no debating her point, although he suspected she would forgive all once she heard about the twist his life had recently taken. Flashing the envelope with the cruise tickets, he said, "I hope these will make up for my negligence."

His mom mellowed with a smile, kissing his cheek before she tugged off the garden gloves and plucked the envelope from his hand. "Your gift is lovely, Jake. Thank you."

"We're looking forward to getting away," his father added.

"Do you all want some help with the mulch? I've got time."

His father shook his head and waved toward the table. "High time for a break. We've been at this all day, and we're not even close to being done. Should have hired professionals."

"And miss being outside getting fresh air and exercise?" his mom countered in a too-familiar argument. "Not likely."

After pouring a glass of iced tea from the sweating pitcher on the patio table, his father motioned Jake to sit with him. "So what's been up with you lately?"

He sat down to visit with his folks, enjoying the familiarity of his childhood home, envisioning Mallory sitting at this table beside him. The thought made him smile.

"I've hired a consultant to work with me on my newest system. She's been helping me get ready to launch."

"She?" his mom asked. "An engineer?"

"A very unusual engineer." Jake explained a few of Mallory's more unique consulting abilities. "She comes at security from such a different perspective that I've already spotted ways to improve my designs. I've decided I want her working exclusively for TSS."

"Really?" his father asked. "What kind of offer can you make her?"

"That's the trouble. I can't figure out what will attract her. Money and perks won't do the trick. I'm sure of that. The only leverage I've got is me. I've been trying to convince her that she wants me around full-time."

Jake waited while the significance of that statement settled in. His father set the iced tea glass back on the table slowly. His mom asked, "Are you dating this woman?"

He nodded.

"You sound very serious about her."

"I am," he admitted, gearing himself up for the real explanation. "Very serious. I want to convince her to marry me. I like being around her."

"Then give her some time, son," his father cautioned, and Jake suspected by his frown that he was questioning whether his son had lost his mind. "You've only been together what…a few weeks?"

He nodded, and his mom reached across the table and slipped her hand over his, a gesture that revealed worry more than words ever could.

"It's not like you to be this impatient," she said.

Jake smiled to reassure her. "No, it's not. I've fallen for her in a big way."

"A woman you just met?" his father asked as though he still hadn't decided whether he was hearing Jake right.

Here it was—the truth. "Actually I met her ten years ago."

"Who is she, Jake?" his mom asked. "Do we know her?"

"Not personally, but I did tell you about her. She was the woman I met during the break-in at Innovative Engineering."

Jake twisted his hand around to grasp his mom's, squeezed lightly and waited. His father put two and two together first.

"You're not referring to one of the burglars, are you?"

Jake nodded. "The burglar's daughter. Her name is Mallory Hunt."

The sudden silence contrasted sharply with the bright afternoon sun, and Jake took in his parents' flabbergasted expressions, experiencing a firsthand glimpse of what Duke had referred to about the difficulties in meshing lifestyles.

"I haven't lost my mind, folks, in case you're wondering." Jake gave them a wry smile and proceeded to explain everything he knew about Mallory.

He told them all about how she'd gone legitimate and her friends had gone non-prosecutable. How her father had served his debt to society. He made no apologies for Mallory, her father or their friends. Not for their circumstances or their unusual lifestyles. He didn't feel the need to apologize. Not one of the crew had impressed him as needing an apology. They were candid people who cared about the woman he loved.

A fact that didn't go unnoticed by his parents.

As an only child, Jake had always interacted closely with his parents, had always had the freedom to speak openly, but he honestly wasn't sure what to expect from them right now. He knew they loved him unconditionally, but he really couldn't predict their responses to this unusual situation. He did know his parents would listen and be open-minded. He was counting on it.

And they didn't disappoint. They listened. With his mom still holding his hand, he explained Duke's opinion about Mallory letting people into her life, and his own observations that reinforced this view.

"I'm getting nowhere trying to convince her that we can have a future," he said. "I'm sure she recognizes what we have is special, and I believe she cares about me, but she won't even acknowledge the issues, let alone address them."

His mom searched his face. "Do you love her, Jake?"

"Yes."

Her expression softened. Her hand tightened around his. "Then that's good enough for us."

His father met his gaze and said simply, "Tell us what we can do to help you."

DUKE SAT DOWN at the drafting table in his office, flipped on a desk lamp then dragged a high-power magnifying glass over the blueprints. He hadn't talked to his daughter in days, and after so long with no news about what was happening with her and Trinity, Duke almost regretted calling off his crew from their spying detail.

But after his conversation with Trinity at the gym, he'd decided to give the man some room to maneuver. Duke knew the crew's constant presence would keep Mallory on the defensive, and that would do nothing to further his cause to see his daughter settled and happy. He hadn't been able to back off entirely, though, and had been driving by Mallory's place at odd times to scope out how often Trinity's car was in the driveway.

The man had apparently moved in with her, which made Duke edgy for an update. As a result, his imagination was in overdrive, so he had settled in for a stint of late-night work as a distraction, even though Opal was heading to bed.

She had to work early, and restlessness would have him tossing and turning. See, he could be a considerate partner when he chose; he'd just never given himself the chance before.

And Opal had been making it very rewarding to be considerate.

He smiled. She'd been spending every night with him, and each day when she arrived at his house after work, a few more of her personal items accompanied her. Clothing. Her impressive stock of fashion and fitness magazines. Even her laptop had made an appearance last night so she could pay bills with her checking software. He'd cleared a space beside his own desk unit and hooked her up to the Internet so she could work by his side.

Duke had no doubt that she knew he was using any opportunity, small though it might be, to prove himself. Just as he knew she was testing the water, unwilling to jump in until convinced the temperature was to her liking. He suspected that she didn't trust him yet. She didn't want to marry him only to discover he'd had a change of heart.

But Duke wouldn't have a change of heart. Not when he'd wasted too much time with her already.

Given their history though, she had every right to be cautious, so he didn't say a word. She could handle the details in whatever way made her comfortable. She would accept his proposal when she was ready, and he'd just be grateful that she hadn't turned him down.

The telephone rang, jarring Duke from his thoughts. He reached for the receiver and said, "Hello."

"John Trinity here. I'm calling for Duke Hunt."

"Speaking. I know your last name."

"Jake's father."

Ah. Duke cradled the receiver against his ear and sat back in his chair, his smile widening. Here was an unexpected, and very interesting, turn of events. "What can I do for you, John?"

"Jake just informed me and my wife that he's involved with your daughter. We wanted to introduce ourselves."

Clever. Duke had told Jake to have more than a fling planned for Mallory. What better way to declare his intentions than by getting the families together?

Simple and effective. His estimation of Jake Trinity rose a few notches. "Glad you called, John. The last I talked to Jake, he hadn't made up his mind what he wanted from my daughter. I'm assuming this call means he's made a decision."

"Nothing indecisive about him today." John gave a laugh. "Strolled right into the backyard where my wife was trying to kill me with yard work, and informed us that he intended to marry your daughter. Given the unusual circumstances of how they met, he wanted a little help convincing his reluctant fiancée."

"I see." And Duke did. Jake Trinity was declaring open war on Mallory.

Opal appeared in the office doorway, looking all soft and flowy with her hair tousled around her face, the filmy peignoir catching the light perfectly to outline her flawless form below.

He mouthed, "Trinity's father."

Her eyebrows shot up. "What does he want?"

"What do you have in mind, John?"

"Jake seems to think our families getting to know each other might reassure Mallory that the past is in the past. His mother and I are game, if you are. He also mentioned a woman who's very close with her."

"Opal." He pushed back from the desk so the woman in question could slip into his lap and eavesdrop.

"Your son is rising in my estimation with every word you say. Opal and I are happy to meet with you and your wife."

"Suggest drinks at your club," Opal whispered.

"We could meet for drinks at my club," Duke said into the receiver. "When will be good for you?"

As he worked out the details with John Trinity, Opal threaded her arms around his neck and snuggled against him, clearly pleased he'd taken her suggestion.

Duke was pleased, too. Not only by Jake Trinity's actions, but that he'd taken advantage of another opportunity to prove to Opal that he valued her opinion. By the time he hung up the telephone with a meeting time in place, he found himself ready to head to bed, even though he still wasn't tired.

"SHEESH, JAKE," Mallory said when he entered her workshop, glancing up from her computer desk where she sat calculating totals from the research she'd been conducting all afternoon. "According to my numbers, the Atlanta Safe Exchange paid TSS enough money for protective bars on *every* window of their storage facility. You don't miss a trick."

If she only knew. He'd just returned from an impromptu cell phone conversation with his father, where he'd learned his luck still held with his scheme to bring the families together. After helping Mallory with Lance, he'd been reasonably certain Duke would agree to meet with his folks, but not only had his parents and Duke and Opal met, they'd struck up what seemed to be a very unlikely friendship.

They'd found a number of shared interests and Jake had

just learned they'd gotten together again last night for the opening of a new Broadway play.

The *third* time they'd gotten together this week.

He didn't share that information with Mallory. Wiping the smile from his face, he dropped his cell phone back into his briefcase on the worktable and asked, "Did my company provide you with the actual cost of the bars?"

She flashed a quicksilver grin. "You have the most helpful staff. What I want to know is if this system is cost-effective."

This wasn't the first time during his training that his company's efficiency had proved a double-edged sword. Or that she'd questioned the cost-effectiveness of the Sentex 2000.

He gave his standard reply. "It's cost-effective for businesses that want to keep burglars off the premises."

"Protective bars on every window will deter a good few. Which means we're back to accessing the building through the roof. Write down a power drill on the tool list, would you?"

Jake obliged, reduced to taking advantage of even the smallest opportunity to prove himself an invaluable asset to her life. He would eventually convince her they were an *us,* and he'd stack the deck in every way he could think of.

And he wasn't above playing dirty to get what he wanted.

Mallory.

"Did you get your business taken care of?" she asked.

He nodded, stifling a smile at how she referred to a phone call with his father as "business." She was trying so hard not to cross the line into his personal life. *Too* hard.

"Good. I'm ready to get out of this workshop," she

said. "I think the time has come for a dry run. Are you ready?"

Any urge to smile faded quickly enough when he thought about rappelling. They'd been practicing daily, and, as Mallory had promised, he'd improved. His strength served him well even without much technique. Whether it was enough to test in the real setting remained to be seen.

"An important part of this break-in will be getting across that floor to disable the motion sensor," she said. "I've got a one-hundred-percent success rate, and I intend to maintain it. Having you accidentally trip the alarm isn't part of my plan."

"Fair enough. Where can we practice? TSS?"

She shook her head, sending shiny hair over her shoulders and down the back of the chair. "Home turf. We need to test you out someplace unfamiliar to see how you react under pressure. I've got a place." She powered down her computer system and pushed the chair back from the desk. "Come on."

Jake followed her to the bedroom for a wardrobe change into what he'd termed "burglar black" when they'd recently shopped at a uniform supply house in preparation for the upcoming job.

She dressed in coveralls that molded her slim curves, and he waited until she'd turned back to the closet before sneaking up and wrapping his arms around her waist. She gasped when he pulled her against him, and Jake buried his smile in her hair.

"I'm having the most incredible sense of déjà vu here. You look like this gorgeous thief I ran into about ten years ago." His hand found its way into the Velcro that she'd yet to fasten. Nudging aside her bra, he skimmed her satin skin.

She melted against him and laughed softly. "Never miss an opportunity to feel me up, do you?"

"Never. Especially since I can't guarantee I'll make it back tonight in one piece."

Especially since he'd realized that the only way to get close to Mallory was to take her by surprise. "Will you miss me if I wind up breaking my head open?"

She pressed her breast into his hand. He tweaked her nipple, smiled when she shivered.

"I'll miss sleeping with you."

Here was a classic example of how she delineated those boundaries of their relationship, reminding him that he hadn't taken a step past fling yet.

He caressed her nipple again, and she lifted her arms to slip her hands behind his neck, idly caressing the hairs at his nape, lifting her breasts up and out to invite exploration. Jake pleasured her until she sighed.

"Did you start this up because you're trying to get out of going live tonight?" she asked.

"No, but I'd never miss a chance to peel off these coveralls. It's been a fantasy of mine for ten years."

"Really?"

He filled his hands with the firm swells of her breasts, shifted his hips to nourish the ache of his growing erection against her bottom. "Really. That sexy thief has been the lady of my dreams, and she's finally all mine."

Predictably, Mallory gave a laugh and stepped out of his reach, the intimacy of that statement enough to make her run. Jake didn't think she'd be happy if she knew how predictable she'd become, and how much her predictability looked like panic.

Panic, like her reminders that they were having only a fling, was a good thing. It meant she wasn't only trying to convince him there was no *us*, but trying to convince herself.

And *that* was a big step past fling, whether she admitted it or not.

13

PEACHTREE FINANCIAL reminded Jake of a small Old South bank with its Doric columns and elegant facade. "I'm not familiar with this place. What sort of financial institution is this?" he asked as he pulled into a spot at the rear of the building.

"One that caters to a very select clientele," she replied, which didn't answer his question.

As she was already opening the door before he'd even put the car out of gear, he was deterred from asking her to elaborate.

"FYI." She pulled open the back door to unload her equipment. "Here's another difference between our job and a real job. On a real job we wouldn't be parking in the lot. We'd have someone drop us off and circle until it was time to pick us up."

"Who drove for you on the night you visited Innovative?"

"Polish Paul."

"The getaway driver?"

"Always."

Retrieving his own equipment, Jake locked his car and joined her at the back entrance of the building.

"Here's another big difference between our job and a real job," she whispered.

"Let me guess, you wouldn't have a key?"

"Very good."

That one had been a no-brainer, so he didn't comment but asked instead, "Who does this place belongs to?"

"Worried about winding up in jail?"

"No. Just curious who would trust you to come and go inside their business."

She gave a laugh, stepped inside and used the touchpad to disable the alarm. Then she moved aside to let him enter. "Are you telling me you wouldn't trust me with a key to TSS corporate?"

"Are you telling me you'd need a key?"

Her smile flashed white as she tugged the ski mask over her face. "Come on."

Pulling his own mask into place, he followed her through low-lit corridors in the rear of the building. His senses heightened along with a growing sense of unreality as they moved through the shadowy interior, bringing back visions of the past.

They arrived at a storage area that appeared to be home to miscellany from high-ticket electronic gadgetry to museum-quality art. That these products would be kept *outside* the vault suggested that what was inside would be worth the effort of trying to circumvent the security system. It also told him that Peachtree Financial wasn't a banking institution in any sense of the term he was familiar with.

"Is this Eddie Gibb's pawn shop?" he asked in surprise, glancing at a late-model sound system that he knew from his own recent purchase cost close to ten grand.

"Very good."

Jake had no idea that high-end pawnshops even existed. When he'd first heard about Eddie Gibb, he'd imagined the man's business in a strip plaza with bars on the windows and a name like E-Z Cash.

Upon reflection though, he supposed that all the late-model vehicles parked behind Polish Paul's Tattoo Studio on the night they'd brought Lance home should have clued him in that this pawn business would be more lucrative than most. Upon further reflection, Jake supposed that wealthy folks who had a need to unload their possessions would also need a place that dealt exclusively with high-ticket items.

"Eddie's got quite a place here."

Mallory gave an absent nod and motioned to the open doorway. "Take a good look at the photoelectric sensor array from this angle. We won't be worrying about anything except getting to the floor without triggering the sensors. I'll only be able to block the beams in an area wide enough to create a channel for us to maneuver through. I will disable the voice and temperature sensors for this quadrant, though. That'll make our job a little easier."

He only nodded, not seeing anything easy about the job ahead. Forcing his concentration onto the thin streams of red light that appeared to be criss-crossing in a random pattern, he studied their design. "Exceptional placement. I implement similar patterns with several of my systems."

"I know." Her green eyes flashed. Her whisper filtered through the quiet, adding to his growing sense of unreality.

Jake took in the angle of the closed-circuit surveillance camera that manned the doorway while she keyed in the access codes to arm the system for their trip into the store-room.

"Where will we come through the ceiling?" he asked.

"There's enough room to maneuver through the crawl space with the duct work."

"Obviously you've done this before."

"We tested out every angle of this system before Eddie was satisfied it was ready to go."

"He doesn't mind us cutting through his drywall?"

"Not a problem. The repair falls under the category of additional daily expenses. Polish Paul will patch it up, and you'll pay the bill."

Jake snorted.

They accessed the crawl space through an electrical cabinet that housed the climate control system, and then all his thoughts focused on maneuvering through the dusty passages that ran along the vents with his gear on his back. His knees ached by the time they reached their destination, and he learned that burglary was a far more physical business than he'd ever realized, despite all the hours he'd spent at the rock-climbing gym.

Mallory told him to unload the battery-operated power saw, and then directed him through the process of creating places to fasten clamps around the three-foot section of drywall he'd be cutting away so she could secure it when it detached.

A drop ceiling lay beneath the roof and she had him remove a panel from the frame. "Don't drop it, or our job will be over before it even gets started."

He handed it to her and she set it aside, but still within easy reach, he noticed.

The drop was only twenty feet. Jake had scaled much more distance with Mallory at the rock-climbing gym, but twenty feet took on a whole new meaning with the thin photoelectric beams cutting off his access to the floor below.

Using special equipment that Jake had never seen implemented for this purpose before, Mallory blocked the beam array to allow them a passage to descend, but getting through the slim apertures separating the beams meant not only steering clear of the beam itself, but not disturbing the air around it. Because of her smaller size, she would have more room to maneuver, a fact she'd already factored into her decision to let him descend closest to the vault where she'd been able to widen the channel.

Jake didn't think he should be feeling nerves right now. This was a dry run, and he had no pride left to salvage after weeks at the Vertical Playground proving how inept he could be. But his pulse raced and his heart was pounding hard when he lifted his gaze to Mallory, who looked exhilarated.

"Ready?" she asked in a whisper.

"Ready."

Leaning forward, she surprised him with a soft kiss and a smile. "Just remember if you trigger the alarm, the police come. There's nothing to worry about if you don't trigger the alarm."

"Right." She made it sound so simple.

And that was Jake's last thought before he was strapping on his harness and securing his line. Mallory insisted they check each other's handiwork as an added precaution before she lowered herself through the ceiling and hung there until she'd controlled her line.

Jake followed, his muscles tight as he slipped his boot into the foothold Mallory had insisted he use. Grasping his line, he lowered himself through the ceiling frame and allowed himself a moment to acclimate to the feeling of weightlessness.

Then they began their descent. He lowered himself slowly, his muscles controlled from the effort of keeping the line steady. He kept his gaze focused on the slim opening in the sensors that was his access point below. The only sound in the stillness was their breaths.

Maybe he was paying *too* much attention, because when his feet reached the first sweep of sensor beams, he missed his hold on the line by mere inches, inches that made him sway unsteadily before he contracted his body enough to

egain control. Mallory inhaled sharply behind him, and
he could feel her gaze on him.

Jake couldn't touch down on the floor, where pressure
sensors in the mat in front of the vault formed a circuit to
the floor that would trip a panic siren if he touched it
before disabling the system.

Coming to a stop within easy reach of the touchpad, he
waited for Mallory to provide the access code, pleased
he'd managed the descent.

She flashed him a smile that he interpreted to mean she
was similarly pleased just as her booted foot found the
toehold of her own line. Before he had a chance to consider what she was up to, she pitched forward in a motion
so controlled that she never even came close to touching
the beams that outlined her channel of maneuverable
space.

Suddenly she was crouched in mid-air before him, dangling perfectly still from her harness.

"What the hell—"

"Shh." She slipped a hand away from her line, paused
as though waiting to make sure she wouldn't sway and
then reached straight for his crotch.

Jake sucked in a huge breath, feeling his body spin out
of control before he managed to impose an iron grip on
his muscles to halt the jerky movement that would send
him into the wake of a sensor beam.

His next breath cleared his head enough to recognize
exactly what this was. Another test. She was changing the
script so he was forced to improvise. He had no doubt that
she would love for him to trip the alarm, and he was absolutely determined not to let her make him lose his focus.

That was of course, until she pulled apart the Velcro
fastening of his coveralls and slipped her hand inside.

Given that his adrenaline pumped double-time and he

held his body so tight that his muscles ached, Jake would have guessed it impossible to become aroused. But, just like that night ten years ago, he was mistaken. He could get aroused anywhere around this woman. He was on his way to a promising erection the instant her gloved fingers slipped beneath his waistband, zeroed in on the target and freed the whole deal.

"Mallory," he ground out, desperate in the quiet.

"I can't resist an opportunity to fondle you."

She gave him a reinforcing squeeze, and his body came alive, a mass of conflicting impulses as the two halves of his brain warred for control. The rational half reasoned that if he moved one muscle—other than the one she was currently teasing with strokes of her gloved fingers—he was sure to cross a beam and trip the alarm.

The impulsive half urged his hips to move, to take what she offered. So he hung there, hovering on the edge of indecision long enough for Mallory to get a really good grip and use his stiffening erection as a handhold to pull them together across the weightless distance.

She sucked him into her mouth with a hot wet pull, so deep the ski mask covering her chin came flush against his balls.

A man who'd been servicing his needs regularly should have had more self-control. He didn't. He could only grit his teeth and will himself not to move as she worked him with a liplock that by all rights should have been impossible given that she didn't appear to be moving a muscle.

Except for those above her neck. And those muscles were doing the job.

Maybe it was the excitement of the moment or the challenge of not losing his grip on the line, but she took him from zero to sixty in the time it took his stalled heart to roar through the first few stuttering beats.

When she slipped her gloved fingers around his erection and gave a healthy squeeze, Jake discovered that it was physically impossible for him to come without moving. He tried. Oh man, did he try. But his hips bucked hard, looking for the additional friction to push him over the edge.

Mallory must have realized the same thing, because she let him slide from her mouth just then, making him buck hard against the cool air that assaulted his throbbing skin…making him lose his grip on the line.

To Jake's credit he controlled his fall enough not to infiltrate any beam sensors, but he landed right on the pressure mat in front of the vault, his legs vibrating so hard they almost buckled beneath him.

The panic alarm shrieked to life in an ear-piercing blast.

With a huge burst of motion, Mallory launched herself toward him, swinging right through the beams and releasing her harness as she went. She dropped to her feet in front of the touchpad and her line swung wildly out behind her.

A few glances of her fingers against the display and the panic siren shuddered to an echoing halt.

"You lasted longer than I thought you—"

He had her before she finished turning.

His heart thundered. His crotch throbbed. His throat was so tight he couldn't even contemplate a reply.

But his hands were working just fine.

Dragging her against him, Jake ripped apart the Velcro fastening, tugged the coverall down her arms with jerky movements…down past her hips…down to her thighs… until she stood there clad in nothing more than her burglar black bra and thong.

The thong took nothing more than one well-aimed swipe to move aside before he could position himself exactly where he wanted to be.

Mallory's hands came around his neck, and she sank back against the vault to brace herself, legs parting as far as the tangle of garments would allow. Then she arched toward him, lace-covered breasts thrust out, and though the ski mask concealed her features, Jake knew she was as caught up in the moment as he was.

He found her moist and ready, entered her in one hot stroke. Jake had no problem controlling his movements with both his feet planted firmly on the ground. With his hands on her breasts and his hips riding her in driving thrusts, he made short work of bringing Mallory right to the edge. And only when she trembled in his arms, did he allow himself to go over, too, grinding out his release with a growl that echoed in the quiet.

They stared at each other, looking almost startled by the intensity, the violence of the moment. Mallory stood before him practically naked, lace-covered breasts heaving, the ski mask covering her beautiful face.

She looked like a vision from one of his fantasies, reminded him so much of ten years ago that Jake felt as if he were in time warp. Only this time…this time *he* tugged the ski mask from her face, dragged his own up enough to kiss her.

His mouth came down hard, and he felt her sigh burst against his lips, knew beyond a doubt that this woman was his soul mate, that he would never want another woman the way he wanted her. He'd been waiting ten long years to catch up with her.

And she'd been waiting for him too, whether she allowed herself to believe it or not.

But Jake was determined to make her a believer. He made love to her mouth with his tongue, letting her know with each stroke that he would be relentless and ruthless. He wouldn't stop until she was his. No matter how much she challenged him. No matter how often she tried to turn the tables. No matter how cleverly she tried to gain the upper hand.

He'd still be here no matter what she pulled on him.

And she got the message loud and clear. She was the one who broke their kiss, the panic around her edges proving she was as impacted by their lovemaking in a way she would never admit.

"I'd say you finished what I started," she said with a breathless laugh. "Did that live up to those fantasies you were telling me about?"

"The real thing beats the fantasies cold."

She lowered her gaze, a gesture that told him better than words that she was feeling overwhelmed right now.

"Here. Let me." He brushed aside her hands and helped her pull the coveralls back up.

Then Jake noticed something he'd missed while making love to her against the vault, even though the only thing separating him from the door had been the width of her slim body.

"I designed this vault." He tugged the ski mask off his head completely and ran a hand over the door.

"You're sure?"

He gave a snort. "I hold the patent on this outer coating. Yeah, I'm sure."

Her green eyes gleamed. She was back on comfortable ground again. "I already knew that. Your patent was one of the reasons my dad recommended TSS to make Eddie's vaults."

"Vaults plural, as in more than one?"

"This one's just smoke. He has a two-vault system. There's another one around here. I won't tell you where."

"I'm impressed. Who designed the set-up?"

"My dad and the crew. They were impressed that your

outer coating would make it easier for law enforcement to lift latent fingerprint impressions. Even though you're not a conventional safe manufacturer, my dad believed you offered better features.''

''I'll take that as a compliment.''

Mallory inclined her head in acknowledgment. ''It is.''

Then they got back to business, replacing the ceiling panels, storing the chunk of drywall and otherwise removing all traces of their visit. Finally, they headed to the rear doorway to reactivate the last quadrant of the security system.

''Jake, do you get the feeling that you've forgotten something?'' she asked.

He tossed their gear into the back seat of his SUV and glanced back at her. ''No. Have I?''

''Do the words *surveillance camera* mean anything to you?''

Those two words stopped him dead in his tracks. *Of course* there was a camera on the storeroom, and he'd forgotten about it. ''There's a tape of you giving me a blow job and me—''

She nodded, her face set in an expression of mock apology.

Another test. ''And you have absolutely no intention of going back inside and getting it, do you?''

''*You* tripped the alarm.''

''You'd leave the tape there?''

''Eddie and Opal will get it back to us.''

Us.

At any other time he might have savored the sound of that word, but right now he was too busy deciding whether or not she was bluffing.

Mallory didn't bluff, and an image of what he would look like on film with his erection showcased against burglar black coveralls while she worked her magic was enough to make him slam the car door shut.

Don't tell me you want a fling. That's not what I want to hear, Duke's warning echoed in his memory.

"Damn it, Mallory. Where's the monitoring station?"

"You'll have to find it yourself. And Jake…" She paused, her smile dazzling in the darkness. "Try not to trip the alarm again."

14

SOME INTUITION warned Mallory of trouble the instant Jake turned the corner onto her block. Her skin tingled as though she'd touched a live current and her senses shot into overdrive. When she saw the blockade of law-enforcement vehicles surrounding her house, visibars flashing silently in the late-night darkness, she almost wasn't surprised.

The impulse to tell Jake to keep driving hit her hard. She didn't want to tackle another problem when she wasn't at her best, when she'd already expended so much energy facing her conflicted feelings for Jake. Their encounter at Eddie's had knocked her into the *really* sub-par category. How could she be anything but when her best attempts to convince herself Jake was only a good piece of ass left her wanting him more than she'd ever wanted any man?

Jake wheeled his SUV behind a police car. "Are you sure Eddie didn't mind us breaking into his place?"

"This isn't about Eddie. Trust me." The sight of her front door standing wide open revealed that the trouble had happened inside her house. The fact that her security company hadn't reached her by cell…she glanced down at her purse. She'd turned her cell phone off when they'd arrived at Eddie's.

Slipping out of the car, she walked with Jake toward the officer who stood beside his patrol car talking into a radio.

"This is my place, officer. What happened?"

He lowered his radio. ''A break-in. The perp's inside. Some stoned-out kid we caught in the act.''

Another icy blast of premonition swept along her spine, and she apparently wasn't the only one who had a bad feeling because Jake's hand was suddenly on her shoulder, steadying her.

Mallory took off up the stairs and the minute she stepped through the open door, she saw him, standing against the wall below the stairs, back toward the uniformed officer who fastened cuffs on his wrists.

Lance.

He wasn't struggling, looked as if he would have sunk to the floor in a heap if another man—a plainclothes detective, Mallory guessed—hadn't been holding him against the wall.

She didn't have to see his bloodshot eyes to know he was wasted, and even knowing he was under the influence didn't dull the reality of him standing inside her home. Or the terrible hope that there was a valid explanation for the mess in the kitchen that looked as though he'd rummaged through her cabinets and drawers for something to steal.

''What happened here, officers?'' Jake asked.

''You own this place?'' the uniformed officer asked, his gaze taking note of their matching black coveralls.

Jake nodded before Mallory had a chance to, her response time really thrown off when Lance fixed an imploring gaze on her.

''Caught this kid helping himself to the cash you had laying around,'' the detective explained. ''And some high-ticket equipment. He claims to know you.''

She nodded, glancing into the dining room, where two more uniformed officers and another detective were cataloguing equipment on the table. Her PDA, laptop, cellular radio units, digital camera, portable global positioning system—all items Lance could carry out the door and pawn for a few grand at best. And with the cash she kept around for emergencies…

Somehow the total seemed wildly out of balance to the reality of what was happening right now, the turmoil that was happening inside her.

Jake talked with the detective about what would happen to Lance now, what Mallory's options were, and she felt stupid and slow-witted and unable to focus on anything beyond the way that Lance had been dismissed from the equation. He was someone who'd given up his rights, a lawbreaker who'd created a problem and would have no say in the resolution.

"Why?" she asked him.

He worked to focus his bleary gaze. "Dad said you'd be at Eddie's tonight. He cut me off. Needed some money, Mal."

For drugs, no doubt. And the fact that Lance obviously considered ripping her off a viable way to finance his habit slapped her in the face with another of those liquid boundaries between right and wrong. She'd been reared as a burglar by a professional, yet never once in her life had her father ever let her believe it was okay to steal.

His business was stealing from businesses for other businesses, impersonal. Insurance companies covered the losses. Yes, it was stealing. Yes, it was illegal. Yes, it was wrong. But it was never a personal invasion of someone's life, of the things someone valued, or the place they felt safe…that was out of bounds, especially if that someone was a friend.

Mallory didn't know what to say. She was stunned that Lance had sunk so low, upset for Polish Paul who couldn't seem to help his son. And she was angry. Lance had placed her in an awkward situation not only with law enforcement who would expect her to press charges, but with her own conscience. She didn't want to be the one forced to make a decision of this magnitude about his future.

"Mallory," Jake said, tightening his grip on her elbow. "Detective Carson wants you to do a walk-through to see if anything else is missing."

"This is quite a security arrangement you've got here, Miss Hunt." The detective inclined his head approvingly. "I still don't believe this kid got in. If it hadn't been for your backup system, he'd have been long gone before we got here."

Mallory only nodded. Once they knew who Lance's father and friends were, they wouldn't be so surprised.

With Jake at her side, she searched her workshop then headed upstairs where she found her jewelry untouched. There were several valuable pieces that her dad had given her through the years that she knew would have brought Lance more money: the emerald ring her dad had given her for her sixteenth birthday, the diamond pendant he'd given her for her twenty-first. Items she would have considered losses for their sentimental value alone.

She supposed that the fact Lance hadn't taken them meant there was still some hope for him.

Jake motioned her into the bathroom then closed the door behind them, blocking out the sound of the officers below, of the radio static and the chatter of a crime-scene investigation.

"Are you all right?" he asked.

"Just relieved he didn't have a weapon on him," she said more calmly than she felt. "Those officers walked in on him. If he'd even looked like he was reaching for a weapon, they'd have shot him right in my living room."

The weight of that statement lingered between them for

a moment before Jake asked, "Are you aware of the choice you need to make now?"

"They expect me to press charges."

He nodded. "What do you want to do?"

She retreated to the window and stared out into her small backyard, illuminated only with the fading starlight and the glow of solar path lights along the neat flower beds.

Jake seemed to understand that she needed space, that she wouldn't welcome him trying to comfort her, that she needed distance to manage the turmoil she felt. Turmoil that was wiping away her objectivity and making her options unclear.

"I don't know." She shrugged, feeling stupidly helpless. "I don't want to press charges. I don't want that responsibility."

"That would be easiest."

"Yes, it would. It would be easiest for me and for Lance." Though she sensed no disapproval in Jake, her own words rang in her ears like a cop-out. "I'm not convinced easiest is what's best for him, though."

Silence fell again, the weight of Jake's warm brown stare underscoring the fact that he was respecting her need to puzzle through this alone, to gauge what she should do against what she could live with.

But she knew by the way he leaned back against the vanity, the way he folded his arms across his chest that he was holding back. He had an opinion, but he wouldn't force it on her unless she wanted it.

To Mallory's surprise, she did. He looked so solid and real standing there, so uncomplicated and in that moment she didn't want to struggle with her need, didn't want to resist him.

"What do you think, Jake?"

"I think you need to do whatever will help Lance."

"I don't know what that is."

"You haven't told me enough about what's going on with him to understand the problem, but from where I'm standing, it seems obvious he's out of control and not getting the help he needs."

He didn't mince words, and she respected his honesty.

"He's angry," she said, a catch in her voice. "I don't know why. No one does. And not for lack of trying to figure it out, either. He's been making poor choices and hanging around with the worst kinds of friends. Polish Paul is doing everything he can, but he loves Lance and feels guilty because he's having such a hard time. We've all been trying to convince Paul to get outside help but he won't. He needs to make some tough choices about his son that he hasn't been able to make."

"Why?"

"I think he's scared. If he lets the situation out of his control he might not get it back. The law can be unpredictable with minors. He's afraid they'll think he hasn't been doing his job and put Lance in a juvenile facility."

Jake's frown gave Mallory the impression that he was remembering their discussion about her own stint in foster care.

"Maybe that would be best for Lance right now."

It was a hard truth, but not one Mallory hadn't thought of already. "Maybe, but how do I *know?*"

"You don't. You take a leap of faith and hope for the best. The only thing you can know for sure right now is if Lance continues what he's doing he could wind up in jail. You might not press charges but someone else could. And consider that the next time one of his friends calls you to pick him up from behind a Dumpster, he might not be alive when you get there."

That statement fell flat between them, a cold hard truth. She just stared at him, hands by her sides because she wasn't sure what to do with them. She didn't want to look upset, didn't want to show weakness, but she knew he saw right through her.

"It's not an easy situation, Mallory," he said softly. "But you have an opportunity to help him."

"You think I should press charges."

"Only you know what feels right. But Lance is a minor. Any trouble he gets in now won't go on his permanent record. Maybe the court will order him into a juvenile facility. Maybe they'll force him to get help. Either way, he gets a chance to fix things. I understand Polish Paul's concerns, but once Lance turns eighteen, he won't have any control over his son at all."

What Jake said made sense. She knew it in her head and more importantly, she knew it in her heart. Polish Paul hadn't been able to bring himself to get tough with Lance and she understood. All the people who loved them did. Polish Paul had never gotten over the death of his wife, felt guilty on some level that she'd died and not him, leaving their young son with no mother.

Polish Paul needed his friends to help him now.

And even knowing that in her heart didn't make her feel any better about what she had to do.

She felt fragile and needy when she wasn't a fragile and needy person. She wanted Jake to tell her that everything would work out all right, because somehow if he said it she could believe it. He didn't lie. She wanted to feel his arms around her, wanted so badly to cross the short distance between them and let him hold her.

She couldn't bring herself to take the first step.

Jake must have seen so much more of her struggle than she wanted to reveal because he reached out to her. Taking her hand, he said, "Let's go talk to the officers. They'll be able to give you more information."

No pressure. He just stood by her side when she spoke with the detectives about what to expect if they took Lance down to the station.

He placed a steadying hand on her shoulder when Lance started apologizing, pleading with her to call his dad, heart-breakingly scared and disbelieving that she'd let the officers take him.

And through it all Mallory appreciated Jake's nearness, grateful that he didn't try to make her feel better with empty words because she hadn't had to blink back the first tear. She just stood there watching Lance disappear with a gleam of red taillights into the night, knowing that she'd cried all her tears the last time she'd watched someone she loved driven away in the back of a police cruiser.

"LANCE HAS BEEN BOOKED. He'll have a chance to call his father before we put him in a holding cell," Lieutenant Gregory Dunkel said after hanging up the telephone. He glanced at the statement Mallory had given the officers and stood, circled his desk and took both of her hands. "I'll personally talk to his father and monitor his case, if that will make you feel better."

"It will, Greg. Thanks."

The lieutenant couldn't have been much older than Jake but he had dark hair streaked with silver and an attitude of commanding self-possession that was pure law enforce-ment. And the way he stared at Mallory... They were ob-viously well acquainted, and Lieutenant Dunkel had made it clear throughout the process of delivering her statement and filing a police report that he was very interested in her welfare.

Mallory hadn't seemed to notice. As she had all night,

she went through the motions, looking raw around the edges and very grateful that her police connections would garner some special consideration for Lance. And as Jake had all night, he stood close, watching officers, detectives and certain lieutenants trip over themselves trying to impress her.

"You did the right thing, Mallory," the lieutenant said. "I know it's hard, but let us do our jobs now and see what we can do to turn this kid around."

"I'm counting on you." She squeezed his hands before releasing them. "Now, what about those reports? Any luck yet?"

The lieutenant's gaze flicked over to Jake. "As a matter of fact, yes. Do you want to talk now?"

She followed his gaze, nodded. "It's okay. Jake's…a friend."

Judging from the look on the lieutenant's face, it wasn't okay. The man clearly didn't like that Mallory considered Jake close enough to hang around while they discussed business.

And neither did Jake. He didn't like that the best term she could come up with for him was that of a very tentative *friend.* He intended to be a helluva lot more. But until they crossed that distance, he supposed the fact that she allowed him to stay in the office was a victory of sorts.

The lieutenant swung back around his desk, retrieved a file with a stack of dated documents and motioned for Mallory to sit down. She set the reports on the desk so Jake could view them over her shoulder and began scanning the pages. "These are exactly what I needed, Greg. I was afraid they'd been cleared out a long time ago."

"Technically, they should have been. That's why it took me so long to track them down. They were filed away with others slated to be inputted into our new digital archive.

Of course our 'new' digital archive program is already three years old.''

Mallory gave an absent smile, clearly absorbed in the report. Jake followed her gaze to the yellowed page detailing the transmissions from Innovative Engineering's central monitoring station to the police on that long-ago night.

The panic alarm had been tripped from inside the warehouse.

On the one hand, Jake was glad she had physical proof that he hadn't sounded the alarm, exactly as he'd claimed. On the other, he wasn't thrilled that after working together, making love and generally sharing their lives around the clock, he couldn't be sure whether she'd still needed proof.

But Jake didn't have long to dwell on wounded pride because suddenly Mallory's face drained of color. Her hand trembled when she flipped a page, and he settled his hand on her shoulder.

''You all right?''

She didn't look all right. She looked small and forlorn sitting there, as though the events of this night and those of a decade ago were weighing too heavily on her shoulders.

For a moment Jake glimpsed behind the tough facade she usually wore, glimpsed the very real woman who suffered very real hurts that she didn't like to share.

He wanted to know what she saw in those reports that he didn't understand. He didn't ask in front of the lieutenant, wouldn't ask until they were alone. Glancing up, he found the lieutenant watching her with an equal amount of concern. That the guy seemed genuine didn't come as much of a consolation.

But Mallory didn't give the lieutenant a chance to question her further when she flipped the last page, slid the reports back across the desk and said, "This was what I needed to see. Thank you. I know this was effort to track down. I owe you."

"No, this was payback for the Fine Art thefts," the lieutenant said referring to a series of high-profile burglaries that had taken place in museums and art galleries around Atlanta not long ago. Jake hadn't known she'd been involved with the investigation. "We wouldn't have cracked that case without you."

She gave him a smile that never quite reached her eyes. "I'll stay in touch about Lance."

And then Jake was escorting her back through the police station. It was just after 5:00 a.m. when he wheeled out of the parking lot. If she noticed they weren't heading in the direction of her house, she didn't comment.

"What did you find in those transmission reports?" he asked. "Besides that I was telling the truth."

"I wasn't looking for confirmation that you didn't trip the alarm. I believed you. I wanted to know who did."

"Who?"

"My dad," she said matter-of-factly. But she didn't give him a chance to respond, didn't give him a chance to express his surprise before adding, "He told me he tripped the alarm, but I didn't believe him. I thought he was lying so I wouldn't feel guilty for getting him busted."

"Accidents happen, Mallory. You and I both know burglary and security aren't exact sciences."

Shifting his gaze off the road, he found her watching him with the sort of stark expression he'd come to realize meant she was struggling to keep her composure in place.

"My dad doesn't make those kinds of mistakes, Jake. Not careless ones. Maybe that sounds impossible to you, but trust me, the man is meticulous. That's the only reason he survived for two decades without getting busted."

Jake couldn't argue that point. "Then what happened?"

"I needed to see the reports to figure that out. Ten years ago I was new to the business, too new to know the right things to look for. But that's not the case now. I needed to see the placement of that alarm to understand if an accident was even a possibility."

"Was it?"

"For someone else, but not for my dad," she said with conviction. "He tripped that alarm intentionally after he drilled the safe."

"Are you saying he wanted to get caught?"

She nodded her head. "Yes."

"Why?"

"He wanted to retire the crew."

"Then why not stop working before spending time in prison?"

She turned to stare out the passenger window into the early-morning sky but Jake could see the grief sharpening her beautiful face even in profile. "He wanted to make sure that none of us would consider continuing without him."

"Watching him sit in prison accomplished that."

"It did."

If what Mallory said was true, then her father had acted for the benefit of the people he loved. And judging by the grief he saw in her expression, she knew it, too.

They fell into a silence heavy with revelations that were too immense to absorb all at once, especially not when they'd been on the run throughout the night. Jake maneuvered through the streets, where streetlamps still glowed and only the sporadic gleam of headlights sliced through the darkness.

He wondered how she would handle the situation now that she'd confirmed her suspicions, whether she'd confront her father outright or continue playing hide-and-seek with her secrets. He knew she still hadn't explained to her father about how they'd met on the Innovative job.

Jake hadn't pushed the issue, but the subject wasn't closed yet, either. It weighed heavily as something unpleasant still needing to be dealt with. Dodging the issue hadn't felt right, still didn't, especially since Jake had designs on Mallory that would make the man a part of his life. *If* he got his way.

He intended to get his way.

"When you're talking to your father about tripping the alarm, will you mention that I was on the job or do you still want to wait?"

"I don't have to tell him. He already knows."

Jake frowned, and she turned to face him, looking tired.

"Chalk another one up to my inexperience," she said. "That transmission report documented the positions of the close-circuit surveillance cameras."

"I noticed that. But the tapes were never confiscated."

"Opal took them so none of us could be made. I didn't realize it at the time but there was a camera positioned on the warehouse door."

When Jake thought about it, he knew she was right and understanding finally dawned. "So there was a camera positioned on us in that foyer."

She nodded.

"What happened to the tape?"

"Polish Paul and Eddie usually destroyed that sort of evidence right after a job. Whether that night was any different because of my dad's arrest, I can't say. But it doesn't really matter. Opal would have seen in the monitoring station, and I'm willing to bet she recognized you. Why else would they be leaving us alone?"

If Mallory was right, then the problem of Duke's reacion to his presence at the Innovative job was a non-issue. Given the amount of time his parents, Duke and Opal had been spending together, Jake suspected he had the man's complete support.

He barely got a chance to absorb the thought let alone savor it, because Mallory asked, "Where are you taking me?"

"To my place. We'll deal with straightening out your house tomorrow. Right now we both need to sleep, and I want to do that in my bed."

He didn't add that he couldn't be sure of the general response to pressing charges against Lance. He didn't want her to have to deal with Polish Paul, her father or any of the crew until she'd had a chance to rest and pull herself together.

On some level she must have known though, because he didn't put up a fight. She just lapsed into silence and stared out the window.

"I'm here for you, Mallory." And he would be until he figured out what it would take to get through to her, to earn her devotion and get her to commit to an *us*.

15

MALLORY KNEW Jake wouldn't make any promise he didn't mean. He cared. They might not have discussed how much he cared—because she'd refused to—but there was no missing the way he'd stepped into her life as though he wanted to be there, as though he belonged there.

She knew he wanted to fit her into his life, too, and a few hours ago she wouldn't have considered letting him take her home. She hadn't wanted to see where he lived, had needed to keep distance between them to maintain a grip on her emotions.

But now he would bridge that distance, and she would let him. She didn't feel like fighting how she felt for him anymore. She didn't see the point. He would only hold her, and she would feel as if she belonged in his arms, as if their being together was right. She'd been running from this feeling, promising herself she'd deal with it tomorrow.

Tomorrow had come. She had to deal with Jake now because when the sun came up, she'd need to tackle her dad and what he'd done ten years ago. She'd have to rally the courage to face Polish Paul and the crew once they found out she'd thrown Lance to the wolves.

She couldn't handle struggling with her feelings for Jake, too. Not when she found so much strength in his arms. Not when by his side seemed like the safest place in the world to be.

Tomorrow had *definitely* come.

And the first thing she had to deal with was Jake's house, which was nothing like Mallory had expected. She'd envisioned him living in a suburban home with a large lot and neighbors who mowed their yards religiously on Saturday mornings.

There wasn't a picket fence in sight. His home was a contemporary marvel with huge plate-glass windows overlooking a conservation reserve. Even in the dark it looked streamlined and stark in design, almost rebellious compared to those of his neighbors.

She liked it. And as he silently led her through rooms decorated in subdued tones where the only color came from the elaborate indoor trees and plants, Mallory knew that the floor plan had been cleverly designed to make the view of the conservation reserve the focal point of the whole house.

Through a wall of windows, dawn would transform the understated decor. Midday would flood these rooms with light. Dusk would bath them in an ethereal glow. Now, the waning stars jeweled the rooms in glimmering shadows.

The effect in Jake's second-floor bedroom was even more dramatic, if possible, and she liked that he didn't ask what she thought of his place, that he didn't need to. He just came to stand behind her where she glanced out the windows. Slipping his arms around her, he rested his chin on the top of her head and stared out into the fading starlight.

It was a companionable moment, a lull in a night filled with emotional highs and lows: the adrenaline rush of breaking into Eddie's place, the turmoil of discovering Lance had broken into hers. And finally, finding out the truth that her dad had done what he'd claimed all those years ago—he'd tripped the alarm, an action that sounded

so simple when the implication was so incredibly profound.

He'd sacrificed himself so his loved ones would have a
chance for a future.

And as she considered how much her dad had been willing to do for what he wanted, another thought struck her.

"You lost your job that night, Jake. TSS is a long way
from the career track you were on with Innovative Engineering. Did you blame me?"

He inhaled heavily, and Mallory sensed his resignation
at the inevitably of the question. "At first," he admitted.
"Everything I'd been working for went straight to hell
when I lost my internship. I lost my scholarship money
and for the first time in my life, I didn't have a clue what
to do next."

He laughed softly, a husky sound that sounded so right.
"I learned a lot. About how easy my life had been until
then. About how inflexible I was. I did blame you at first,
but after a while I realized that meeting you was just meant
to be. I might not have understood why, but I was meant
to get off the corporate ladder and go into the security
field. I will admit that I did think you owed me a favor
when I sent my proposal."

"I got that part loud and clear." She'd laughed when
he'd said he wanted to assist her on the job, had been
amused by his lack of trust. Now she wanted to ask him
if he trusted her yet.

And she couldn't bring herself to ask the question.

"I only accepted your job because I felt you owed me
something," she said instead.

"I figured that out when you stripped in the bathroom."

"It was a test. I wanted to see what kind of man you'd
grown up to be."

"You expected me to hop into the shower. You thought I wouldn't be able to resist you, didn't you?"

"I figured you'd either hop into the shower or you'd run screaming."

He gave a hearty laugh. "I'd never back down from that kind of dare."

"I thought I'd offend your self-righteous sensibilities. But of course, that was when I thought you'd tripped the alarm."

"Meaning you don't think I'm self-righteous anymore."

"No, I don't, as a matter of fact. I've placed you in a difficult situation, and you've handled yourself very well."

He'd taken what she'd offered that day, only on his own terms, blowing all her preconceived ideas about him right out of the water. She wouldn't admit that, knew she didn't have to. This man read her with an ability that had made her uneasy.

She wouldn't admit that either.

"So you don't think I'm self-righteous anymore," he said. "That's a good thing. I'm guessing you also think I'm adequate in bed and less than adequate as a rock climber."

"Definitely less than adequate as a rock climber. You're a nightmare. I'm still not believing you tripped the alarm at Eddie's tonight."

"I'm still not believing you didn't. You gave me a blow job in mid-air."

Mallory resisted the urge to smile. "You're more than adequate in bed, Jake."

"Mmm." The sound rumbled deep in his chest, told her he was very satisfied that she thought so. "Exceptional lover, lame rock climber. I can live with that. What else do you think?"

Here it was, the place where he'd segue the conversation

around to their relationship and try to manipulate her into
an emotionally honest corner. She recognized the maneuver after dodging it so often lately.

Tonight she'd surprise him.

"I think you've been having as good a time challenging
me as I've been having challenging you."

"Oh, you do?" he said, but there was no surprise in his
voice, only amusement. "How have I been challenging
you?"

"You keep trying to get me to deal with our relationship."

He shifted position, bracing his legs a little farther apart
so she was forced to sink back against him for balance.
His arms tightened around her, and he said, "You noticed."

"I did."

"I thought it was only fair to let you know where I was.
That the more time we spend together, the more convinced
I am we should be an *us*."

He presented her own words with tremendous new
meaning, words that proved how much he did trust her.
He laid his heart between them when she'd done nothing
to prove that she might be willing or able to handle it
carefully.

A thoughtful silence claimed the moment, a silence
where she considered whether she was worthy of his trust
when until this very moment she hadn't even been honest
with herself about how she felt about him.

"Why security, Jake?" she asked, not sure this wasn't
another diversionary tactic but suddenly needing an answer.

He held her close, his big body surrounding hers with
warmth, enveloping her as though she'd been designed to
fit in the shelter of his broad chest. "I wanted to keep

beautiful thieves from screwing up other young men's lives.''

His answer was light, not personal or emotional, and Mallory realized he thought she was running again. He was giving her a place to retreat to in case she couldn't handle his honesty.

His willingness to put aside what he wanted for what she could handle humbled her.

''You're making very good progress,'' was all she could say.

''I have more work to do on securing ceiling access. Any suggestions?''

''I'll make my recommendations in my summary report, after we see how the Atlanta Safe Exchange job goes.''

He didn't reply, and they fell back into that silence again, a silence where she recognized that he was letting her take the lead, a silence where she didn't want him continuing to make concessions because she was too weak to deal with her feelings.

''What do you want from me, Jake?''

''The truth?''

On the surface he asked a simple question, one that should have had an easy answer, but Mallory understood the subtext, knew the answer wasn't simple at all.

He'd been honest with her from the start. No matter what trick she pulled, he'd risen to her challenges and met them with challenges of his own. His question was perhaps the greatest one of all. To meet this challenge, she'd have to be honest not only with him, but with herself.

Honesty meant facing that he would ask something of her she wasn't sure she had to give. Honesty meant looking at everything her dad had been willing to do for the people he loved and knowing she hadn't had the courage to do the same. She'd wanted Jake and had been dodging that very truth since the minute she'd stripped for him in her bathroom.

"Yes. The truth please." More simple words that changed everything.

"I want a chance for a future." His voice was rich and warm and completely certain. "I want you to work with me at TSS and perform your magic on every system I put on the market. I want you to live with me. I don't really care where. And I want you to love me, Mallory."

A flip comment about wanting a fantasy sprang to her lips, but she bit it back, knowing it was nothing more than a defense to distance them, to stop feeling vulnerable when her heart was coming apart with every word he spoke.

Then he lowered his head until their cheeks were pressed together, his breath flowing gently against her skin. "I want you to make a leap of faith and trust that allowing yourself to love me will be the best challenge of all."

Each word crumbled away a few more pieces of her heart, made her voice waver uncertainly when she said, "You sound convinced I love you already."

He laughed. "You do. You just haven't accepted it yet. It's obvious in the way you respond to me, in the way we can spend twenty-four seven together without getting on each other's nerves. Why else do you think you've been trying so hard to scare me off?"

She didn't have an answer for that, hadn't realized she'd been so transparent.

"Let me be a part of your life. You won't be sorry."

"My life has a few rough places right now." She knew he'd see right through this stall tactic, knew he would overcome yet another obstacle she tossed into his path.

And it surprised her how much she needed him to.

"Whose doesn't?" he said. "I haven't met anyone out there living the perfect life."

"We're from two totally different worlds."

"Are you sure? You've refused to look at mine."

More honesty, only this honesty shamed her with the truth of how weak she'd been. She hadn't looked at his life. She'd refused even to take a peek.

"I don't know how to let you in," she admitted honestly. "An important part of me closed off a long time ago. I don't think I realized how much until tonight when I watched Lance drive off in that cruiser."

"There's nothing closed off inside you that you can't open up to someone you trust," he said fiercely, his voice reflecting such utter conviction that she squeezed her eyes shut as if she could somehow dim the blinding glare of his faith.

"You might have closed down and not let anyone inside so you wouldn't be hurt again, but look at the people you love, Mallory, look at how you care for them and how much they love you in return. If you choose to let me in, you will. It's that simple. Trust me."

She did. That was the simplest truth she'd had to face all night. She did trust Jake, trusted him not to lie, not to push. She trusted him to ask only for what she had to give. He wasn't expecting promises or guarantees. He only wanted her to accept him, wanted her to give them a shot at a future.

"I love you, Mallory."

More simple words. Slipping his hands over her shoulders, he forced her to turn around until she faced him, saw the truth in his handsome face, a truth that made her yearn for a future she'd been afraid to believe in.

She needed to feel his hands on her, needed to find her courage in the ecstasy she knew only in his arms.

''Take me to bed, Jake. Make love to me.''

Without a word, he scooped her into his arms and gave her what she wanted.

BY THE TIME Mallory opened her eyes, the sun shone brightly through the floor-to-ceiling windows. She blinked to clear away sleep, to gather her thoughts as she remembered all that had transpired through the night and the courage she'd found in Jake's arms while the sun had risen.

Before she had a chance to mull through the enormity of the changes the night had brought, she heard what must have awakened her—voices.

''Jake, wake up.'' She shook his shoulder. ''Were you expecting company this morning? There's a party downstairs.''

He sat up, eyes heavy with sleep, tawny hair rumpled, a drowsy look that made her smile.

She tried again. ''Do you have any friends who have access to your security system?''

''Just my folks.''

''I think they've come to visit.''

But then she heard a familiar female voice and the sound of laughter that made her glance in the direction of the stairs. That couldn't be...*Opal?*

Jake apparently recognized the voice, too, because he whipped off the covers and shot out of bed in an impressive display of sun-kissed skin and shifting muscle.

He disappeared into the hallway only to reappear a second later. ''Opal, your father and my parents.'' At her look of surprise, he crossed the room, retrieved a robe from inside his bathroom and tossed it to her. ''Here, put this on.'' Then he rummaged through his dresser and pulled on sweats.

Her dad, Opal and...*Jake's parents?*

They descended the stairs quietly and Mallory found her heart galloping as they crouched low on the risers, peering through the balustrade to see what was taking place....

"They're in the dining room," he whispered.

A burst of deep laughter confirmed that her dad was indeed one of the unexpected guests, but before she could comment on how her dad and Opal might have wound up in Jake's dining room with his parents, the doorbell rang.

Heels rapped on the wooden floor, and Mallory made a wild leap to her feet, felt Jake shoot into motion right behind her, but she hadn't gained the first step before a pleasant female voice called out, "The kids are awake."

An impeccably dressed woman with tawny hair and flawless golden skin that labeled her as Jake's mother appeared at the foot of the stairs.

"Good morning, Jake. We have guests. We didn't think you'd mind." She tipped up a cheek for a kiss. "And you're Mallory." She smiled warmly, a smile that Mallory recognized from seeing often on her son's face. "I'm Rosalyn, dear. Jake's mother. I'm so pleased to finally meet you. We've heard so much about you."

Mallory wasn't sure who the *we* was, but she forced what must have been an absurdly shell-shocked smile on her face. "From Jake?"

Rosalyn shot Jake an amused look disguised as displeasure. "Yes, and from your father and Opal and your friends."

"Oh." Mallory wasn't sure how to respond with thoughts of killing her dad and his crew crowding her head. "Pleased to meet you."

She settled for a civility, and fortunately the ringing bell interrupted their exchange. Jake pulled open the door to find Polish Paul, holding a large bag from a well-known bagel bakery.

He looked bleary-eyed from what Mallory guessed was lack of sleep, but he'd donned a short-sleeved button-down shirt, the tails of which hung out over his great belly, a shocking departure from his ritual T-shirts. Miraculously, a stogie was poking out of his front pocket and not dangling from his lips.

Before Mallory had a chance to absorb this amazing transformation, he asked, "Did I miss brunch?"

"No, you're right on time, Paul," Rosalyn said as if they were already acquainted. "Please come in."

Polish Paul's gaze shot up to Mallory, and she forced herself to meet his gaze, even though her heart had leapt into her throat and threatened to choke her.

He absently passed off the bag to Jake's mother and marched straight up to Mallory, pulled her down the last steps and folded her in his beefy embrace.

"You did the right thing," he said in a gruff voice. "Don't question it for a second."

"Is he okay?"

"He will be." Polish Paul shook his grizzled head with a certainty Mallory hadn't seen for far too long when it came to discussing Lance. "Lieutenant Dunkel said you'd talked to him, so he's going to recommend the judge order Lance into a treatment program before I can bail him out. Lance feels so bad, Mallory...I think he'll cooperate. This'll all work out for the best, you'll see."

She hugged him hard, blinking back tears when he released her and extended his hand to Jake. "Thanks for all your help."

Jake didn't reply, only shook Polish Paul's hand, which was exactly the right thing to do to segue through the difficult moment.

Rosalyn demonstrated further insight when she said, "Come on, Paul. Let's get something to eat. And you kids, too. Jake, your father's wowing everyone with his special Western omelets.'' She rolled her gaze. ''And Eddie has been whipping up hash browns that are just delicious. He let me nibble from the skillet.''

Then she linked arms with Polish Paul and led him away, leaving Mallory staring after her in stunned silence.

''How does she know Polish Paul?'' When Jake didn't reply, she added, ''And what are special Western omelets?''

''My father's specialty. He makes them on holidays.''

''Oh.''

A burst of laughter issued from the dining room. Her dad, probably laughing about the two of them getting caught on the stairs like kids trying to peek at Santa in the act. ''If there's a party, I'd better go get dressed.''

She was too emotionally overwhelmed to handle facing her dad, the crew *and* Jake's parents dressed in his overlarge robe.

''At least it's not a towel.''

''You didn't have a choice. I do. This is *your* house and those people are *your* guests.'' She started back up the stairs, tossing him a grin over her shoulder. ''Make my apologies. I'll be down in five minutes.''

Mallory's five minutes turned into ten by the time she appeared in the dining room freshly groomed and wearing her coveralls. Jake's dining room backed up to the windows, and the view of the conservation reserve in daylight was spectacular.

Eddie and a man who could only be Jake's dad, given his brawny size, worked companionably in the full-size kitchen that was separated from the dining area by a huge island bar currently housing an array of fresh fruits that Eddie was arranging on platters.

He caught sight of her first, raked his gaze over her

clothing and flashed a gold-toothed grin. "Good morning, sunshine. Came straight from work I see. I heard you had an eventful night."

"Definitely eventful." Eddie didn't know the half of it. She shifted her gaze to Jake's dad who'd pulled a skillet off the burner and extended his hand.

"Hello, Mallory. I'm John."

His eyes were a steely blue color, but Mallory felt as though she could have been staring into Jake's eyes so solid and steady was his gaze. "A pleasure, sir."

Everyone else sat around a long oak picnic table—her dad, Opal, Polish Paul and Rosalyn—all drinking coffee and enjoying what appeared to be an impressive brunch.

"Good morning," she said.

Her dad stood. She acknowledged Opal and Jake's mother with a smile before making her way to her dad.

She gave him a hug. "So you heard?"

He only nodded. His dark gaze said everything else, how sorry he was she'd had to deal with the situation, how he'd approved of the hard choice she'd made.

"Are you all right, honey?" Opal asked.

Mallory glanced down at Polish Paul, who encouraged her with a salute of his coffee mug. "I'm fine."

Her dad motioned to an empty space beside Jake and said, "Join us. We're all one big happy family. Surprised?"

Surprised didn't quite cover it. Eddie appeared with a mug of coffee, which she gratefully accepted.

"Just out of idle curiosity," she said, pointedly glancing around the table as she sat down. "Exactly how did all this big-happy-family stuff transpire?"

"Jake told us he'd met you," Rosalyn said. "He asked if we'd introduce ourselves to your family and friends."

"Oh, he did, did he?"

Jake nodded, looking completely unfazed as he reached for a platter stacked with bagels. "I did."

"John and Rosalyn gave us a call so we decided to meet for drinks at my club," her dad added. "Given the circumstances, it seemed appropriate. The least I could do was apologize for all the trouble we'd caused for Jake ten years ago."

Mallory took a fortifying sip of coffee and stared over the rim of her mug. "When did you figure out who he was?"

"I didn't. Opal did after she met him at your place."

Mallory shot Jake a look that translated into "I told you so" before confronting Opal. "So you're the culprit."

She smiled brightly. "Of course, honey. You know I don't ever forget a handsome man. Or the back of his head as it was."

"I asked you to run interference with Daddy."

She spread her hands in entreaty. "I tried to get him to 'fess up, but you know him. He had to do things his own way. So I've been coordinating social visits with Rosalyn. This has been the perfect opportunity to get to know Jake's parents."

"And we always enjoy getting to know Jake's friends," Rosalyn said with a pointed gaze and a thoughtful smile.

Mallory didn't miss the subtext. Rosalyn didn't have any problems with the past or their disparate backgrounds, and she wanted to make her position clear. Jake's father backed her up with a nod, and Mallory could only meet their gazes and accept their approval with a smile of her own.

Jake nudged her knee beneath the table as if to say, "I told you so," and then began to fight a losing battle against laughter as her dad began a convoluted tale of meetings that had started with drinks at the club and wound up at Polish Paul's Tattoo Studio.

John shoved up his sleeve to display a newly acquired "Polish Paul," a circlet of gold-brushed angel's wings around his bicep with the name Rosalyn showcased in the center.

"I've always wanted one but your mother hasn't been impressed with anything we've seen through the years."

"Polish Paul does beautiful work," Rosalyn said. "So I gave him a tattoo for an anniversary gift."

She smiled so lovingly at her husband that Mallory suspected she glimpsed the reason Jake believed in soul mates.

"So this solves the mystery of where everyone has been lately," Mallory said dryly. "But I have a question, Jake. Why did you feel the need to suggest our parents get together?"

He slathered cream cheese on a bagel with that same look of calm deliberation. "You were such a challenge to win over that I didn't have time to work on your father and the crew. You wouldn't even tell them who I was, and I knew I didn't stand a chance with you without your family and friends' support. I had no choice but to call in the big guns."

"The big guns?" Mallory glanced at his parents—Rosalyn, seated on the bench clasping her husband's hand on her shoulder, and John, who stood behind her still holding a skillet—and her confusion must have been obvious to everyone at the table.

Jake smiled. "Remember when you mentioned my lack of any long-term relationships?"

Mallory nodded.

"You weren't the first person to mention it."

"We want grandbabies while we're still young enough

to enjoy them," Rosalyn said. "So when Jake said he'd finally met the right woman, we wanted to do everything we could to help."

"Hear, hear." Duke raised his coffee mug.

Mallory found herself the recipient of every gaze around the table. Setting her mug down, she turned to Jake. "So while I was training you in good faith as per our contract, you were siccing the posse on me. Does that sum it up?"

His gaze cut through her, made her feel absurdly fluttery inside. "I wasn't willing to take chances with you. And you haven't exactly been a pushover. I needed help. I asked for it."

She sat back, feeling as though the wind had been knocked out of her, unable to drag her gaze away from the truth so evident in his handsome face.

When he leaned toward her, Mallory's heart actually tripped over another beat. "Let me love you," he whispered for her ears alone, such intimate, honest words that heat flooded her cheeks.

Whether this was a function of the promise in his voice or that everyone stared at them, Mallory couldn't say, but when her dad laughed, the heat in her cheeks flared even hotter.

"Babe, I don't think I've ever seen you blush."

"Oh, this is too romantic." Opal gave a sigh, and Mallory scowled, even though her blush undermined the effect.

Underneath the table, Jake slipped his hand over her knee, gave a reassuring squeeze and then questioned Eddie about Peachtree Financial's security system. He wanted to know exactly when TSS had designed the safe and how the crew had farmed out the work.

The change of conversation had the desired effect, diverting everyone's attention from Mallory and the potential for grandbabies, when she and Jake hadn't even discussed what the reality of an *us* would involve yet.

So Mallory sipped her coffee, listening to the conversations happening around the table, trying to catch her breath. But there was still one more thing that needed settling.

Leaning close to her father, she whispered, "You tripped the alarm that night on purpose."

He met her gaze and the wealth of emotion in his eyes had her blinking back tears. "Do you understand why I did?"

She nodded.

He reached up to brush his thumb along her jaw, a tender gesture that made Mallory feel so loved that those tears threatened to fall.

"Good," he said softly. "I just want you to be happy." Then he held out his coffee mug to Opal, who'd just stood to take her plate into the kitchen, and said, "Would you mind, gorgeous?"

Opal went to get more coffee. Polish Paul asked Eddie to pass the butter and got a lecture about saturated fats and arteries. The moment passed, easily.

Mallory liked that about her dad. He didn't angst about radically changing all their lives. He didn't hold up his sacrifice for a standing ovation, either. He'd done what he'd thought was best for the people he loved, and he expected them to understand. It was uncomplicated, *right*.

Sort of like the way she felt about Jake.

"I have a new development you'll be happy to hear about," she told him. "I'll be limiting my work for law enforcement in the future."

Duke held a forkful of John Trinity's special Western omelet poised above his plate. "Really? And what has brought about this remarkable change of heart? Nothing I've said, I'm sure.''

"Jake offered me a position with TSS. I've agreed to give up my consulting business to work for him.''

The fork descended slowly to the plate. "Really?''

"You look surprised.''

"I am.''

"He offered me stock options and health benefits and an obscene amount of money. I could hardly pass his offer up.''

Now it was Jake's turn to stop with his fork poised in mid-air. "Oh, I did, did I?''

She nodded. "TSS needs my particular expertise. You should have seen this man on the job last night, Eddie. He fell right on the pressure mat and activated the panic alarm. It's loud.''

Eddie hooted with laughter.

Jake frowned. "What she's not telling you is that she was directly responsible for making me fall.''

Duke raised a skeptical brow. "I'll take your word for it, Jake, but remember that I've seen you rappel.''

"Ha, ha.'' Jake wrapped his arm around her. "Go ahead, tell them your other surprise.''

"What other surprise?''

His smug smile made her brace herself. "Mallory has agreed to marry me.''

"Oh, I did, did I?''

"Yes,'' he said. "You did.''

Leave it to Jake to spring this on her in public, although Mallory supposed she'd brought it on herself with her announcement about accepting his job offer. Glancing around the table at the family and friends awaiting her reaction, she found that she didn't know what to say.

She'd already agreed to work for the man. This morning

in his arms, she'd also agreed to be an *us*. She supposed there was no reason why marriage couldn't be a part of the future.

"Honey, I haven't seen you this quiet since the fourth grade when Denny McKenna told you he didn't like you anymore after you beat up that bully boy for picking on him." Opal placed two mugs on the table and slipped onto the bench. "Marriage to a man as handsome as Jake is a *good* thing."

It wasn't Opal's declaration that kicked Mallory's brain into gear again, but the sight of her hand.

"Where's the black opal?" She referred to Opal's signature ring that she'd worn for as long as Mallory could remember.

"Here." She held up her right hand. "I needed a change."

"What's that on your left hand?"

"Oh, I wasn't going to say anything yet." Opal heaved a dramatic sigh and looked close to bursting. "You know me, honey, I wouldn't dream of stealing your thunder, and I don't care to share mine. But since you've asked…"

She let her statement trail off while displaying her left hand, where a platinum band rested on her elegantly manicured ring finger. Twisting the band, she revealed a solitaire diamond that flashed in the sunlight flooding the room.

"That's not what I think it is, is it?" Mallory reached for her hand to inspect the ring. "This is Mrs. McGillivray's diamond. It's got to be close to eight carats."

"It *is* eight carats," Opal said proudly.

"Didn't she swear she'd never part with this?"

"Which positively broke my heart because it was her only piece of jewelry worth owning," Eddie said, guiding Opal's hand away from Mallory so he could gaze longingly at the stone. "I would have had them lining up at the door for this ring."

"As soon as Mrs. McGillivray heard your dad had finally asked me to marry him after *thirty years,* the dear lady took it off her finger and insisted I have it. She gave your dad a great deal because she wanted to make sure it went to a good home. Of course she knew how much I admired it."

"Of course," Duke said with a dashing grin. "And whatever the lady wants…"

"The lady wants an intimate wedding and a very expensive honeymoon," Opal informed him in a tone that brooked no refusal. "I've earned it."

Her dad nodded. "That you have, gorgeous."

And before Mallory had a chance to react to this news, Rosalyn said, "We mentioned the cruise that you're sending us on for our anniversary, Jake, so we've decided to go together."

"On your anniversary cruise?"

His dad nodded. "You know those cruises. So much more fun if you actually know someone on board."

Rosalyn agreed. "Especially when I want to visit the casino. Your father always refuses to go. Damage control, he says."

Duke laughed and Opal warned him not to bother trying to curtail the damage that she could do in a casino, all the while gazing at him with that same sort of contented look that Rosalyn wore whenever she looked at her husband.

"About time, Daddy." Mallory blew him and Opal a kiss. She wouldn't mention how pleased she was that Opal would officially be her stepmother, didn't think Opal would appreciate the title even if she had been doing the job all along.

Jake's hand found hers beneath the table, and as they

listened to their respective families make plans for upcoming weddings, anniversaries and honeymoons, Mallory met his warm gaze and felt that crazy flutter of excitement again.

Jake was right. Loving him would be the best challenge of all. She'd wanted a piece of this man's ass for ten long years, and she'd finally gotten it. *Forever.*

Epilogue

The kiss—ten days later

MALLORY MOVED as if she were making love, slim curves gathering and unfolding in a sinuous display as she descended a rope with nothing more than the strength of her upper body to lower her and long sleek legs to anchor her. She wore all black, from her form-fitting coveralls to her soft-soled boots.

She was *his* woman now, and her effect on him was almost overwhelming as Jake stood beyond a doorway that led into the warehouse of the Atlanta Safe Exchange. She was his fantasy come to life, and two very primitive impulses warred with each other. One urged him to stand there and enjoy the sight of her shimmying down that line, while the other caught him up in the thrill of sensor-washed darkness and rushing adrenaline. He wanted to do a lot more than watch.

His breath caught and held as she maneuvered her slim body through a particularly narrow passage in the sensor array. Her every muscle was compacted, yet liquid enough to slip between the narrow channel of free space without making contact.

Perhaps with another decade or so of practice at the rock-climbing gym, Jake might be able to accomplish such controlled moves. At the moment he was content to stand back and marvel at her skill and his own ingenuity at the

sensor design, which would make it impossible for any
thief with less than Mallory's skill to penetrate the infrared
web leading to the Atlanta Safe Exchange vault.

His woman had been so impressed by his sensor design
that she'd asked him to limit his involvement during this
part of the job to observation. He'd agreed, conceding to
her greater ability and understanding her reluctance to
jeopardize her impeccable record on her last job in private
practice.

Trust was no longer an issue between them. Mallory had
committed to him, and he was content with the path his
life had taken and hopeful that her affiliation with TSS
would yield equally amazing results.

He knew it would. She hadn't completed this job yet,
and as promised, she was already pinpointing places he
could tighten his new system. And she hadn't made him
wait for her summary report, either. She was a part of his
team, and Jake knew with her on his side, he'd realize his
lofty goals for TSS.

As soon as she officially came to work for him, they'd
create her position for real and the negotiation would begin. She'd already been making demands. While he could
live with the stock options and pension plan, the salary
she'd quoted him *was* obscene.

But he looked forward to the negotiating, which had
proven to be another challenge for them—the type that
frequently landed them in bed. Or against a vault. Or any-
place he could remind her that he found her irresistible.

And how much he loved her.

Their first negotiation had involved setting their wedding date. The Hunt/Trinity nuptials would take place three
months hence, enough time to establish Mallory's new position at TSS—her requirement—and to plan a wedding

that would satisfy the expectations of the groom's mother and the bride's stepmother.

There was another friendship that continued to surprise everyone. His parents and the new Mr. and Mrs. Duke Hunt genuinely liked each other and were currently out cruising the high seas, availing themselves of the sun, the island tours and the casinos. Apparently they were having the time of their lives, according to their latest e-mail.

His mom had reported that his father had taken to sunning himself at the upper deck pool to catch the attention of the other cruisers—mostly bikini-clad women—who frequently commented on the unusual design of his "Polish Paul."

His mom also reported that Opal had been crusading to disabuse her new husband of all thoughts of impending old age by keeping him on the dance floor every night until the wee hours.

Life was working out between them, and Jake knew it would get even better once Mallory became his wife.

He watched as she dropped to her feet without a sound, her body absorbing the impact with an effortless motion that brought to mind a cat landing on all fours. She stood barely a foot away, sandwiched between thin slivers of infrared, the criss-crossing web of light that was the only barrier between them.

And while that web effectively blocked them from one another, there was a place that was the perfect size for…he thrust his hand through a triangular wedge of free space between the beams, caught her face.

"Jake!" she hissed.

"Don't move a muscle or you'll disturb the beam and trip the alarm."

The wild look in her eyes proved she hadn't needed the reminder, and he liked that he'd shocked her. She was worried. *Very* worried. Her chest rose and fell sharply as he eased her head to the side, aligned her face to that triangular space and drew her toward him with agonizing slowness.

Then he lowered his mouth to hers. His own heartbeat spiked sharply as he brushed those luscious lips in a kiss. A kiss that promised she'd made the right choice by loving him.

His employee.

His woman.

His love.

The thief who'd stolen his heart.

HARLEQUIN® Blaze™

In L.A., nothing remains confidential for long...

KISS & TELL

Don't miss

Tori Carrington's

exciting new miniseries featuring four
twentysomething friends—
and the secrets they *don't* keep.

Look for:

#105—NIGHT FEVER
October 2003

#109—FLAVOR OF THE MONTH
November 2003

#113—JUST BETWEEN US...
December 2003

Available wherever Harlequin books are sold.

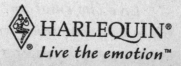

HARLEQUIN®
Live the emotion™

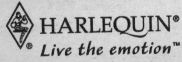

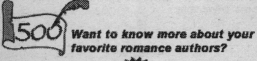

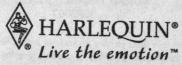